About the Novel

"A real writer, with the true comic spirit. A really funny book."—JAMES JOYCE

"A book in a thousand . . . in the line of *Tristram Shandy* and *Ulysses*."—GRAHAM GREENE

About the Author

FLANN O'BRIEN was one of the two pseudonyms of Brian O'Nolan. The other was Myles na gCopaleen, which he used as a celebrated Irish newspaper columnist. Born in County Tyrone before the First World War, the author settled in Dublin, and in 1939, *At Swim-Two-Birds* established him as a major novelist. His other notable works include *The Third Policeman* (also available in a Plume edition), *The Hard Life*, and *The Dalkey Archive*. Of him John Updike has written: "He was five years younger than Samuel Beckett, sounded his genius earlier, husbanded it less thriftily, and died young, at the age of fifty-four. As with Scott Fitzgerald, there is a brilliant ease in his prose, a poignant grace glimmering off every page . . . Like Beckett, he has the gift of the perfect sentence, the art, which they both learned from Joyce, of turning plain language to a lyric pitch."

'Εξίσταται γὰρ πάντ' ἀπ' ἀλλήλων δίχα

"All things fleet and yield each other place"

multiple voices in text

transparent style vs. obvious style

noticing style causes detachment —
    reader is forced into outside ~~position~~ position

"tissue paper of plagerisms," "self-evident sham"
figures who have control are brought down

At Swim-Two-Birds

by Flann O'Brien

A PLUME BOOK

PLUME
Published by the Penguin Group
Penguin Books USA Inc., 375 Hudson Street, New York, New York 10014,
U.S.A.
Penguin Books Ltd, 27 Wrights Lane, London W8 5TZ, England
Penguin Books Australia Ltd, Ringwood, Victoria, Australia
Penguin Books Canada Ltd, 2801 John Street, Markham,
Ontario, Canada L3R 1B4
Penguin Books (N.Z.) Ltd, 182-190 Wairau Road, Auckland 10, New Zealand

Penguin Books Ltd, Registered Offices: Harmondsworth, Middlesex, England

Published by Plume, an imprint of New American Library, a division of
Penguin Books USA Inc.

BOOKS ARE AVAILABLE AT QUANTITY DISCOUNTS WHEN USED TO PROMOTE
PRODUCTS OR SERVICES. FOR INFORMATION PLEASE WRITE TO PREMIUM
MARKETING DIVISION, PENGUIN BOOKS USA INC., 375 HUDSON STREET,
NEW YORK, NEW YORK 10014.

All the characters and events portrayed in this book are fictitious.

Library of Congress Catalog Card Number: 66-17221

This is an authorized reprint of a hardcover edition
published by Walker and Company.

 REGISTERED TRADEMARK—MARCA REGISTRADA

First Plume Printing, October, 1976

10 11 12 13 14 15 16

PRINTED IN THE UNITED STATES OF AMERICA

1939

CHAPTER I

HAVING placed in my mouth sufficient bread for three minutes' chewing, I withdrew my powers of sensual perception and retired into the privacy of my mind, my eyes and face assuming a vacant and preoccupied expression. I reflected on the subject of my spare-time literary activities. One beginning and one ending for a book was a thing I did not agree with. A good book may have three openings entirely dissimilar and inter-related only in the prescience of the author, or for that matter one hundred times as many endings.

Examples of three separate openings—the first: The Pooka MacPhellimey, a member of the devil class, sat in his hut in the middle of a firwood meditating on the nature of the numerals and segregating in his mind the odd ones from the even. He was seated at his diptych or ancient two-leaved hinged writing-table with inner sides waxed. His rough long-nailed fingers toyed with a snuff-box of perfect rotundity and through a gap in his teeth he whistled a civil cavatina. He was a courtly man and received honour by reason of the generous treatment he gave his wife, one of the Corrigans of Carlow.

The second opening: There was nothing unusual in the

9

appearance of Mr. John Furriskey but actually he had one distinction that is rarely encountered—he was born at the age of twenty-five and entered the world with a memory but without a personal experience to account for it. His teeth were well-formed but stained by tobacco, with two molars filled and a cavity threatened in the left canine. His knowledge of physics was moderate and extended to Boyle's Law and the Parallelogram of Forces.

The third opening: Finn Mac Cool was a legendary hero of old Ireland. Though not mentally robust, he was a man of superb physique and development. Each of his thighs was as thick as a horse's belly, narrowing to a calf as thick as the belly of a foal. Three fifties of fosterlings could engage with handball against the wideness of his backside, which was large enough to halt the march of men through a mountain-pass.

I hurt a tooth in the corner of my jaw with a lump of the crust I was eating. This recalled me to the perception of my surroundings.

It is a great pity, observed my uncle, that you don't apply yourself more to your studies. The dear knows your father worked hard enough for the money he is laying out on your education. Tell me this, do you ever open a book at all?

I surveyed my uncle in a sullen manner. He speared a portion of cooked rasher against a crust on the prongs of his fork and poised the whole at the opening of his mouth in a token of continued interrogation.

Description of my uncle: Red-faced, bead-eyed, ball-bellied. Fleshy about the shoulders with long swinging arms giving ape-like effect to gait. Large moustache. Holder of Guinness clerkship the third class.

I do, I replied.

He put the point of his fork into the interior of his mouth and withdrew it again, chewing in a coarse manner.

Quality of rasher in use in household: Inferior, one and two the pound.

Well faith, he said, I never see you at it. I never see you at your studies at all.

I work in my bedroom, I answered.

Whether in or out, I always kept the door of my bedroom locked. This made my movements a matter of some secrecy and enabled me to spend an inclement day in bed without disturbing my uncle's assumption that I had gone to the College to attend to my studies. A contemplative life has always been suitable to my disposition. I was accustomed to stretch myself for many hours upon my bed, thinking and smoking there. I rarely undressed and my inexpensive suit was not the better for the use I gave it, but I found that a brisk application with a coarse brush before going out would redeem it somewhat without quite dispelling the curious bedroom smell which clung to my person and which was frequently the subject of humorous or other comment on the part of my friends and acquaintances.

Aren't you very fond of your bedroom now, my uncle continued. Why don't you study in the dining-room here where the ink is and where there is a good book-case for your books? Boys but you make a great secret about your studies.

My bedroom is quiet, convenient and I have my books there. I prefer to work in my bedroom, I answered.

My bedroom was small and indifferently lighted but it contained most of the things I deemed essential for existence—my bed, a chair which was rarely used, a table and a washstand. The washstand had a ledge upon which I had arranged a number of books. Each of them was generally recognized as indispensable to all who aspire to an appreciation of the nature of contemporary literature and my small collection contained works ranging from those of Mr. Joyce to the widely-read books of Mr. A. Huxley, the eminent English writer. In my bedroom also were certain porcelain articles related more to utility than ornament. The mirror at which I shaved every second day was of the type supplied gratis by Messrs. Watkins, Jameson and Pim and bore brief letter-press in reference to a proprietary brand of ale between the words of which I had acquired considerable skill in inserting the reflection of my countenance. The mantel-piece contained forty buckskin volumes comprising a Conspectus of the Arts and Natural Sciences. They were published in 1854 by a reputable Bath house for a guinea the volume. They bore their years bravely and retained in their interior the kindly seed of knowledge intact and without decay.

I know the studying you do in your bedroom, said my uncle. Damn the studying you do in your bedroom.

I denied this.

Nature of denial: Inarticulate, of gesture.

My uncle drained away the remainder of his tea and arranged his cup and saucer in the centre of his bacon plate in a token that his meal was at an end. He then blessed himself and sat for a time drawing air into his mouth with a hissing sound in an attempt to extract foodstuff from the crevices of his dentures. Subsequently he pursed his mouth and swallowed something.

A boy of your age, he said at last, who gives himself up to the sin of sloth—what in God's name is going to happen to him when he goes out to face the world? Boys but I often wonder what the world is coming to, I do indeed. Tell me this, do you ever open a book at all?

I open several books every day, I answered.

You open your granny, said my uncle. O I know the game you are at above in your bedroom. I am not as stupid as I look, I'll warrant you that.

He got up from the table and went out to the hall, sending back his voice to annoy me in his absence.

Tell me this, did you press my Sunday trousers?

I forgot, I said.

What?

I forgot, I shouted.

Well that is very nice, he called, very nice indeed. Oh, trust you to forget. God look down on us and pity us this night and day. Will you forget again to-day?

13

Contrast between narrative voice & uncle's voice

No, I answered.

As he opened the hall-door, he was saying to himself in a low tone:

Lord save us!

The slam of the door released me from my anger. I finished my collation and retired to my bedroom, standing for a time at the window and observing the street-scene arranged below me that morning. Rain was coming softly from the low sky. I lit my cigarette and then took my letter from my pocket, opened it and read it.

Mail from V. Wright, Wyvern Cottage, Newmarket, Suffolk. V. Wright, the backer's friend. Dear Friend and member. Thanks for your faith in me, it is very comforting to know that I have clients who are sportsmen who do not lose heart when the luck is "the wrong way." Bounty Queen was indeed a great disappointment tho' many were of opinion that she had dead-heated with the leaders but more of that anon. Considering I have been posting information from the same address since 1926, anybody leaving me now because of bad luck would indeed be a "puzzler." You had the losers why not "row in" and make a packet over the winners that are now our due. So much for the past now for the future. SENSATIONAL NEWS has reached me that certain interests have planned a gigantic coup involving a certain animal who has been saved for the past month. INFORMATION from the RIGHT QUARTER notifies me that a sum of £5,000 at least will be wagered. The animal in question will be slipped at the right moment with the right man up and there will be a

14

GOLDEN OPPORTUNITY to all who act "pronto" and give their bookmaker the shock of his life. To all my friends forwarding 6d. and two S.A.E.'s I will present this THREE-STAR CAST-IRON PLUNGER and we will have the win of our lives and all the bad luck forgotten. We will feel "bucked" when this animal flashes past the post at a fancy price. This will be my only treble nap for the week and old friends will know that my STRICTLY OCCA-SIONAL LETTERS are always "the goods". Act now! Yours in sport and best of luck together, V. Wright. Order Form. To V. Wright, Turf Correspondent, Wyvern Cottage, Newmarket, Suffolk. Herewith please find P.O. for £   s.   d. and hoping to obtain by return your exclusive three-star Plunger for Thursday and I hereby promise to remit the odds thereon to one shilling. Name. Address. No business transacted with minors or persons at College. P.S. The above will be the business, have the win of your life. Yours, Verney.

I put the letter with care into a pocket at my right buttock and went to the tender trestle of my bed, arrang-ing my back upon it in an indolent horizontal attitude. I closed my eyes, hurting slightly my right stye, and retired into the kingdom of my mind. For a time there was complete darkness and an absence of movement on the part of the cerebral mechanism. The bright square of the window was faintly evidenced at the juncture of my lids. One book, one opening, was a principle with which I did not find it possible to concur. After an interval Finn Mac Cool, a hero of old Ireland, came out before me from his shadow, Finn the wide-hammed, the heavy-eyed, Finn that could spend a Lammas morning with girdled girls at far-from-simple chess-play.

Extract from my typescript descriptive of Finn Mac Cool and his people, being humorous or quasi-humorous incursion into ancient mythology: Of the musics you have ever got, asked Conán, which have you found the sweetest?

I will relate, said Finn. When the seven companies of my warriors are gathered together on the one plain and the truant clean-cold loud-voiced wind goes through them, too sweet to me is that. Echo-blow of a goblet-base against the tables of the palace, sweet to me is that. I like gull-cries and the twittering together of fine cranes. I like the surf-roar at Tralee, the songs of the three sons of Meadhra and the whistle of Mac Lughaidh. These also please me, man-shouts at a parting, cuckoo-call in May. I incline to like pig-grunting in Magh Eithne, the bellowing of the stag of Ceara, the whinging of fauns in Derrynish. The low warble of water-owls in Loch Barra also, sweeter than life that. I am fond of wing-beating in dark belfries, cow-cries in pregnancy, trout-spurt in a lake-top. Also the whining of small otters in nettle-beds at evening, the croaking of small-jays behind a wall, these are heart-pleasing. I am friend to the pilibeen, the red-necked chough, the parsnip land-rail, the pilibeen móna, the bottle-tailed tit, the common marsh-coot, the speckle-toed guillemot, the pilibeen sléibhe, the Mohar gannet, the peregrine plough-gull, the long-eared bush-owl, the Wicklow small-fowl, the bevil-beaked chough, the hooded tit, the pilibeen uisce, the common corby, the fish-tailed mud-piper, the crúiskeen lawn, the carrion sea-cock, the green-lidded parakeet, the brown bog-martin, the maritime wren, the dove-tailed wheatcrake, the beaded daw, the Galway hill-bantam and the pilibeen cathrach. A satisfying ululation is the contending of a river with the sea. Good to hear is the chirping of little red-breasted men in bare winter and distant hounds giving tongue in the secrecy of fog. The lamenting of a wounded otter in a black hole, sweeter than harpstrings that. There is no torture so narrow as to be bound and beset in a dark cavern without food or music, without the bestowing of gold on bards. To be chained by night in a dark pit without company of chessmen—evil destiny! Soothing to my ear is the shout of a hidden blackbird, the squeal of a troubled mare, the complaining of wild-hogs caught in snow.

Relate further for us, said Conán.

It is true that I will not, said Finn.

With that he rose to a full tree-high standing, the sable cat-guts which held his bog-cloth drawers to the hems of his jacket of pleated fustian clanging together in melodious discourse. Too great was he for standing. The neck to him was as the bole of a great oak, knotted and seized together with muscle-humps and carbuncles of tangled sinew, the better for good feasting and contending with the bards. The chest to him was wider than the poles of a good chariot, coming now out, now in, and pastured from chin to navel with meadows of black man-hair and meated with layers of fine man-meat the

17

better to hide his bones and fashion the semblance of his
twin bubs. The arms to him were like the necks of beasts,
ball-swollen with their bunched-up brawnstrings and
blood-veins, the better for harping and hunting and contending with the bards. Each thigh to him was to the
thickness of a horse's belly, narrowing to a green-veined
calf to the thickness of a foal. Three fifties of fosterlings
could engage with handball against the wideness of his
backside, which was wide enough to halt the march of
warriors through a mountain-pass.

> I am a bark for buffeting, said Finn,
> I am a hound for thornypaws.
> I am a doe for swiftness.
> I am a tree for wind-siege.
> I am a windmill.
> I am a hole in a wall.

On the seat of the bog-cloth drawers to his fork was
shuttled the green alchemy of mountain-leeks from Slieve
an Iarainn in the middle of Erin; for it was here that he
would hunt for a part of the year with his people, piercing
the hams of a black hog with his spears, birds-nesting, hole-
drawing, vanishing into the fog of a small gully, sitting on
green knolls with Fergus and watching the boys at ball-
throw.

On the kerseymere of the gutted jacket to his back
was the dark tincture of the ivory sloes and the pubic
gooseberries and the manivaried whortles of the ditches
of the east of Erin; for it was here that he would spend a
part of the year with his people, courting and rummaging

generous women, vibrating quick spears at the old stag
of Slieve Gullian, hog-baiting in thickets and engaging
in sapient dialectics with the bag-eyed brehons.

The knees and calves to him, swealed and swathed
with soogawns and Thomond weed-ropes, were smutted
with dungs and dirt-daubs of every hue and pigment,
hardened by stainings of mead and trickles of metheglin
and all the dribblings and drippings of his medher, for
it was the custom of Finn to drink nightly with his
people

> I am the breast of a young queen, said Finn,
> I am a thatching against rains.
> I am a dark castle against bat-flutters.
> I am a Connachtman's ear.
> I am a harpstring.
> I am a gnat.

The nose to his white wheyface was a headland against
white seas with height to it, in all, the height of ten
warriors man on man and with breadth to it the breadth
of Erin. The caverns to the butt of his nose had fulness
and breadth for the instanding in their shade of twenty
arm-bearing warriors with their tribal rams and dove-
cages together with a generous following of ollavs and
bards with their law-books and their verse-scrolls, their
herb-pots and their alabaster firkins of oil and unguent.

Relate us further, said Diarmuid Donn, for the love of
God.

Who is it? said Finn.

It is Diarmuid Donn, said Conán, even Diarmuid

O'Diveney of Ui bhFailghe and of Cruachna Conalath in the west of Erin, it is Brown Dermot of Galway.

It is true, said Finn, that I will not.

The mouth to his white wheyface had dimensions and measurements to the width of Ulster, bordered by a red lip-wall and inhabited unseen by the watchful host of his honey-yellow teeth to the size, each with each, of a cornstack; and in the dark hollow to each tooth was there home and fulness for the sitting there of a thorny dog or for the lying there of a spear-pierced badger. To each of the two eyes in his head was there eye-hair to the fashion of a young forest, and the colour to each great eyeball was as the slaughter of a host in snow. The lid to each eye of them was limp and cheese-dun like ship-canvas in harbour at evening, enough eye-cloth to cover the whole of Erin.

Sweet to me your voice, said Caolcrodha Mac Morna, brother to sweet-worded sweet-toothed Goll from Sliabh Riabhach and Brosnacha Bladhma, relate then the attributes that are to Finn's people.

Who is it? said Finn.

It is Caolcrodha Mac Morna from Sliabh Riabhach, said Conán, it is Calecroe MacMorney from Baltinglass.

I will relate, said Finn. Till a man has accomplished twelve books of poetry, the same is not taken for want of poetry but is forced away. No man is taken till a black hole is hollowed in the world to the depth of his two oxters and he put into it to gaze from it with his lonely head and nothing to him but his shield and a stick of hazel. Then must nine warriors fly their spears at him, one with the other and together. If he be spear-holed past his shield, or spear-killed, he is not taken for want of shield-skill. No man is taken till he is run by warriors through the woods of Erin with his hair bunched-loose about him for bough-tangle and briar-twitch. Should branches disturb his hair or pull it forth like sheep-wool on a hawthorn, he is not taken but is caught and gashed. Weapon-quivering hand or twig-crackling foot at full run, neither is taken. Neck-high sticks he must pass by vaulting, knee-high sticks by stooping. With the eyelids to him stitched to the fringe of his eye-bags, he must be run by Finn's people through the bogs and the marsh-swamps of Erin with two odorous prickle-backed hogs ham-tied and asleep in the seat of his hempen drawers. If he sink beneath a peat-swamp or lose a hog, he is not accepted of Finn's people. For five days he must sit on the brow of a cold hill with twelve-pointed stag-antlers hidden in his seat, without food or music or chessmen. If he cry out or eat grass-stalks or desist from the constant recital of sweet poetry and melodious Irish, he is not taken but is wounded. When pursued by a host, he must stick a spear in the world and hide behind it and vanish in its narrow shelter or he is not taken for want of sorcery. Likewise he must hide beneath a twig, or behind a dried leaf, or under a red stone, or vanish at full speed into the seat of his hempen drawers without changing his course or abating his pace or angering the men of Erin. Two young fosterlings he must carry under the armpits to his jacket through the whole of Erin, and six arm-bearing warriors in his seat together. If he be

delivered of a warrior or a blue spear, he is not taken.
One hundred head of cattle he must accommodate with
wisdom about his person when walking all Erin, the half
about his armpits and the half about his trews, his mouth
never halting from the discoursing of sweet poetry. One
thousand rams he must sequester about his trunks with
no offence to the men of Erin, or he is unknown to Finn.
He must swiftly milk a fat cow and carry milk-pail and
cow for twenty years in the seat of his drawers. When
pursued in a chariot by the men of Erin he must dismount,
place horse and chariot in the slack of his seat and hide
behind his spear, the same being stuck upright in Erin.
Unless he accomplishes these feats, he is not wanted of
Finn. But if he do them all and be skilful, he is of Finn's
people.

What advantages are to Finn's people? asked Liagan
Luaimneach O Luachair Dheaghaidh.

Who is it? said Finn.

It is Liagan Luaimneach O Luachair Dheaghaidh, said
Conán, the third man of the three cousins from Cnoc
Sneachta, Lagan Lumley O'Lowther-Day from Elphin
Beg.

I will relate three things and nothing above three, said
Finn. Myself I can get wisdom from the sucking of my
thumb, another (though he knows it not) can bring to
defeat a host by viewing it through his fingers, and another
can cure a sick warrior by judging the smoke of the house
in which he is.

Wonderful for telling, said Conán, and I know it.
Relate for us, after, the tale of the feast of Bricriú.

I cannot make it, said Finn.

Then the tale of the Bull of Cooley.

It goes beyond me, said Finn, I cannot make it.

Then the tale of the Giolla Deacar and his old horse of the world, said Gearr mac Aonchearda.

Who is it? said Finn.

Surely it is Gearr mac Aonchearda, said Conán, the middle man of the three brothers from Cruach Conite, Gar MacEncarty O'Hussey from Phillipstown.

I cannot make it, said Finn.

Recount then for the love of God, said Conán, the Tale of the Enchanted Fort of the Sally Tree or give shanachy's tidings of the Little Brawl at Allen.

They go above me and around me and through me, said Finn. It is true that I cannot make them.

Oh then, said Conán, the story of the Churl in the Puce Great-coat.

Evil story for telling, that, said Finn, and though itself I can make it, it is surely true that I will not recount it. It is a crooked and dishonourable story that tells how Finn spoke honey-words and peace-words to a stranger who came seeking the high-rule and the high-rent of this kingdom and saying that he would play the sorrow of death and small-life on the lot of us in one single day if his wish was not given. Surely I have never heard (nor have I seen) a man come with high-deed the like of that to Erin that there was not found for him a man of his own equality. Who has heard honey-talk from Finn before strangers, Finn that is wind-quick, Finn that is a better man than God? Or who has seen the like of

Finn or seen the living semblance of him standing in the
world, Finn that could best God at ball-throw or wrestling
or pig-trailing or at the honeyed discourse of sweet Irish
with jewels and gold for bards, or at the listening of
distant harpers in a black hole at evening? Or where is
the living human man who could beat Finn at the making
of generous cheese, at the spearing of ganders, at the
magic of thumb-suck, at the shaving of hog-hair, or at the
unleashing of long hounds from a golden thong in the
full chase, sweet-fingered corn-yellow Finn, Finn that
could carry an armed host from Almha to Slieve Luachra
in the craw of his gut-hung knickers.

Good for telling, said Conan.

Who is it? said Finn.

It is I, said Conán.

I believe it for truth, said Finn.

Relate further then.

I am an Ulsterman, a Connachtman, a Greek, said Finn,
I am Cuchulainn, I am Patrick.
I am Carbery-Cathead, I am Goll.
I am my own father and my son.
I am every hero from the crack of time.

Melodious is your voice, said Conán.

Small wonder, said Finn, that Finn is without honour
in the breast of a sea-blue book, Finn that is twisted and
trampled and tortured for the weaving of a story-teller's
book-web. Who but a book-poet would dishonour the
God-big Finn for the sake of a gap-worded story? Who
could have the saint Ceallach carried off by his four acolytes

and he feeble and thin from his Lent-fast, laid in the timbers of an old boat, hidden for a night in a hollow oak tree and slaughtered without mercy in the morning, his shrivelled body to be torn by a wolf and a scaldcrow and the Kite of Cluain-Eo? Who could think to turn the children of a king into white swans with the loss of their own bodies, to be swimming the two seas of Erin in snow and ice-cold rain without bards or chess-boards, without their own tongues for discoursing melodious Irish, changing the fat white legs of a maiden into plumes and troubling her body with shameful eggs? Who could put a terrible madness on the head of Sweeney for the slaughter of a single Lent-gaunt cleric, to make him live in tree-tops and roost in the middle of a yew, not a wattle to the shielding of his mad head in the middle of the wet winter, perished to the marrow without company of women or strains of harp-pluck, with no feeding but stag-food and the green branches? Who but a story-teller? Indeed, it is true that there has been ill-usage to the men of Erin from the book-poets of the world and dishonour to Finn, with no knowing the nearness of disgrace or the sorrow of death, or the hour when they may swim for swans or trot for ponies or bell for stags or croak for frogs or fester for the wounds on a man's back.

True for telling, said Conán.

Conclusion of the foregoing.

Biographical reminiscence, part the first: It was only a few months before composing the foregoing that I had my first experience of intoxicating beverages and their strange intestinal chemistry. I was walking through the Stephen's Green on a summer evening and conducting a conversation with a man called Kelly, then a student, hitherto a member of the farming class and now a private in the armed forces of the King. He was addicted to unclean expressions in ordinary conversation and spat continually, always fouling the flowerbeds on his way through the Green with a mucous deposit dislodged with a low grunting from the interior of his windpipe. In some respects he was a coarse man but he was lacking in malice or ill-humour. He purported to be a medical student but he had failed at least once to satisfy a body of examiners charged with regulating admission to the faculty. He suggested that we should drink a number of *jars* or pints of plain porter in Grogan's public house. I derived considerable pleasure from the casual quality of his suggestion and observed that it would probably do us no harm, thus expressing my whole-hearted concurrence by a figure of speech.

Name of figure of speech: Litotes (or Meiosis).

He turned to me with a facetious wry expression and showed me a penny and a sixpence in his rough hand.

I'm thirsty, he said. I have sevenpence. Therefore I buy a pint.

I immediately recognized this as an intimation that I should pay for my own porter.

The conclusion of your syllogism, I said lightly, is fallacious, being based on licensed premises.

Licensed premises is right, he replied, spitting heavily.

26

I saw that my witticism was unperceived and quietly replaced it in the treasury of my mind.

We sat in Grogan's with our faded overcoats finely disarrayed on easy chairs in the mullioned snug. I gave a shilling and two pennies to a civil man who brought us in return two glasses of black porter, imperial pint measure. I adjusted the glasses to the front of each of us and reflected on the solemnity of the occasion. It was my first taste of porter. Innumerable persons with whom I had conversed had represented to me that spirituous liquors and intoxicants generally had an adverse effect on the senses and the body and that those who became addicted to stimulants in youth were unhappy throughout their lives and met with death at the end by a drunkard's fall, expiring ingloriously at the stair-bottom in a welter of blood and puke. Indian tonic-waters had been proposed to me by an aged lay-brother as an incomparable specific for thirst. The importance of the subject had been impressed upon me in a school-book which I read at the age of twelve.

Extract from Literary Reader, the Higher Class, by the Irish Christian Brothers: And in the flowers that wreathe the sparkling bowl, fell adders hiss and poisonous serpents roll—Prior. What is alcohol? All medical authorities tell us it is a double poison—an irritant and a narcotic poison. As an irritant it excites the brain, quickens the action of the heart, produces intoxication and leads to degeneration of the tissues. As a narcotic, it chiefly affects the nervous system; blunts the sensibility of the brain, spinal cord and nerves; and when taken in sufficient quantity, produces death. When alcohol is taken into the system, an extra amount of work is thrown on various organs, particularly the lungs. The lungs, being overtaxed, become degenerated, and this is why so many inebriates suffer from a peculiar form of consumption called alcoholic phthisis—many, many cases of which are, alas, to be found in our hospitals, where the unhappy victims await the slow but sure march of an early death. It is a well-established fact that alcohol not only does not give strength but lessens it. It relaxes the muscles or instruments of motion and consequently their power decreases. This muscular depression is often followed by complete paralysis of the body, drink having unstrung the whole nervous system, which, when so unstrung leaves the body like a ship without sails or ropes—an unmovable or unmanageable thing. Alcohol may have its uses in the medical world, to which it should be relegated; but once a man becomes its victim, it is a terrible and a merciless master, and he finds himself in that dreadful state when all will-power is gone and he becomes a helpless imbecile, tortured at times by remorse and despair. Conclusion of the foregoing.

On the other hand, young men of my acquaintance who were in the habit of voluntarily placing themselves under the influence of alcohol had often surprised me with a recital of their strange adventures. The mind may be impaired by alcohol, I mused, but withal it may be pleasantly impaired. Personal experience appeared to me to be the only satisfactory means to the resolution of my doubts. Knowing it was my first one, I quietly fingered the butt of my glass before I raised it. Lightly I subjected myself to an inward interrogation.

Nature of interrogation: Who are my future cronies, where our mad carousals? What neat repast shall feast us light and choice of Attic taste with wine whence we may rise to hear the lute well touched or artful voice warble immortal notes or Tuscan air? What mad pursuit? What pipes and timbrels? What wild ecstasy?

steal from romantic poets - keats?

Here's to your health, said Kelly.
Good luck, I said.
The porter was sour to the palate but viscid, potent. Kelly made a long noise as if releasing air from his interior.
I looked at him from the corner of my eye and said:
You can't beat a good pint.
He leaned over and put his face close to me in an earnest manner.
Do you know what I am going to tell you, he said with his wry mouth, a pint of plain is your only man.
Notwithstanding this eulogy, I soon found that the mass of plain porter bears an unsatisfactory relation to its toxic content and I became subsequently addicted to brown stout in bottle, a drink which still remains the one that I prefer the most despite the painful and blinding fits of vomiting which a plurality of bottles has often induced in me.
I proceeded home one evening in October after leaving a gallon of half-digested porter on the floor of a public-

house in Parnell Street and put myself with considerable difficulty into bed, where I remained for three days on the pretence of a chill. I was compelled to secrete my suit beneath the mattress because it was offensive to at least two of the senses and bore an explanation of my illness contrary to that already advanced.

The two senses referred to: Vision, smell.

On the evening of the third day, a friend of mine, Brinsley, was admitted to my chamber. He bore miscellaneous books and papers. I complained on the subject of my health and ascertained from him that the weather was inimical to the well-being of invalids. . . . He remarked that there was a queer smell in the room.

Description of my friend: Thin, dark-haired, hesitant; an intellectual Meath-man; given to close-knit epigrammatic talk; weak-chested, pale.

I opened wide my windpipe and made a coarse noise unassociated with the usages of gentlemen.

I feel very bad, I said.

By God you're the queer bloody man, he said.

I was down in Parnell Street, I said, with the Shader Ward, the two of us drinking pints. Well, whatever happened me, I started to puke and I puked till the eyes nearly left my head. I made a right haimes of my suit. I puked till I puked air.

Is that the way of it? said Brinsley.

Look at here, I said.

I arose in my bed, my body on the prop of an elbow.

I was talking to the Shader, I said, talking about God and one thing and another, and suddenly I felt something inside me like a man trying to get out of my stomach. The next minute my head was in the grip of the Shader's hand and I was letting it out in great style. O Lord save us. . . .

Here Brinsley interposed a laugh.

I thought my stomach was on the floor, I said. Take it easy, says the Shader, you'll be better when you get that off. Better? How I got home at all I couldn't tell you.

Well you did get home, said Brinsley.

I withdrew my elbow and fell back again as if exhausted by my effort. My talk had been forced, couched in the accent of the lower or working classes. Under the cover of the bed-clothes I poked idly with a pencil at my navel. Brinsley was at the window giving chuckles out.

Nature of chuckles: Quiet, private, averted.

What are you laughing at? I said.

You and your book and your porter, he answered.

Did you read that stuff about Finn, I said, that stuff I gave you?

Oh, yes, he said, that was the pig's whiskers. That was funny all right.

This I found a pleasing eulogy. The God-big Finn. Brinsley turned from the window and asked me for a cigarette. I took out my "butt" or half-spent cigarette and showed it in the hollow of my hand.

That is all I have, I said, affecting a pathos in my voice.

By God you're the queer bloody man, he said.

He then brought from his own pocket a box of the twenty denomination, lighting one for each of us.

There are two ways to make big money, he said, to write a book or to make a book.

It happened that this remark provoked between us a discussion on the subject of Literature—great authors living and dead, the character of modern poetry, the predilections of publishers and the importance of being at all times occupied with literary activities of a spare-time or recreative character. My dim room rang with the iron of fine words and the names of great Russian masters were articulated with fastidious intonation. Witticisms were canvassed, depending for their utility on a knowledge of the French language as spoken in the medieval times. Psycho-analysis was mentioned—with, however, a somewhat light touch. I then tendered an explanation spontaneous and unsolicited concerning my own work, affording an insight as to its aesthetic, its daemon, its argument, its sorrow and its joy, its darkness, its sun-twinkle clearness.

Nature of explanation offered: It was stated that while the novel and the play were both pleasing intellectual exercises, the novel was inferior to the play inasmuch as it lacked the outward accidents of illusion, frequently inducing the reader to be outwitted in a shabby fashion and caused to experience a real concern for the fortunes of illusory characters. The play was consumed in wholesome fashion by large masses in places of public resort; the novel was self-administered in private. The novel,

32

in the hands of an unscrupulous writer, could be despotic. In reply to an inquiry, it was explained that a satisfactory novel should be a self-evident sham to which the reader could regulate at will the degree of his credulity. It was undemocratic to compel characters to be uniformly good or bad or poor or rich. Each should be allowed a private life, self-determination and a decent standard of living. This would make for self-respect, contentment and better service. It would be incorrect to say that it would lead to chaos. Characters should be interchangeable as between one book and another. The entire corpus of existing literature should be regarded as a limbo from which discerning authors could draw their characters as required, creating only when they failed to find a suitable existing puppet. The modern novel should be largely a work of reference. Most authors spend their time saying what has been said before—usually said much better. A wealth of references to existing works would acquaint the reader instantaneously with the nature of each character, would obviate tiresome explanations and would effectively preclude mountebanks, upstarts, thimbleriggers and persons of inferior education from an understanding of contemporary literature. Conclusion of explanation.

That is all my bum, said Brinsley.

But taking precise typescript from beneath the book that was at my side, I explained to him my literary intentions in considerable detail—now reading, now discoursing, oratio recta and oratio obliqua.

Extract from Manuscript as to nature of Red Swan premises,

oratio recta: The Red Swan premises in Lower Leeson Street
are held in fee farm, the landlord whosoever being pledged
to maintain the narrow lane which marks its eastern boun-
dary unimpeded and free from nuisance for a distance of
seventeen yards, that is, up to the intersection of Peter
Place. New Paragraph. A terminus of the Cornelscourt
coach in the seventeenth century, the hotel was rebuilt
in 1712 and afterwards fired by the yeomanry for reasons
which must be sought in the quiet of its ruined garden,
on the three-perch stretch that goes by Croppies' Acre.
To-day, it is a large building of four stories. The title is
worked in snow-white letters along the circumference
of the fanlight and the centre of the circle is concerned
with the delicate image of a red swan, pleasingly conceived and carried out by a casting process in Birmingham
delf. Conclusion of the foregoing.

*Further extract descriptive of Dermot Trellis rated occupier
of the Red Swan Hotel, oratio recta*: Dermot Trellis was a
man of average stature but his person was flabby and
unattractive, partly a result of his having remained in bed
for a period of twenty years. He was voluntarily bed-
ridden and suffered from no organic or other illness. He
occasionally rose for very brief periods in the evening to
pad about the empty house in his felt slippers or to interview the slavey in the kitchen on the subject of his food
or bedclothes. He had lost all physical reaction to bad
or good weather and was accustomed to trace the seasonal
changes of the year by inactivity or virulence of his
pimples. His legs were puffed and affected with a prickly

heat, a result of wearing his woollen undertrunks in bed. He never went out and rarely approached the windows.

Tour de force by Brinsley, vocally interjected, being a comparable description in the Finn canon: The neck to Trellis is house-thick and house-rough and is guarded by night and day against the coming of enemies by his old watchful boil. His bottom is the stern of a sea-blue schooner, his stomach is its mainsail with a filling of wind. His face is a snowfall on old mountains, the feet are fields.

There was an interruption, I recall, at this stage. My uncle put his head through the door and looked at me in a severe manner, his face flushed from walking and an evening paper in his hand. He was about to address me when he perceived the shadow of Brinsley by the window.

Well, well, he said. He came in in a genial noisy manner, closed the door with vigour and peered at the form of Brinsley. Brinsley took his hands from his pockets and smiled without reason in the twilight.

Good evening to you, gentlemen, said my uncle.

Good evening, said Brinsley.

This is Mr. Brinsley, a friend of mine, I said, raising my shoulders feebly from the bed. I gave a low moan of exhaustion.

My uncle extended an honest hand in the grip of friendship.

Ah, Mr. Brinsley, how do you do? he said. How do you do, Sir? You are a University man, Mr. Brinsley?

Oh, yes.

Ah, very good, said my uncle. It's a grand thing, that
—a thing that will stand to you. It is certainly. A good
degree is a very nice thing to have. Are the masters hard
to please, Mr. Brinsley?

Well, no. As a matter of fact they don't care very
much.

Do you tell me so! Well it was a different tale in the
old days. The old schoolmasters believed in the big stick.
Oh, plenty of that boyo.

He gave a laugh here in which we concurred without
emotion.

The stick was mightier than the pen, he added, laughing again in a louder way and relapsing into a quiet chuckle.
He paused for a brief interval as if examining something
hitherto overlooked in the interior of his memory.

And how is our friend? he inquired in the direction of
my bed.

Nature of my reply: Civil, perfunctory, uninformative.

My uncle leaned over towards Brinsley and said to him
in a low, confidential manner:

Do you know what I am going to tell you, there is a
very catching cold going around. Every second man you
meet has got a cold. God preserve us, there will be plenty
of 'flu before the winter's out, make no mistake about
that. You would need to keep yourself well wrapped up.

As a matter of fact, said Brinsley in a crafty way, I have
only just recovered from a cold myself.

You would need to keep yourself well wrapped up,
rejoined my uncle, you would, faith.

Here there was a pause, each of us searching for a word with which it might be broken.

Tell me this, Mr. Brinsley, said my uncle, are you going to be a doctor?

I am not, said Brinsley.

Or a schoolmaster?

Here I interposed a shaft from my bed.

He hopes to get a job from the Christian Brothers, I said, when he gets his B.A.

That would be a great thing, said my uncle. The Brothers, of course, are very particular about the boys they take. You must have a good record, a clean sheet.

Well I have that, said Brinsley.

Of course you have, said my uncle. But doctoring and teaching are two jobs that call for great application and love of God. For what is the love of God but the love of your neighbour?

He sought agreement from each of us in turn, reverting a second to Brinsley with his ocular inquiry.

It is a grand and a noble life, he said, teaching the young and the sick and nursing them back to their God-given health. It is, faith. There is a special crown for those that give themselves up to that work.

It is a hard life, but, said Brinsley.

A hard life? said my uncle. Certainly so, but tell me this: Is it worth your while?

Brinsley gave a nod.

Worth your while and well worth it, said my uncle. A special crown is a thing that is not offered every day of the week. Oh, it's a grand thing, a grand life. Doctoring and teaching, the two of them are marked out for special graces and blessings.

He mused for a while, staring at the smoke of his cigarette. He then looked up and laughed, clapping his hand on the top of the washstand.

But long faces, he said, long faces won't get any of us very far. Eh, Mr. Brinsley? I am a great believer in the smile and the happy word.

A sovereign remedy for all our ills, said Brinsley.

A sovereign remedy for all our ills, said my uncle. Very nicely put. Well . . .

He held out a hand in valediction.

Mind yourself now, he said, and mind and keep the coat buttoned up. The 'flu is the boy I'd give the slip to.

He was civilly replied to. He left the room with a pleased smile but was not gone for three seconds till he was back again with a grave look, coming upon us suddenly in the moment of our relaxation and relief.

Oh, that matter of the Brothers, he said in a low tone to Brinsley, would you care for me to put in a word for you?

Thanks very much, said Brinsley, but——

No trouble at all, said my uncle. Brother Hanley, late of Richmond Street, he is a very special friend of mine. No question of pulling strings, you know. Just a private word in his ear. He is a special friend.

Well, that is very good of you, said Brinsley.

Oh, not in the least, said my uncle. There is a way of doing things, you understand. It is a great thing to have a friend in court. And Brother Hanley, I may tell you privately, is one of the best—Oh, one of the very best in the world. It would be a pleasure to work with a man like Brother Hanley. I will have a word with him to-morrow.

The only thing is, but, said Brinsley, it will be some time before I am qualified and get my parchment.

Never mind, said my uncle, it is always well to be in early. First come, first called.

At this point he assembled his features into an expression of extreme secrecy and responsibility:

The Order, of course, is always on the look-out for boys of education and character. Tell me this, Mr. Brinsley, have you ever . . .

I never thought of that, said Brinsley in surprise.

Do you think would the religious life appeal to you?

I'm afraid I never thought much about it.

Brinsley's tone was of a forced texture as if he were labouring in the stress of some emotion.

It is a good healthy life and a special crown at the end of it, said my uncle. Every boy should consider it very carefully before he decides to remain out in the world. He should pray to God for a vocation.

Not everybody is called, I ventured from the bed.

Not everybody is called, agreed my uncle, perfectly true. Only a small and a select band.

Perceiving then that the statement had come from me, he looked sharply in the direction of my corner as if to verify the honesty of my face. He turned back to Brinsley.

I want you to make me a promise, Mr. Brinsley, he said. Will you promise me that you will think about it?

I will certainly, said Brinsley.

My uncle smiled warmly and held out a hand.

Good, he said. God bless you.

Description of my uncle: Rat-brained, cunning, concerned-that-he-should-be-well-thought-of. Abounding in pretence, deceit. Holder of Guinness clerkship the third class.

In a moment he was gone, this time without return. Brinsley, a shadow by the window, performed perfunctorily the movements of a mime, making at the same time a pious ejaculation.

Nature of mime and ejaculation: Removal of sweat from brow; holy God.

I hope, said Brinsley, that Trellis is not a replica of the uncle.

I did not answer but reached a hand to the mantelpiece and took down the twenty-first volume of my *Conspectus of the Arts and Natural Sciences*. Opening it, I read a passage which I subsequently embodied in my manuscript as being suitable for my purpose. The passage had in fact reference to Doctor Beatty (now with God) but boldly I took it for my own.

Extract from "A Conspectus of the Arts and Natural Sciences," being a further description of Trellis's person, and with a reference to a failing: In person he was of the middle size, of a broad square make, which seemed to indicate a more robust constitution than he really possessed. In his gait there was something of a slouch. During his later years he grew corpulent and unwieldy; his features were very regular and his complexion somewhat high. His eyes were black, brilliant, full of a tender and melancholy expression, and, in the course of conversation with his friends, became extremely animated. It is with regret that it is found expedient to touch upon a reported failing of so great a man. It has been asserted that towards the close of his life he indulged to excess in the use of wine. In a letter to Mr. Arbuthnot he says: With the present pressure upon my mind, I should not be able to sleep if I did not use wine as an opiate; it is less hurtful than laudanum but not so effectual. Conclusion of extract from letter to Mr. Arbuthnot. He may, perhaps, have had too frequent a recourse to so palatable a medicine, in the hope of banishing for a time the recollection of his sorrows; and if, under any circumstances, such a fault is to be regarded as venial, it may be excused in one who was a more than widowed husband and a childless father. Some years after his son's death, he occupied himself in the melancholy yet pleasing task of editing a volume of the compositions of the deceased. From a pardonable partiality for the writings of a beloved child, and from his own not very accurate attainments in classical scholarship, he admitted into the collection several pieces, both English and Latin, which fall considerably below mediocrity. A few copies of the work were privately printed and offered as presents to those friends with whom the author was particularly acquainted. Conclusion of extract.

Further extract from my Manuscript, descriptive. Oratio recta: Trellis stirred feebly in his room in the stillness of

41

the second floor. He frowned to himself quietly in the gloom, flickering his heavy lids and wrinkling his brow into pimpled corrugations. He twitched with his thick fingers at the quilts.

His bed was a timber article of great age in which many of his forefathers had died and been born; it was delicately made and embellished with delicately carved cornices. It was of Italian manufacture, an early excursion of the genius of the great Stradivari. On one side of it was a small table with books and type-darkened papers and on the other a cabinet containing two chambers. Also there was a deal wardrobe and two chairs. On the window-ledge there was a small bakelite clock which grappled with each new day as it entered his room through the window from Peter Place, arranging it with precision into twenty-four hours. It was quiet, servile and emasculated; its twin alarming gongs could be found if looked for behind the dust-laden books on the mantelpiece.

Trellis had three separate suits of sleeping-clothes and was accustomed to be extremely fastidious as to the manner in which they were washed. He supervised the weekly wash, which was carried out by his servant-girl on Tuesdays.

A Tuesday evening at the Red Swan, example of: In the darkness of the early night Trellis arose from his bed and drew a trousers over the bulging exuberance of his night-clothes, swaying on his white worthless legs.

Nature of trousers: Narrow-legged, out-moded, the pre-War class.

He groped for his slippers and went out to the dark stairs, stretching an arm for guidance to the banister. He reached the hall-way and continued towards the dark stone stairs to the basement, peering before him with apprehension. Strong basement smells assailed his nostrils, the odours of a washerwoman's fete from a kitchen beflagged with the steamy bunting of underclothes drying. He entered and looked about him from the door. The ceiling was decked with the rectangular banners of his long-tailed shirts, the ensigns of his sheets, the flags of his bed-bibs, the great buff pennants of his drawers.

The figure of Teresa was visible at the stove, her thick thighs presented to the penetration of the fire. She was a stout girl of high colour, attired in grey and divided at the centre by the terminal ridge of a corset of inferior design.

Interjection on the part of Brinsley: He commented at some length on the similarity between the ridge referred to and the moulding-ridge which circumscribed the image of the red swan in the fanlight. Both ridges he advanced as the ineluctable badge of mass-production. Slaveys, he considered, were the Ford cars of humanity; they were created to a standard pattern by the hundred thousand. But they were grand girls and there was nothing he liked better, he said.

Penultimum, continued: Trellis examined his wools with appraising fingers, turning them tenderly in his hands.

Nature of wools: Soft, lacked chafing hardness.

He smiled gratefully on his servant and laboured back to his bedroom, reflectively passing a hand across the pimples of his face. Fearing his bed would cool, he hastened past the emptiness of the hall, where a handsome girl stood poised without her clothes on the brink of a blue river. Napoleon peered at her in a wanton fashion from the dark of the other wall.

Biographical reminiscence, part the second: Some days later I said to my uncle in the morning at breakfast-time:

Could you give me five shillings to buy a book, please?

Five shillings? Well, dear knows it must be a great book altogether that can cost five shillings. What do they call it?

Die Harzreise by Heine, I answered.

Dee . . . ?

Die Harzreise, a German book.

I see, he said.

His head was bent, his two eyes engaged on a meticulous observation of the activities of his knife and fork as they dissected between them a fried haddock. Suddenly disengaging his right hand, he dipped in his waistcoat and put two half-crowns on the table-cloth.

After a time, he said:

So long as the book is used, well and good. So long as it is read and studied, well and good.

The redness of his fingers as he handed out his coins, his occupation with feeding for the nourishment of his body, these were two things that revealed for an instant

44

his equal humanity. I left him there, going quickly to the street in my grey coat and bending forward through the cold rain to the College.

Description of College: The College is outwardly a rectangular plain building with a fine porch where the mid-day sun pours down in summer from the Donnybrook direction, heating the steps for the comfort of the students, The hallway inside is composed of large black and white squares arranged in the orthodox chessboard pattern, and the surrounding walls, done in an unpretentious cream wash, bear three rough smudges caused by the heels, buttocks and shoulders of the students.

The hall was crowded by students, some of them deporting themselves in a quiet civil manner. Modest girls bearing books filed in and out in the channels formed by the groups of boys. There was a hum of converse and much bustle and activity. A liveried attendant came out of a small office in the wall and pealed a shrill bell. This caused some dispersal, many of the boys extinguishing their cigarettes by manual manipulation and going up a circular stairway to the lecture-halls in a brave, arrogant way, some stopping on the stairs to call back to those still below a message of facetious or obscene import.

I perused a number of public notices attached to the wall and then made my way without offence to the back of the College, where there was another old ruined College containing an apartment known as the Gentlemen's Smoke-room. This room was usually occupied by card-players, hooligans and rough persons. Once they made an attempt to fire the complete building by igniting a number of arm-chairs and cane stools, but the attempt was foiled by reason of the dampness of the season—it was October—and the intervention of the porters.

I sat alone in a retired corner in the cold, closely wrapping the feeble citadel of my body with my grey coat. Through the two apertures of my eyes I gazed out in a hostile manner. Strong country boys were planking down cards and coins and roaring out the name of God. Occasionally there was a sudden burst of horseplay, scuffling and kicking, and a chair or a man would crash across the floor. Newspapers were widely read and notices posted on the wall were being torn down or altered by deletion of words or letters so as to impart to them an obscene or facetious import.

A friend of mine, Brinsley, came in and looked about him at the door. He came forward at my invitation and asked me to give him a cigarette. I took out my "butt" and showed it to him in the hollow of my hand.

That is all I have, I said, affecting a pathos in my voice.

By God you're the queer bloody man, he said. Are you sitting on a newspaper?

No, I said. I struck a match and lit my "butt" and also another "butt", the property of Brinsley. We smoked there together for a time. The floor was wet from foot-falls and a mist covered the high windows. Brinsley utilized an unclean expression in a random fashion and added that the weather was very bad, likening it, in fact, to a harlot.

I was talking to a friend of yours last night, I said drily.

I mean Mr. Trellis. He has bought a ream of ruled foolscap and is starting on his story. He is compelling all his characters to live with him in the Red Swan Hotel so that he can keep an eye on them and see that there is no boozing.

I see, said Brinsley.

Most of them are characters used in other books, chiefly the works of another great writer called Tracy. There is a cowboy in Room 13 and Mr. McCool, a hero of old Ireland, is on the floor above. The cellar is full of leprechauns.

What are they going to all do? asked Brinsley.

Nature of his tone: Without intent, tired, formal.

Trellis, I answered steadily, is writing a book on sin and the wages attaching thereto. He is a philosopher and a moralist. He is appalled by the spate of sexual and other crimes recorded in recent times in the newspapers—particularly in those published on Saturday night.

Nobody will read the like of that, said Brinsley.

Yes they will, I answered. Trellis wants this salutary book to be read by all. He realizes that purely a moralizing tract would not reach the public. Therefore he is putting plenty of smut into his book. There will be no less than seven indecent assaults on young girls and any amount of bad language. There will be whisky and porter for further orders.

I thought there was to be no boozing, Brinsley said.

No unauthorized boozing, I answered. Trellis has absolute control over his minions but this control is abandoned when he falls asleep. Consequently he must make sure that they are all in bed before he locks up and goes to bed himself. Now do you understand me?

You needn't shout, said Brinsley.

His book is so bad that there will be no hero, nothing but villains. The central villain will be a man of unexampled depravity, so bad that he must be created *ab ovo et initio*. A small dark man called Furriskey.

I paused to examine my story, allowing a small laugh as a just tribute. Then whipping typescript from a pocket, I read an extract quickly for his further entertainment.

Extract from Manuscript where Trellis is explaining to an unnamed listener the character of his projected labour: . . . It appeared to him that a great and a daring book—a green book—was the crying need of the hour—a book that would show the terrible cancer of sin in its true light and act as a clarion-call to torn humanity. Continuing, he said that all children were born clean and innocent. (It was not by chance that he avoided the doctrine of original sin and the theological profundities which its consideration would entail.) They grew up to be polluted by their foul environment and transformed—was not the word a feeble one!—into bawds and criminals and harpies. Evil, it seemed to him, was the most contagious of all known diseases. Put a thief among honest men and they will eventually relieve him of his watch. In his book he would present two examples of humanity—a man of great depravity and a woman of unprecedented virtue. They meet. The woman is corrupted, eventually ravished and done to death in a back lane. Presented in its own *milieu*, in the timeless conflict of grime and beauty, gold and black, sin and grace, the tale would be a moving and a salutary one. *Mens sana in corpore sano*. What a keen discernment had the old philosopher! How well he knew that the beetle was of the dunghill, the butterfly of the flower! Conclusion of extract.

Looking up in triumph, I found Brinsley standing very straight and staring at the floor, his neck bent. A newspaper, soiled and damp, was on the floor at his feet and his eyes strained narrowly at the print.

Gob I see that horse of Peacock's is going to-day, he said.

I folded my manuscript without a word and replaced it in my clothing.

Eight stone four, he said.

Listen here, he continued looking up, we'd be bloody fools if we didn't have something on this.

He stooped and peeled the paper from the floor, reading it intently.

What horse is this? I asked.

What horse? Grandchild. Peacock's horse.

Here I uttered an exclamation.

Nature of exclamation: Inarticulate, of surprise, recollection.

Wait till I show you something, I said groping in my pocket. Wait till you read this. I got this yesterday. I am in the hands of a man from Newmarket.

I handed him a letter.

Mail from V. Wright, Wyvern Cottage, Newmarket, Suffolk:
V. Wright, the Backer's Friend. Dear friend and member.
Many thanks for yours to hand. As promised I send you
my promised "good thing" which is GRANDCHILD in the
4.30 at Gatwick on Friday. Do not hesitate to plunge and
put on an extra shilling for me towards my heavy expenses.
This animal has been saved *for this race only* for the past
two months and is a certain starter, ignore newspaper
probabilities and GO IN FOR THE WIN OF YOUR LIFE. This
horse is my treble nap CAST-IRON PLUNGER for the week
—no other selection given—and I know all there is to
be known about it. Old friends will know that I do not
send "guessworks" but only STRICTLY OCCASIONAL advices
over animals already as good as past the post. Of course
I have to pay heavily for my information, each winner
costs me a packet so do not fail to remit the odds to a
"bob" promptly so as to make sure to not miss my next
CAST-IRON PLUNGER and remain permanently on my
books. Those not clear on my books by Tuesday next
will be in danger of missing *the cream of racing information*
which I expect to have available next week. So do not
hesitate to plunge to your limit on GRANDCHILD on Friday
and remit immediately after the race, on the same evening
if possible. Excuses over winners will be ignored. If
going away please do not fail to send me your new address
so as not to miss my good things. Please have a good bet
on Grandchild. Yours and best of luck together, V.
Wright. Remittance Form. To V. Wright, Wyvern
Cottage, Newmarket, Suffolk. Herewith please find P.O.
for £   s.   d. being the odds to 1/- over Grandchild

(thus 4 to 1, 4/-), and hoping to receive further winners of the same kind. Name, address.

Do you know this man? asked Brinsley.

I do not, I said.

Do you intend to back the horse?

I have no money, I answered.

Nothing at all? I have two shillings.

In the interior of my pocket I fingered the smooth disks of my book-money.

I have to buy a book to-day, I said. I got five shillings for it this morning.

The price given here, said Brinsley from the paper, is ten to one and say that's seven to one at a half-a-crown each way that's twenty-one bob. Buy your book and you have sixteen shillings change.

More by accident than by any mastery of the body, I here expressed my doubts on the proposal by the means of a noise.

Title of noise, the Greek version: πορδή.

That same afternoon I was sitting on a stool in an intoxicated condition in Grogan's licensed premises. Adjacent stools bore the forms of Brinsley and Kelly, my two true friends. The three of us were occupied in putting glasses of stout into the interior of our bodies and expressing by fine disputation the resulting sense of physical and mental well-being. In my thigh pocket I had eleven and eightpence in a weighty pendulum of mixed coins. Each of the arrayed bottles on the shelves before me, narrow or squat-bellied, bore a dull picture of the gas

bracket. Who can tell the stock of a public-house?
Many no doubt are dummies, those especially within an
arm-reach of the snug. The stout was of superior quality,
soft against the tongue but sharp upon the orifice of the
throat, softly efficient in its magical circulation through
the conduits of the body. Half to myself, I said:
Do not let us forget that I have to buy *Die Harzreise*.
Do not let us forget that.

Harzreise, said Brinsley. There is a house in Dalkey
called Heartrise.

Brinsley then put his dark chin on the cup of a palm
and leaned in thought on the counter, overlooking his
drink, gazing beyond the frontier of the world.

What about another jar? said Kelly.

Ah, Lesbia, said Brinsley. The finest thing I ever wrote.
How many kisses, Lesbia, you ask, would serve to sate
this hungry love of mine?—As many as the Libyan sands
that bask along Cyrene's shore where pine-trees wave,
where burning Jupiter's untended shrine lies near to old
King Battus' sacred grave:

Three stouts, called Kelly.

Let them be endless as the stars at night, that stare upon
the lovers in a ditch—so often would love-crazed Catullus
bite your burning lips, that prying eyes should not have
power to count, nor evil tongues bewitch, the frenzied
kisses that you gave and got.

Before we die of thirst, called Kelly, will you bring us
three more stouts. God, he said to me, it's in the desert
you'd think we were.

That's good stuff, you know, I said to Brinsley.

A picture came before my mind of the lovers at their hedge-pleasure in the pale starlight, no sound from them, his fierce mouth burying into hers.

Bloody good stuff, I said.

Kelly, invisible to my left, made a slapping noise.

The best I ever drank, he said.

As I exchanged an eye-message with Brinsley, a wheezing beggar inserted his person at my side and said:

Buy a scapular or a stud, Sir.

This interruption I did not understand. Afterwards, near Lad Lane police station a small man in black fell in with us and tapping me often about the chest, talked to me earnestly on the subject of Rousseau, a member of the French nation. He was animated, his pale features striking in the starlight and his voice going up and falling in the lilt of his argumentum. I did not understand his talk and was personally unacquainted with him. But Kelly was taking in all he said, for he stood near him, his taller head inclined in an attitude of close attention. Kelly then made a low noise and opened his mouth and covered the small man from shoulder to knee with a coating of unpleasant buff-coloured puke. Many other things happened on that night now imperfectly recorded in my memory but that incident is still very clear to me in my mind. Afterwards the small man was some distance from us in the lane, shaking his divested coat and rubbing it along the wall. He is a little man that the name of Rousseau will always recall to me. Conclusion of reminiscence.

Further extract from my Manuscript wherein Mr. Trellis

commences the writing of his story: Propped by pillows in his bed in the white light of an incandescent petrol lamp, Dermot Trellis adjusted the pimples in his forehead into a frown of deep creative import. His pencil moved slowly across the ruled paper, leaving words behind it of every size. He was engaged in the creation of John Furriskey, the villain of his tale.

Extract from Press regarding Furriskey's birth: We are in position to announce that a happy event has taken place at the Red Swan Hotel, where the proprietor, Mr. Dermot Trellis, has succeeded in encompassing the birth of a man called Furriskey. Stated to be doing "very nicely", the new arrival is about five feet eight inches in height, well-built, dark, and clean-shaven. The eyes are blue and the teeth well-formed and good, though stained somewhat by tobacco; there are two fillings in the molars of the left upperside and a cavity threatened in the left canine. The hair, black and of thick quality, is worn plastered back on the head with a straight parting from the left temple. The chest is muscular and well-developed while the legs are straight but rather short. He is very proficient mentally, having an unusually firm grasp of the Latin idiom and a knowledge of Physics extending from Boyle's Law to the Leclanche Cell and the Greasespot Photometer. He would seem to have a special aptitude for mathematics. In the course of a brief test conducted by our reporter, he solved a "cut" from an advanced chapter of Hall and Knight's Geometry and failed to be mystified by an intricate operation involving the calculus. His voice is light and pleasant, although from his fingers it is obvious that he is a heavy smoker. He is apparently not a virgin, although it is admittedly difficult to establish this attribute with certainty in the male.

Our Medical Correspondent writes:

The birth of a son in the Red Swan Hotel is a fitting tribute to the zeal and perseverance of Mr. Dermot Trellis, who has won international repute in connection with his researches into the theory of aestho-autogamy. The event may be said to crown the savant's life-work as he has at last realized his dream of producing a living mammal from an operation involving neither fertilization nor conception.

Aestho-autogamy with one unknown quantity on the male side, Mr. Trellis told me in conversation, has long been a commonplace. For fully five centuries in all parts of the world epileptic slavies have been pleading it in extenuation of uncalled-for fecundity. It is a very familiar phenomenon in literature. The elimination of conception and pregnancy, however, or the reduction of these processes to the same mysterious abstraction as that of the paternal factor in the commonplace case of unexplained maternity, has been the dream of every practising psycho-eugenist the world over. I am very happy to have been fortunate enough to bring a century of ceaseless experiment and endeavour to a triumphant conclusion. Much of the credit for Mr. Furriskey's presence on this planet to-day must go to my late friend and colleague William Tracy, whose early researches furnished me with invaluable data and largely determined the direction of my experiments. The credit for the achievement of a successful act of procreation involving two unknown quantities is as much his as mine.

This graceful reference on the part of Mr. Trellis to the late Mr. William Tracy, the eminent writer of Western romances—his *Flower o' the Prairie* is still read—is apparently directed at the latter's gallant efforts to change the monotonous and unimaginative process by which all children are invariably born young.

Many social problems of contemporary interest, he wrote in 1909, could be readily resolved if issue could be born already matured, teethed, reared, educated, and ready to essay those competitive plums which make the Civil Service and the Banks so attractive to the younger bread-winners of to-day. The process of bringing up children is a tedious anachronism in these enlightened times. Those mortifying stratagems collectively known as birth-control would become a mere memory if parents and married couples could be assured that their legitimate diversion would straightway result in finished bread-winners or marriageable daughters.

He also envisaged the day when the breeding and safe deliverance of Old Age Pensioners and other aged and infirm persons eligible for public money would transform matrimony from the sordid struggle that it often is to an adventurous business enterprise of limitless possibilities.

It is noteworthy that Mr. Tracy succeeded, after six disconcerting miscarriages, in having his own wife delivered of a middle-aged Spaniard who lived for only six weeks. A man who carried jealousy to the point of farce, the

novelist insisted that his wife and the new arrival should
occupy separate beds and use the bathroom at divergent
times. Some amusement was elicited in literary circles
by the predicament of a woman who was delivered of a son
old enough to be her father but it served to deflect
Mr. Tracy not one tittle from his dispassionate quest for
scientific truth. His acumen and pertinacity have, in fact,
become legendary in the world of psycho-eugenics. Conclusion of the foregoing.

*Shorthand Note of a cross-examination of Mr. Trellis at a
later date on the occasion of his being on trial for his life, the
birth of Furriskey being the subject of the examination referred
to:*

In what manner was he born?

He awoke as if from sleep.

His sensations?

Bewilderment, perplexity.

Are not these terms synonymous and one as a consequence
redundant?

Yes: but the terms of the inquiry postulated unsingular
information.

(At this reply ten of the judges made angry noises on
the counter with the butts of their stout-glasses. Judge
Shanahan put his head out through a door and issued
a severe warning to the witness, advising him to conduct
himself and drawing his attention to the serious penalties
which would be attendant on further impudence.)

His sensations? Is it not possible to be more precise?

It is. He was consumed by doubts as to his own identity,

as to the nature of his body and the cast of his countenance.

In what manner did he resolve these doubts?

By the sensory perception of his ten fingers.

By feeling?

Yes.

Did you write the following: Sir Francis Thumb Drake, comma, with three inquiring midshipmen and a cabin boy, comma, he dispatched in a wrinkled Mayflower across the seas of his Braille face?

I did.

I put it to you that the passage was written by Mr. Tracy and that you stole it.

No.

I put it to you that you are lying.

No.

Describe this man's conduct after he had examined his face.

He arose from his bed and examined his stomach, lower chest and legs.

What parts did he not examine?

His back, neck and head.

Can you suggest a reason for so imperfect a survey?

Yes. His vision was necessarily limited by the movement of his neck.

(At this point Judge Shanahan entered the court adjusting his dress and said: That point was exceedingly well taken. Proceed.)

Having examined his stomach, legs and lower chest, what did he do next?

He dressed.

He dressed? A suit of the latest pattern, made to measure?

No. A suit of navy-blue of the pre-War style.

With a vent behind?

Yes.

The cast-aways of your own wardrobe?

Yes.

I put it to you that your intention was purely to humiliate him.

No. By no means.

And after he was dressed in his ludicrous clothes . . .?

He spent some time searching in his room for a looking-glass or for a surface that would enable him to ascertain the character of his countenance.

You had already hidden the glass?

No. I had forgotten to provide one.

By reason of his doubts as to his personal appearance, he suffered considerable mental anguish?

It is possible.

You could have appeared to him—by magic if necessary—and explained his identity and duties to him. Why did you not perform so obvious an errand of mercy?

I do not know.

Answer the question, please.

(At this point Judge Sweeny made an angry noise with a crack of his stout-glass on the counter and retired in a hurried petulant manner from the court.)

I suppose I fell asleep.

I see. You fell asleep.

Conclusion of the foregoing.

Biographical reminiscence, part the third: The early winter in which these matters were occupying my attention was a season of unexampled severity. The prevailing wind (according to the word of Brinsley) was from the eastern point and was not infrequently saturated with a fine chilly rain. From my bed I had perceived the sodden forms of travellers lurking behind the frosted windows of the tram-tops. Morning would come slowly, decaying to twilight in the early afternoon.

A congenital disposition predisposing me to the most common of the wasting diseases—a cousin had died in Davos—had induced in me what was perhaps a disproportionate concern for pulmonary well-being; at all events I recall that I rarely left my room for the first three months of the winter except on occasions when my domestic circumstances made it necessary for me to appear casually before my uncle attired in my grey street-coat. I was, if possible, on worse terms than ever with him, my continued failure to produce for his examination a book called *Die Harzreise* being a sore point. I cannot recall that I ever quitted the four walls of the house. Alexander, who had chosen a scheme of studies similar to my own, answered with my voice at lecture roll-calls.

It was in the New Year, in February, I think, that I discovered that my person was verminous. A growing irritation in various parts of my body led me to examine my bedclothes and the discovery of lice in large numbers was the result of my researches. I was surprised and experienced also a sense of shame. I resolved at the time to make an end of my dissolute habits and composed mentally a régime of physical regeneration which included bending exercises.

One consequence of my resolve, at any rate, was that I attended at the College every day and walked through the Green and up and down the streets, conducting conversations with my acquaintances and occasionally talking with strangers on general topics.

It was my custom to go into the main hall of the College and stand with my back to one of the steam-heating devices, my faded overcoat open and my cold hostile eyes flitting about the faces that passed before me. The younger students were much in evidence, formless and ugly in adolescence; others were older, bore themselves with assurance and wore clothing of good quality. Groups would form for the purpose of disputation and dissolve again quickly. There was much foot-shuffling, chatter and noise of a general or indeterminate character. Students emerging from the confinement of an hour's lecture would grope eagerly for their cigarettes or accept one with gratitude from a friend. Clerical students from Blackrock or Rathfarnham, black clothes and bowler hats, would file past civilly and leave the building by a door opening the back where they were accustomed to leave the iron pedal-cycles. Young postulants or nuns would also pass, their eyes upon the floor and their fresh young faces dimmed in the twilight of their hoods, passing to a private cloakroom where they would spend the intervals between their lectures in meditation and pious practices. Occasion-

ally there would be a burst of horse-play and a sharp cry
from a student accidentally hurt. On wet days there
would be an unpleasant odour of dampness, an aroma of
overcoats dried by body-heat. There was a clock plainly
visible but the hours were told by a liveried attendant
who emerged from a small office in the wall and pealed a
shrill bell similar to that utilized by auctioneers and street-
criers; the bell served this purpose, that it notified
professors—distant in the web of their fine thought—that
their discourses should terminate.

One afternoon I saw the form of Brinsley bent in
converse with a small fair-haired man who was fast acquiring a reputation in the Leinster Square district on account
of the beauty of his poems and their affinity with the
high-class work of another writer, Mr. Pound, an American gentleman. The small man had an off-hand way with
him and talked with jerks. I advanced without diffidence
and learnt that his name was Donaghy. We talked together
in a polished manner, utilizing with frequency words from
the French language, discussing the primacy of America
and Ireland in contemporary letters and commenting on
the inferior work produced by writers of the English
nationality. The Holy Name was often taken, I do not
recollect with what advertence. Brinsley, whose education and maintenance was a charge on the rates of his
native county—the product of a farthing in the pound
applied for the purpose of enabling necessitous boys of
promising intellect to enjoy the benefits of University
learning—Brinsley said that he was prepared to give
myself and Donaghy a pint of stout apiece, explaining that

he had recently been paid. I rejoined that if his finances warranted such generosity, I would raise no objection, but that I (for my part) was no Rockefeller, thus utilizing a figure of speech to convey the poverty of my circumstances.

Name of figure of speech: Synecdoche (or Autonomasia).

The three of us walked slowly down to Grogan's, our three voices interplaying in scholarly disputations, our faded overcoats finely open in the glint of the winter sun.

Isn't there a queer smell off this fellow? said Brinsley, directing his inquiring face to that of Donaghy.

I sniffed at my person in mock appraisement.

You're in bad odour, said Donaghy.

Well it's not the smell of drink, I answered. What class of a smell is it?

Did you ever go into a room early in the morning, asked Brinsley, where there had been a hooley the night before, with cigars and whisky and food and crackers and women's scent? Well that's the smell. A stale spent smell.

There's a hum off yourself, I said.

We entered the tavern and ordered our dark drinks.

To convert stout into water, I said, that is a simple process. Even a child can do it, though I would not stand for giving stout to children. Is it not a pity that the art of man has not attained the secret of converting water into stout?

Donaghy gave a laugh but Brinsley restrained me from drinking by the weight of his hand upon my arm and named a proprietary brand of ale.

Did you ever taste it? he asked.

I did not, I said.

Well that crowd have the secret if you like, he said. By God I never tasted anything like it. Did *you* ever try it?

No, said Donaghy.

Keep away from it if you value your life.

Here there was a pause as we savoured the dull syrup.

We had a great feed of wine at the Inns the other night, observed Donaghy, a swell time. Wine is better than stout. Stout sticks. Wine is more grateful to the intestines, the digestive viscera, you know. Stout sticks and leaves a scum on the interior of the paunch.

Raising my glass idly to my head, I said:

If that conclusion is the result of a mental syllogism, it is fallacious, being based on licensed premises.

Two laughs in unison, these were my rewards. I frowned and drank unheedingly, savouring the dull oaten aftertaste of the stout as it lingered against my palate. Brinsley tapped me sharply on the belly.

Gob you're getting a paunch, he said.

Leave my bag alone, I answered. I protected it with my hand.

We had three drinks in all in respect of each of which Brinsley paid a sixpence without regret.

The ultimate emptors: Meath County Council, rural rating authority.

The sun was gone and the evening students—many of them teachers, elderly and bald—were hurrying towards the College through the gathering dusk on foot and on pedal-cycles. We closed our coats closely about us and stood watching and talking at the corner. We went eventually to the moving pictures, the three of us, travelling to the centre of the city in the interior of a tramcar.

The emptors: Meath County Council.

Three nights later at about eight o'clock I was alone in Nassau Street, a district frequented by the prostitute class, when I perceived a ramrod in a cloth cap on the watch at the corner of Kildare Street. As I passed I saw that the man was Kelly. Large spits were about him on the path and carriage-way. I poked him in a manner offensive to propriety and greeted his turned face with a facetious ejaculation:

How is the boy! I said.

My hard man, he answered.

I took cigarettes from my pocket and lit one for each of us, frowning. With my face averted and a hardness in my voice, I put this question in a casual manner:

Anything doing?

O God no, he said. Not at all, man. Come away for a walk somewhere.

I agreed. Purporting to be an immoral character, I accompanied him on a long walk through the environs of Irishtown, Sandymount and Sydney Parade, returning by Haddington Road and the banks of the canal.

Purpose of walk: Discovery and embracing of virgins.

We attained nothing on our walk that was relevant to the purpose thereof but we filled up the loneliness of our souls with the music of our two voices, dog-racing, betting and offences against chastity being the several subjects of our discourse. We walked many miles together on other nights on similar missions—following matrons, accosting strangers, representing to married ladies that we were their friends, and gratuitously molesting members of the public. One night we were followed in our turn by a member of the police force attired in civilian clothing. On the advice of Kelly we hid ourselves in the interior of a church until he had gone. I found that the walking was beneficial to my health.

The people who attended the College had banded themselves into many private associations, some purely cultural and some concerned with the arrangement and conduct of ball games. The cultural societies were diverse in their character and aims and measured their vitality by the number of hooligans and unprincipled persons they attracted to their deliberations. Some were devoted to English letters, some to Irish letters and some to the study and advancement of the French language. The most important was a body that met every Saturday night for the purpose of debate and disputation; its meetings, however, were availed of by many hundreds of students for shouting, horseplay, singing and the use of words, actions and gestures contrary to the usages of Christians. The society met in an old disused lecture theatre capable of accommodating the seats of about two hundred and fifty persons. Outside the theatre there was a spacious lobby or ante-room and it was here that the rough boys would gather and make their noises. One gas-jet was the means of affording light in the lobby and when a paroxysm of fighting and roaring would be at its height, the light would be extinguished as if by a supernatural or diabolic agency and the effect of the darkness in such circumstances afforded me many moments of physical and spiritual anxiety, for it seemed to me that the majority of the persons present were possessed by unclean spirits. The lighted rectangle of the doorway to the debate-hall was regarded by many persons not only as a receptacle for the foul and discordant speeches which they addressed to it, but also for many objects of a worthless nature—for example spent cigarette ends, old shoes, the hats of friends, parcels of damp horse dung, wads of soiled sacking and discarded articles of ladies' clothing not infrequently the worse for wear. Kelly on one occasion confined articles of his landlady's small-clothes in a neatly done parcel of brown paper and sent it through a friend to the visiting chairman, who opened it *coram populo* (in the presence of the assembly), and examined the articles fastidiously as if searching among them for an explanatory note, being unable to appraise their character instantaneously for two reasons, his failing sight and his station as a bachelor.

Result of overt act mentioned: Uproar and disorder.

When I attended these meetings I maintained a position where I was not personally identified, standing quietly without a word in the darkness. Conclusion of the foregoing.

Further extract from my Manuscript on the subject of Mr. Trellis's Manuscript on the subject of John Furriskey, his first steps in life and his first meeting with those who were destined to become his firm friends; the direct style: He remarked to himself that it was a nice pass when a man did not know the shape of his own face. His voice startled him. It had the accent and intonation usually associated with the Dublin lower or working classes.

He commenced to conduct an examination of the walls of the room he was in with a view to discovering which of them contained a door or other feasible means of egress. He had completed the examination of two of the walls when he experienced an unpleasant sensation embracing blindness, hysteria and a desire to vomit—the last a circumstance very complex and difficult of explanation, for in the course of his life he had never eaten. That this visitation was miraculous was soon evidenced by the appearance of a supernatural cloud or aura resembling steam in the vicinity of the fire-place. He dropped on one knee in his weakness and gazed at the long gauze-like wisps of vapour as they intermixed and thickened about the ceiling, his eyes smarting and his pores opening as a result of the dampness. He saw faces forming faintly and resolving again without perceptible delay. He heard the measured beat of a good-quality time-piece coming from the centre of the cloud and then the form of a chamber-pot was evidenced to his gaze, hanging without support and invested with a pallid and indeed ghostly aspect; it was slowly transformed as he watched it until it appeared to be the castor of a bed-leg, magnified to roughly 118 diameters. A voice came from the interior of the cloud.

Are you there, Furriskey? it asked.

Furriskey experienced the emotion of fear which distorted for a time the character of his face. He also experienced a return of his desire for enteric evacuation.

Yes, sir, he answered.

Biographical reminiscence, part the fourth: The further obtrusion of my personal affairs at this stage is unhappily not entirely fortuitous. It happens that a portion of my manuscript containing an account (in the direct style) of the words that passed between Furriskey and the voice is lost beyond retrieval. I recollect that I abstracted it from the portfolio in which I kept my writings—an article composed of two boards of stout cardboard connected by a steel spine containing a patent spring mechanism— and brought it with me one evening to the College in order that I might obtain the opinion of Brinsley as to its style and the propriety of the matters which were the subject of the discussion set out therein. In the many mental searches which I conducted subsequently in an effort to ascertain where the manuscript was mislaid in the first instance, I succeeded in recalling the circumstances of my meeting and dialogue with Brinsley with perfection of detail and event.

Attired in my grey street-coat, I entered the College in the early afternoon by the side-portal and encountered a group of four ladies in the passage to the main hall. I recall that I surmised that they were proceeding to an underground cloakroom or lavatory for the purpose of handwash or other private act. A number of male students, the majority of whom were unacquainted with me, were present in the hall in the vicinity of the steam-heaters, conversing together in low tranquil tones. I inspected the features of each but could not identify the face of Brinsley. I saw, however, a man who I knew was acquainted with him, a Mr. Kerrigan, a slim young man of moustached features usually attired in inexpensive clothing. He came forward quickly when he saw me and enunciated and answered an obscene conundrum. He then looked away and frowned, waiting intently for my laugh. I gave this without reluctance and asked where Mr. Brinsley was. Kerrigan said that he had seen him going in the direction of the billiard-hall, he (Kerrigan) then walking away from me with a strange sidewise gait and saluting in a military fashion from the distance. The billiard-hall referred to was in the basement of the building and separated by a thin wall from another hall containing gentlemen's retiring rooms. I halted at the doorway of the billiard-hall. Fifty youths were present, some moving at the conduct of their games in the murk of the tobacco smoke, a hand or a face pallidly illuminated here or there in the strong floods of light which were pouring from green containers on the flat of the tables. The majority of those present had accommodated themselves in lazy attitudes on chairs and forms and occupied themselves in an indolent inspection of the balls. Brinsley was present, eating bread from a paper in his pocket and following the play of a small friend called Morris with close attention, making comments of a derisive or facetious character.

As I advanced, he hailed me, utilizing a gesture for the purpose. He chewed thickly, pointing to the play. The craft of billiards was unfamiliar to me but in politeness I watched the quick darting of the balls, endeavouring to deduce from the results of a stroke the intentions which preceded it.

Gob, *there's* a kiss, said Brinsley.

Extract from Concise Oxford Dictionary: Kiss, n. Caress given with lips; (Billiards) impact between moving balls; kind of sugar plum.

Diverting his attention with difficulty from the affairs of the table, I persuaded him to peruse my manuscript, a matter of some nine pages. He read idly at first, subsequently with some attention. He then turned to me and praised me, commenting favourably on my literary talent.

This is the shield, he said.

The subject-matter of the dialogue in question was concerned (as may be inferred) with the turpitude and moral weakness of Mr. Furriskey. It was pointed out to him by the voice that he was by vocation a voluptuary concerned only with the ravishing and destruction of the fair sex. His habits and physical attributes were explained to him in some detail. It was stated, for example, that his drinking capacity, speaking roughly and making allowance for discrepancies in strength as between the products of various houses, was six bottles of stout; and that any quantity taken in excess of such six bottles would not be retained. At the conclusion of the interview, the voice administered a number of stern warnings as to the penalties which would befall him should he deviate, even in the secrecy of his own thought, from his mission of debauchery. His life was to be devoted without distraction to the attainment of his empirical lusts. The talking then stopped and the steam-like cloud grew thinner and thinner and finally disappeared, the last wisps going quickly up the chimney as a result of the draught. Mr. Furriskey then found that his blue clothing was slightly damp but as the cloud receded from the room, he found his strength returning to him; and after an interval of about eighteen minutes, he was sufficiently strong to continue his search for the door. He found it in the third wall he examined and it may be valuable to state—as an indication of the growing acuteness of his reasoning powers—that he neglected investigating one of the walls as a result of a deduction to the effect that the door of a room in the upper storey of a house is rarely to be found in the same wall which contains the window.

He opened the door and went out to the passage. He opened one of the many other doors which he found there and entered a room in which (scarcely by accident) he found Mr. Paul Shanahan and Mr. Antony Lamont, two men of his own social class who were destined to become his close friends. Strange to say, they were already acquainted with his name and his congenital addiction to the delights of the flesh. Mr. Furriskey detected a faint odour of steam in this room also. He conversed with the two other men, rather diffidently at first but subsequently in an earnest sincere manner. Mr. Shanahan introduced himself and Mr. Lamont by name, explained their respective offices and duties and was kind enough to produce his costly fifteen-jewel hunter watch and permit Mr. Furriskey to appraise the character of his countenance on the polish of its inner lid. This relieved Mr. Furriskey of some anxiety and facilitated further conversation, which now turned on such subjects as politics foreign and domestic, the acceleration due to gravity, gunnery, parabolics and public health. Mr. Lamont recounted an adventure which once befell him in a book when teaching French and piano-playing to a young girl of delicate and refined nature. Mr. Shanahan, who was an older man and who had appeared in many of the well-known tales of Mr. Tracy, then entertained his hearers with a brief though racy account of his experiences as a cow-puncher in the Rings-end district of Dublin city.

Substance of reminiscence by Mr. Shanahan, the comments of his hearers being embodied parenthetically in the text; with relevant excerpts from the public press: Do you know what I am going to tell you, there was a rare life in Dublin in the old days. (There was certainly.) That was the day of the great O'Callaghan, the day of Baskin, the day of Tracy that brought cowboys to Ringsend. I knew them all, man.

Relevant excerpt from the Press: We regret to announce the passing of Mr. William Tracy, the eminent novelist, which occurred yesterday under painful circumstances at his home in Grace Park Gardens. Early in the afternoon, deceased was knocked down in Weavers' Square by a tandem cycle proceeding towards the city. He got up unaided, however, laughed heartily, treated the accident as a joke in the jolly way that was peculiarly his own and made his way home on a tram. When he had•smoked six after-dinner pipes, he went to ascend the stairs and dropped dead on the landing. A man of culture and old-world courtesy, his passing will be regretted by all without distinction of creed or class and in particular by the world of letters, which he adorned with distinction for many years. He was the first man in Europe to exhibit twenty-nine lions in a cage at the same time and the only writer to demonstrate that cow-punching could be economically carried on in Ringsend. His best known works were *Red Flanagan's Last Throw, Flower o' the Prairie,* and *Jake's Last Ride.* Deceased was fifty-nine. Conclusion of excerpt.

One day Tracy sent for me and gave me my orders and said it was one of his cowboy books. Two days later I was cow-punching down by the river in Ringsend with Shorty Andrews and Slug Willard, the toughest pair of boyos you'd meet in a day's walk. Rounding up steers, you know, and branding, and breaking in colts in the corral with lassoes on our saddle-horns and pistols at our hips. (O the real thing. Was there any drink to be had?) There certainly was. At night we would gather in the bunk-house with our porter and all our orders, cigarettes and plenty there on the chiffonier to be taken and no questions asked, school-marms and saloon-girls and little black maids skivvying there in the galley. (That was the place to be, now.) After a while be damned but in would walk a musicianer with a fiddle or a pipes in the hollow of his arm and there he would sit and play *Ave Maria* to bring the tears to your eyes. Then the boys would take up an old come-all-ye, the real old stuff, you know, *Phil the*

Fluter's Ball or the *Darling Girl from Clare*, a bloody lovely thing. (That was very nice certainly.) O we had the right time of it. One morning Slug and Shorty and myself and a few of the boys got the wire to saddle and ride up to Drumcondra to see my nabs Mr. Tracy to get our orders for the day. Up we went on our horses, cantering up Mountjoy Square with' our hats tilted back on our heads and the sun in our eyes and our gun-butts swinging at our holsters. When we got the length, go to God but wasn't it a false alarm. (A false alarm! Lord save us! What brought that about now?) Wait till I tell you. Get back to hell, says Tracy, I never sent any message. Get back to hell to your prairies, says he, you pack of lousers that can be taken in by any fly-be-night with a fine story. I'm telling you that we were small men when we took the trail again for home. When we got the length, be damned but wasn't the half of our steers rustled across the border in Irishtown by Red Kiersay's gang of thieving ruffians. (Well that was a kick for you where-you-know.) Certainly it was. Red Kiersay, you understand, was working for another man by the name of Henderson that was writing another book about cattle-dealers and jobbing and shipping bullocks to Liverpool. (Likely it was he sent you the false message?) Do you mind the cuteness of it? Get yourselves fed, says I to Shorty and Slug, we're goin' ridin' to-night. Where? says Slug. Right over to them thar rustlers' roost, says I, before Tracy finds out and skins us. Where's the nigger skivvies? says Shorty. Now go to God, says I, don't tell me they have taken the lot with them. (And had they?) Every one.

Relevant excerpt from the Press: An examination of the galley and servants' sleeping-quarters revealed no trace of the negro maids. They had been offered lucrative inducements to come from the United States and had at no time expressed themselves as being dissatisfied with their conditions of service. Detective-Officer Snodgrass found a pearl-handled shooting-iron under the pillow in the bed of Liza Roberts, the youngest of the maids. No great importance is attached by the police to this discovery, however, as ownership has been traced to Peter (Shorty) Andrews, a cowboy, who states that though at a loss to explain the presence of his property in the maid's bed, it is possible that she appropriated the article in order to clean it in her spare time in bed (she was an industrious girl) or in order to play a joke. It is stated that the former explanation is the more likely of the two as there is no intercourse of a social character between the men and the scullery-maids. A number of minor clues have been found and an arrest is expected in the near future. Conclusion of excerpt.

I'm not what you call fussy when it comes to women but damn it all I draw the line when it comes to carrying off a bunch of black niggers—human beings, you must remember—and a couple of thousand steers, by God. So when the moon had raised her lamp o'er the prairie grasses, out flies the bunch of us, Slug, Shorty and myself on a buckboard making like hell for Irishtown with our ears back and the butts of our six-guns streaming out behind us in the wind. (You were out to get your own?) We were out to get our own. I tell you we were travelling in

great style. Shorty drew out and gave the horses an un-
merciful skelp across the where-you-know and away with
us like the wind and us roaring and cursing out of us like
men that were lit with whisky, our steel-studded holsters
swaying at our hips and the sheep-fur on our leg-chaps
lying down like corn before a spring-wind. Be damned to
the lot of us, I roared, flaying the nags and bashing the
buckboard across the prairie, passing out lorries and trams
and sending poor so-and-so's on bicycles scuttling down
side-lanes with nothing showing but the whites of their
eyes. (By God you were travelling all right.) Certainly,
going like the hammers of hell. I smell cattle, says Slug
and sure enough there was the ranch of Red Kiersay the
length of a turkey-trot ahead of us sitting on the moonlit
prairie as peaceful as you please.

Relevant excerpt from the Press: The Circle N is reputed to
be the most venerable of Dublin's older ranches. The
main building is a gothic structure of red sandstone
timbered in the Elizabethan style and supported by
corinthian pillars at the posterior. Added as a lean-to
at the south gable is the wooden bunk-house, one of the
most up-to-date of its kind in the country. It contains
three holster-racks, ten gas fires and a spacious dormitory
fitted with an ingenious apparatus worked by compressed
air by which all verminous beds can be fumigated instantaneously by the mere pressing of a button, the operation
occupying only the space of forty seconds: The old Dublin
custom of utilizing imported negroid labour for operating
the fine electrically-equipped cooking-galley is still

observed in this time-hallowed house. On the land adjacent, grazing is available for 10,000 steers and 2,000 horses, thanks to the public spirit of Mr. William Tracy, the indefatigable novelist, who had 8,912 dangerous houses demolished in the environs of Irishtown and Sandymount to make the enterprise possible. Visitors can readily reach the ranch by taking the Number 3 tram. The exquisitely laid out gardens of the ranch are open for inspection on Thursdays and Fridays, the nominal admission fee of one and sixpence being devoted to the cause of the Jubilee Nurses' Fund. Conclusion of excerpt.

Down we got offa the buckboard to our hands and knees and up with us towards the doss-house on our bellies, our silver-mounted gun-butts jiggling at our hips, our eyes narrowed into slits and our jaws set and stern like be damned. (By God you weren't a party to meet on a dark night). Don't make a sound, says I *viva voce* to the boys, or its kiss my hand to taking these lousers by surprise. On we slithered with as much sound out of us as an eel in a barrel of tripes, right up to the bunk-house on the flat of our three beilies. (Don't tell me you were seen?) Go to hell but a lad pulls a gun on us from behind and tells us to get on our feet and no delay or monkey-work. Be damned but wasn't it Red Kiersay himself, the so-and-so, standing there with an iron in each hand and a Lucifer leer on his beery face. What are you at, you swine, he asks in a real snotty voice. Don't come it, Kiersay, says I, we're here for our own and damn the bloody thing else. (You were in the right, of course. What was the upshot?) Come across, Kiersay, says I, come across with our steers

and our black girls or down I go straight to Lad Lane
and get the police up. Keep your hands up or I'll paste
your guts on that tree, says he, you swine. You can't
cow the like of us with your big gun, says Slug, and don't
think it my boyo. (O trust Slug.) You dirty dog, says I
between my teeth, you dirty swine you, Kiersay, you
bastard. My God I was in the right temper and that's
a fact. (You had good reason to be. If I was there I
don't know what I'd do.) Well the upshot was that he
gave us three minutes to go home and home we went like
boys because Kiersay would think nothing of shooting the
lights out of us and that's the God's truth. (You had a
right to go for the police.) That's the very thing we done.
Out we crept to the buggy and down Londonbridge
Road and across the town to Lad Lane. It was good gas
all right. The station sergeant was with us from the start
and gave us over to the superintendent, a Clohessy from
Tipp. Nothing would do him but give us a whole detachment of the D.M.P. to see fair play and justice done, and
the fire-brigade there for the calling. (Well that was
very decent of him now.) Do you know what it is, says
Slug, Tracy is writing another book too and has a crowd of
Red Indians up in the Phoenix Park, squaws and wigwams
and warpaint an' all, the real stuff all right, believe me.
A couple of bob to the right man there and the lot are
ours for the asking, says he. Go to hell, says I, you don't
tell me. As sure as God, says he. Right, says I, let yourself go for the Indians, let Shorty here go back for our
own boys and let myself stop where I am with the police.
Let the lot of us meet at Kiersay's at a quarter past eight.

(Fair enough, fair enough.) Off went the two at a half-
canter on the buckboard and the super and myself got
stuck into a dozen stout in the back-room. After a while,
the policemen were rounded up and marched across the
prairies to the Circle N, as fine a body of men as you'd
hope to see, myself and the super as proud as be damned
at the head of them. (Well that was a sight to see.)
When we got the length, there was Slug with his Red
Indians, Shorty and his cowboys, the whole shooting
gallery waiting for the word. The super and myself put
our heads together and in no time we had everything
arranged. In behind the buckboards and food wagons
with the policemen and the cowboys to wait for the sweet
foe. Away with the Red Indians around the ranch-house
in circles, the braves galloping like red hell on their Arab
ponies, screaming and shrieking and waving their bloody
scalp-hatchets and firing flaming rods into the house from
their little bows. (Boys-a-dear.) I'm telling you it was
the business. The whole place was burning like billyo
in no time and out came Red with a shot-gun in his hand
and followed by his men, prepared if you please to make
a last stand for king and country. The Indians got windy
and flew back to us behind the buckboards and go to
God if Red doesn't hold up a passing tram and take cover
behind it, firing all the people out with a stream of dirty
filthy language. (Well dirty language is a thing I don't like.
He deserved all he got.) Lord save us but it was the right
hard battle. I fired off my six bullets without stopping.
A big sheet of plate-glass crashed from the tram to the
roadway. Then with a terrible scutter of oaths, the

boys began to get busy. We broke every pane of glass in
that tram, raked the roadway with a death-dealing rain of
six-gun shrapnel and took the tip off an enemy cowboy's
ear, by God. In no time wasn't there a crowd around
the battlefield and them cheering and calling and asking
every man of us to do his duty. (O you'll always get those
boys to gather. Sneeze in the street and they're all around
you.) The bloody Indians started squealing at the back
and slapping their horses on the belly, the policemen were
firing off their six-guns and their batons in the air and
Shorty and myself behind a sack of potatoes picking off the
snipers like be damned. On raged the scrap for a half an
hour, the lot of us giving back more than we got and never
thinking of the terrible danger we were in, every man
jack of us, loading and shooting off our pistols like divils
from below. Be damned but the enemy was weakening.
Now is your chance, says I to the super, now is your chance
to lead your men over the top, says I, and capture the
enemy's stronghold for good and all. Right you are, says
he. Over the top with my brave bobbies, muttered oaths
flying all over the place, as bold as brass with their batons
in their hands. The crowd gave a big cheer and the
Indians shrieked and flayed the bellies offa their horses
with their hands. (Well did the dodge work?) Certainly.
The battle was over before you could count your fingers
and here were my brave men handcuffed hand and foot
and marched down to Lad Lane like a bunch of orphans
out for a Sunday walk. Did you get Red? says I to the
super. Didn't see him at all at all, says he. As sure as
God, says I, he's doing the Brian Boru in his bloody tent.

(What, at the prayers?) Round I searched till I found the
tent and here was my bold man inside on his two knees
and him praying there for further orders. Where's our
girls, Red, says I. Gone home, says he. Take yourself
out of here, says he, and bring your steers with you, says
he, can't you see I'm at my prayers. Do you mind the
cuteness of it? I could do nothing, of course, him there
in front of me on his two knees praying. There wasn't a
thing left for me to do but go off again and choke down
my rising dander. Come on away with me, says I to
Slug and Shorty till we get our stolen steers. Next day
didn't the super bring the enemy punchers up before the
bench and got every man of them presented free with
seven days hard without the option. Cool them down,
says Slug.

Relevant excerpt from the Press: A number of men, stated to
be labourers, were arraigned before Mr. Lamphall in the
District Court yesterday morning on charges of riotous
assembly and malicious damage. Accused were described
by Superintendent Clohessy as a gang of corner-boys
whose horse-play in the streets was the curse of the Ringsend district. They were pests and public nuisances whose
antics were not infrequently attended by damage to
property. Complaints as to their conduct were frequently
being received from residents in the area. On the occasion
of the last escapade, two windows were broken in a tramcar the property of the Dublin United Tramway Company.
Inspector Quin of the Company stated that the damage
to the vehicle amounted to £2 11s. od. Remarking that

no civilized community could tolerate organized hooliganism of this kind, the justice sentenced the accused to
seven days hard labour without the option of a fine, and
hoped that it would be a lesson to them and to other
playboys of the boulevards. Conclusion of excerpt.

Biographical reminiscence, part the fifth: The weather in
the following March was cold, with snow and rain, and
generally dangerous to persons of inferior vitality. I kept
to the house as much as possible, reclining safe from ill
and infection in the envelope of my bed. My uncle had
taken to the studying of musical scores and endeavouring,
by undertoned hummings, to make himself proficient in
the vocal craft. Conducting researches in his bedroom one
day in an attempt to find cigarettes, I came upon a policeman's hat of the papier mâché type utilized by persons
following the dramatic profession. A result of this
departure in his habits was absence from the house on three
nights a week and temporary indifference—amounting
almost to unconcern—for my temporal and spiritual welfare. This I found convenient.

I recall that at the time of the loss of portion of my
day-papers, I found myself one day speculating as to the
gravity of the situation which would arise if the entirety
of my papers were lost in the same manner. My literary
or spare-time compositions, written not infrequently with
animation and enjoyment, I always found tedious of subsequent perusal. This sense of tedium is so deeply seated in
the texture of my mind that I can rarely suffer myself to
endure the pain of it. One result is that many of my shorter

works, even those made the subject of extremely flattering *encomia* on the part of friends and acquaintances, I have never myself read, nor does my indolent memory enable me to recall their contents with a satisfactory degree of accuracy. A hasty search for syntactical solecism was the most I could perform.

With regard to my present work, however, the forty pages which follow the lost portion were so vital to the operation of the ingenious plot which I had devised that I deemed it advisable to spend an April forenoon—a time of sun-glistening showers—glancing through them in a critical if precipitate manner. This was fortunate for I found two things which caused me considerable consternation.

The first thing: An inexplicable chasm in the pagination, four pages of unascertained content being wanting.

The second thing: An unaccountable omission of one of the four improper assaults required by the ramification of the plot or argument, together with an absence of structural cohesion and a general feebleness of literary style.

I recall that these discoveries caused me concern for many days and were mainly the subjects turned over in my mind in the pauses which occurred in the casual day-to-day conversations which I conducted with my friends and acquaintances. Without seeking independent advice on the matter, I decided—foolishly perhaps—to delete the entire narrative and present in its place a brief résumé (or summary) of the events which it contained, a device frequently employed by newspapers to avoid the trouble and expense of reprinting past portions of their serial stories. The synopsis is as follows:

Synopsis, being a summary of what has gone before, FOR THE BENEFIT OF NEW READERS: DERMOT TRELLIS, an eccentric author, conceives the project of writing a salutary book on the consequences which follow wrong-doing and creates for the purpose

THE POOKA FERGUS MACPHELLIMEY, a species of human Irish devil endowed with magical powers. He then creates

JOHN FURRISKEY, a depraved character, whose task is to attack women and behave at all times in an indecent manner. By magic he is instructed by Trellis to go one night to Donnybrook where he will by arrangement meet and betray

PEGGY, a domestic servant. He meets her and is much surprised when she confides in him that Trellis has fallen asleep and that her virtue has already been assailed by an elderly man subsequently to be identified as

FINN MACCOOL, a legendary character hired by Trellis on account of the former's venerable appearance and experience, to act as the girl's father and chastise her for her transgressions against the moral law; and that her virtue has also been assailed by

PAUL SHANAHAN, another man hired by Trellis for performing various small and unimportant parts in the story, also for running messages, &c. &c. Peggy and Furriskey then have a long discussion on the roadside in which she explains to him that Trellis's powers are suspended when he falls asleep and that Finn and Shanahan were taking advantage of that fact when they came to see her because they would not dare to defy him when he is awake. Furriskey then inquires whether she yielded to them and she replies that indeed she did not. Furriskey then praises her and they discover after a short time that they have fallen in love with each other at first sight. They arrange to lead virtuous lives, to simulate the immoral actions, thoughts and words which Trellis demands of them on pain of the severest penalties. They also arrange that the first of them who shall be free shall wait for the other with a view to marriage at the earliest opportunity. Meanwhile Trellis, in order to show how an evil man can debase the highest and the lowest in the same story, creates a very beautiful and refined girl called

SHEILA LAMONT, whose brother,

ANTONY LAMONT he has already hired so that there will be somebody to demand satisfaction off John Furriskey for betraying her—all this being provided for in the plot. Trellis creates Miss Lamont in his own bedroom and he is so blinded by her beauty (which is naturally the type of beauty nearest to his heart), that he so far forgets himself as to assault her himself. Furriskey in the meantime returns to the Red Swan Hotel where Trellis lives and compels all those working for him to live also. He (Furriskey) is determined to pretend that he faithfully carried out the terrible mission he was sent on. Now read on.

Further extract from Manuscript. Oratio recta: With a key in his soft nervous hand, he opened the hall door and removed his shoes with two swift spells of crouching on the one leg. He crept up the stairs with the noiseless cat-tread of his good-quality woollen socks. The door of Trellis was dark and sleeping as he passed up the stairs to his room. There was a crack of light at Shanahan's door and he placed his shoes quietly on the floor and turned the handle.

The hard Furriskey, said Shanahan.

Here was Shanahan stretched at the fire, with Lamont on his left and the old greybeard seated beyond dimly on the bed with his stick between his knees and his old eyes staring far into the red fire like a man whose thought was in a distant part of the old world or maybe in another world altogether.

By God you weren't long, said Lamont.

Shut the door, said Shanahan, but see you're in the room before you do so. Shut the door and treat yourself to a chair, Mr. F. You're quick off the mark all right. Move up there, Mr. L.

It's not what you call a full-time occupation, said Furriskey in a weary way. It's not what you call a life sentence.

It is not, said Lamont. You're right there.

Now don't worry, said Shanahan in a pitying manner, there's plenty more coming. We'll keep you occupied now, don't you worry, won't we, Mr. Lamont?

We'll see that he gets his bellyful, said Lamont.

You're decent fellows the pair of ye, said Furriskey.

He sat on a stool and extended his fan to the fire, the fan of his ten fingers.

You can get too much of them the same women, he said.

Is that a fact, said Shanahan in unbelief. Well I never heard that said before. Come here, Mr. Furriskey, did you. . . .

O it was all right, I'll tell you sometime, said Furriskey. Didn't I tell you it was all right? Didn't I?

You did, said Furriskey.

He took a sole cigarette from a small box.

I'll tell you the whole story sometime but not now, he said. He nodded towards the bed.

Is your man asleep or what?

Maybe he is, said Shanahan, but by God it didn't sound like it five minutes ago. Mr. Storybook was wide awake.

He was wide awake, said Lamont.

Five minutes ago he was giving out a yarn the length of my arm, said Shanahan. Right enough he is a terrible man for talk. Aren't you now? He'd talk the lot of us into the one grave if you gave him his head, don't ask me how I know, look at my grey hairs. Isn't that a fact, Mr. Lamont?

For a man of his years, said Lamont slowly and authoritatively, he can do the talking. By God he can do the talking. He has seen more of the world than you or me, of course, that's the secret of it.

That's true, said Furriskey, a happy fire-glow running about his body. He carefully directed the smoke of his cigarette towards the flames and up the chimney. Yes, he's an old man, of course.

His stories are not the worst though, I'll say that, said Lamont, there's always a head and a tail on his yarns, a beginning and an end, give him his due.

O I don't know, said Furriskey.

O he can talk, he can talk, I agree with you there, said Shanahan, credit where credit is due. But you'd want what you'd call a grain of *salo* with more than one of them if I know anything.

A pinch of salt? said Lamont.

A grain of *salo*, Mr. L.

I don't doubt it, said Furriskey.

Relate, said hidden Conán, the tale of the Feasting of Dún na nGedh.

Finn in his mind was nestling with his people.

I mean to say, said Lamont, whether a yarn is tall or small I like to hear it well told. I like to meet a man that can take in hand to tell a story and not make a balls of it while he's at it. I like to know where I am, do you know. Everything has a beginning and an end.

It is true, said Finn, that I will not.

O that's right too, said Shanahan.

Relate then, said Conán, the account of the madness of King Sweeny and he on a madman's flight through the length of Erin.

That's a grand fire, said Furriskey, and if a man has that, he can't want a lot more. A fire, a bed, and a roof over his head, that's all. With a bite to eat, of course.

It's all very fine for you to talk, now, said Lamont, you had something for your tea to-night that the rest of us hadn't, eh, Mr. Shanahan. Know what I mean?

Keep the fun clean, said Shanahan.

I beg, Mr. Chairman, said Furriskey, to be associated with them sentiments. What's clean, keep it clean.

There was a concerted snigger, harmonious, scored for three voices.

I will relate, said Finn.

We're off again, said Furriskey.

The first matter that I will occupy with honey-words and melodious recital, said Finn, is the reason and the first cause for Sweeny's frenzy.

Draw in your chairs, boys, said Shanahan, we're right for the night. We're away on a hack.

Pray proceed, Sir, said Lamont.

Now Sweeny was King of Dal Araidhe and a man that was easily moved to the tides of anger. Near his house was the cave of a saint called Ronan—a shield against evil was this gentle generous friendly active man, who was out in the matin-hours taping out the wall-steads of a new sun-bright church and ringing his bell in the morning.

Good for telling, said Conán.

Now when Sweeny heard the clack of the clergyman's bell, his brain and his spleen and his gut were exercised by turn and together with the fever of a flaming anger. He made a great run out of the house without a cloth-stitch to the sheltering of his naked nudity, for he had run out of his cloak when his wife Eorann held it for restraint and deterrence, and he did not rest till he had snatched the beauteous light-lined psalter from the cleric and put it in the lake, at the bottom; after that he took the hard grip of the cleric's hand and ran with a wind-swift stride to the lake without a halting or a letting go of the hand because he had a mind to place the cleric by the side of his psalter in the lake, on the bottom, to speak precisely.

But, evil destiny, he was deterred by the big storm-voiced hoarse shout, the shout of a scullion calling him to the profession of arms at the battle of Magh Rath. Sweeny then left the cleric sad and sorrowful over the godless battery of the king and lamenting his psalter. This, however, an otter from the murk of the lake returned to him unharmed, its lines and its letters unblemished. He then returned with joyous piety to his devotions and put a malediction on Sweeny by the uttering of a lay of eleven melodious stanzas.

Thereafter he went himself with his acolytes to the plain of Magh Rath for the weaving of concord and peace between the hosts and was himself taken as a holy pledge, the person of the cleric, that fighting should cease at sundown and that no man should be slain until fighting would be again permitted, the person of the cleric a holy hostage and exchange between the hosts. But, evil destiny, Sweeny was used to violating the guarantee by the slaughter of a man every morning before the hour when fighting was permitted. On the morning of a certain day, Ronan and his eight psalmists were walking in the field and sprinkling holy water on the hosts against the incidence of hurt or evil when they sprinkled the head of Sweeny with the rest. Sweeny in anger took a cast and reddened his spear in the white side of a psalmist and broke Ronan's bell whereupon the cleric uttered this melodious lay:

> My curse on Sweeny!
> His guilt against me is immense,
> he pierced with his long swift javelin
> my holy bell.

The holy bell that thou hast outraged
will banish thee to branches,
it will put thee on a par with fowls—
the saint-bell of saints with sainty-saints.

Just as it went prestissimo
the spear-shaft skyward,
you too, Sweeny, go madly mad-gone
skyward.

Eorann of Conn tried to hold him
by a hold of his smock
and though I bless her therefore,
my curse on Sweeny.

Thereafter when the hosts clashed and bellowed like stag-herds and gave three audible world-wide shouts till Sweeny heard them and their hollow reverberations in the sky-vault, he was beleaguered by an anger and a darkness, and fury and fits and frenzy and fright-fraught fear, and he was filled with a restless tottering unquiet and with a disgust for the places that he knew and with a desire to be where he never was, so that he was palsied of hand and foot and eye-mad and heart-quick and went from the curse of Ronan bird-quick in craze and madness from the battle. For the nimble lightness of his tread in flight he did not shake dewdrops from the grass-stalks and staying not for bog or thicket or marsh or hollow or thick-sheltering wood in Erin for that day, he travelled till he reached Ros Bearaigh in Glenn Earcain where he went into the yew-tree that was in the glen.

In a later hour his kin came to halt beneath the tree for a spell of discourse and melodious talk about Sweeny and no tidings concerning him either in the east or the west; and Sweeny in the yew-tree above them listened till he made answer in this lay:

> O warriors approach,
> warriors of Dal Araidhe,
> you will find him in the tree he is
> the man you seek.
>
> God has given me life here,
> very bare, very narrow,
> no woman, no trysting,
> no music or trance-eyed sleep.

When they noticed the verses from the tree-top they saw Sweeny in branches and then they talked their honey-words, beseeching him that he should be trustful, and then made a ring around the tree-bole. But Sweeny arose nimbly and away to Cell Riagain in Tir Conaill where he perched in the old tree of the church, going and coming between branches and the rain-clouds of the skies, trespassing and wayfaring over peaks and summits and across the ridge-poles of black hills, and visiting in dark mountains, ruminating and searching in cavities and narrow crags and slag-slits in rocky hidings, and lodging in the clump of tall ivies and in the cracks of hill-stones, a year of time from summit to summit and from glen to glen and from river-mouth to river till he arrived at ever-delightful Glen Bolcain. For it is thus that Glen Bolcain is, it has four gaps to the four winds and a too-fine too-pleasant wood and fresh-banked wells and cold-clean fountains and sandy pellucid streams of clear water with green-topped watercress and brooklime long-streamed on the current, and a richness of sorrels and wood-sorrels, *lus-bian* and *biorragan* and berries and wild garlic, *melle* and *miodhbhun*, inky sloes and dun acorns. For it was here that the madmen of Erin were used to come when their year of madness was complete, smiting and lamming each other for choice of its watercress and in rivalry for its fine couches.

In that glen it was hard for Sweeny to endure the pain of his bed there on the top of a tall ivy-grown hawthorn in the glen, every twist that he would turn sending showers of hawy thorns into his flesh, tearing and rending and piercing him and pricking his blood-red skin. He thereupon changed beds to the resting of another tree where there were tangles of thick fine-thorned briars and a solitary branch of blackthorn growing up through the core of the brambles. He settled and roosted on its slender perch till it bowed beneath him and bent till it slammed him to the ground, not one inch of him from toe to crown that was not red-prickled and blood-gashed, the skin to his body being ragged and flapping and thorned, the tattered cloak of his perished skin. He arose death-weak from the ground to his standing for the recital of this lay.

> A year to last night
> I have lodged there in branches
> from the flood-tide to the ebb-tide
> naked.
>
> Bereft of fine women-folk,
> the brooklime for a brother—
> our choice for a fresh meal
> is watercress always.

Without accomplished musicians
without generous women,
no jewel-gift for bards—
respected Christ, it has perished me.

The thorntop that is not gentle
has reduced me, has pierced me,
it has brought me near death
the brown thorn-bush.

Once free, once gentle,
I am banished for ever,
wretch-wretched I have been
a year to last night.

He remained there in Glen Bolcain until he elevated
himself high in the air and went to Cluain Cille on the
border of Tir Conaill and Tir Boghaine. He went to the
edge of the water and took food against the night, watercress and water. After that he went into the old tree of
the church where he said another melodious poem on the
subject of his personal hardship.

After another time he set forth in the air again till he
reached the church at Snámh-dá-én (or Swim-Two-
Birds) by the side of the Shannon, arriving there on a
Friday, to speak precisely; here the clerics were engaged
at the observation of their nones, flax was being beaten and
here and there a woman was giving birth to a child; and
Sweeny did not stop until he had recited the full length of
a further lay.

For seven years, to relate precisely, was Sweeny at the air
travel of all Erin, returning always to his tree in charming
Glen Bolcain, for that was his fortress and his haven, it

was his house there in the glen. It was to this place that his foster-brother Linchehaun came for tidings concerning him, for he carried always a deep affection for Sweeny and had retrieved him three times from madness before that. Linchehaun went seeking him in the glen with shouts and found toe-tracks by the stream-mud where the madman was wont to appease himself by the eating of cresses. But track or trace of Sweeny he did not attain for that day and he sat down in an old deserted house in the glen till the labour and weariness of his pursuit brought about his sleep. And Sweeny, hearing his snore from his tree-clump in the glen, uttered this lay in the pitch darkness.

> The man by the wall snores
> a snore-sleep that's beyond me,
> for seven years from that Tuesday at Magh Rath
> I have not slept a wink.
>
> O God that I had not gone
> to the hard battle!
> thereafter my name was Mad—
> Mad Sweeny in the bush.
>
> Watercress from the well at Cirb
> is my lot at terce,
> its colour is my mouth,
> green on the mouth of Sweeny.
>
> Chill chill is my body
> when away from ivy,
> the rain torrent hurts it
> and the thunder.

I am in summer with the herons of Cuailgne
with wolves in winter,
at other times I am hidden in a copse—
not so the man by the wall.

And thereafter he met Linchehaun who came visiting
to his tree and they parleyed there the two of them
together and the one of them talkative and unseen in
branches and prickle-briars. And Sweeny bade Linchehaun
to depart and not to pursue or annoy him further because
the curse of Ronan stopped him from putting his trust or
his mad faith in any man.

Thereafter he travelled in distant places till he came at
the black fall of a night to Ros Bearaigh and lodged himself
in a hunched huddle in the middle of the yew-tree of the
church in that place. But being besieged with nets and
hog-harried by the caretaker of the church and his false
wife, he hurried nimbly to the old tree at Ros Eareain
where he remained hidden and unnoticed the length of a
full fortnight, till the time when Linchehaun came and
perceived the murk of his shadow in the sparse branches
and saw the other branches he had broken and bent in his
movements and in changing trees. And the two of them
parleyed together until they had said between them
these fine words following.

Sad it is Sweeny, said Linchehaun, that your last extremity
should be thus, without food or drink or raiment like a
fowl, the same man that had cloth of silk and of satin
and the foreign steed of the peerless bridle, also comely
generous women and boys and hounds and princely
people of every refinement; hosts and tenants and men-at-

arms, and mugs and goblets and embellished buffalo-
horns for the savouring of pleasant-tasted fine liquors. Sad
it is to see the same man as a hapless air-fowl.

Cease now, Linchehaun, said Sweeny, and give me
tidings.

Your father is dead, said Linchehaun.

That has seized me with a blind agony, said Sweeny.

Your mother is likewise dead.

Now all the pity in me is at an end.

Dead is your brother.

Gaping open is my side on account of that.

She has died too your sister.

A needle for the heart is an only sister.

Ah, dumb dead is the little son that called you
pop.

Truly, said Sweeny, that is the last blow that brings a
man to the ground.

When Sweeny heard the sorry word of his small son still
and without life, he fell with a crap from the middle of the
yew to the ground and Linchehaun hastened to his thorn-
packed flank with fetters and handcuffs and manacles and
locks and black-iron chains and he did not achieve a resting
until the lot were about the madman, and through him
and above him and over him, roundwise and about.
Thereafter there was a concourse of hospitallers and
knights and warriors around the trunk of the yew, and
after melodious talk they entrusted the mad one to the
care of Linchehaun till he would take him away to a
quiet place for a fortnight and a month, to the quiet
of a certain room where his senses returned to him, the

one after the other, with no one near him but the old mill-hag.

O hag, said Sweeny, searing are the tribulations I have suffered; many a terrible leap have I leaped from hill to hill, from fort to fort, from land to land, from valley to valley.

For the sake of God, said the hag, leap for us now a leap such as you leaped in the days of your madness.

And thereupon Sweeny gave a bound over the top of the bedrail till he reached the extremity of the bench.

My conscience indeed, said the hag, I could leap the same leap myself.

And the hag gave a like jump.

Sweeny then gathered himself together in the extremity of his jealousy and threw a leap right out through the skylight of the hostel.

I could vault that vault too, said the hag and straightway she vaulted the same vault. And the short of it is this, that Sweeny travelled the length of five cantreds of leaps until he had penetrated to Glenn na nEachtach in Fiodh Gaibhle with the hag at her hag's leaps behind him; and when Sweeny rested there in a huddle at the top of a tall ivy-branch, the hag was perched there on another tree beside him. He heard there the voice of a stag and he thereupon made a lay euologizing aloud the trees and the stags of Erin, and he did not cease or sleep until he had achieved these staves.

> Bleating one, little antlers,,
> O lamenter we like
> delightful the clamouring
> from your glen you make.

O leafy-oak, clumpy-leaved,
you are high above trees,
O hazlet, little clumpy-branch—
the nut-smell of hazels.

O alder, O alder-friend,
delightful your colour,
you don't prickle me or tear
in the place you are.

O blackthorn, little thorny-one,
O little dark sloe-tree;
O watercress, O green-crowned,
at the well-brink.

O holly, holly-shelter,
O door against the wind,
O ash-tree inimical,
you spearshaft of warrior.

O birch clean and blessed,
O melodious, O proud,
delightful the tangle
of your head-rods.

What I like least in woodlands
from none I conceal it—
stirk of a leafy-oak,
at its swaying.

O faun, little long-legs,
I caught you with grips,
I rode you upon your back
from peak to peak.

Glen Bolcain my home ever,
it was my haven,
many a night have I tried
a race against the peak.

I beg your pardon for interrupting, said Shanahan, but you're after reminding me of something, brought the thing into my head in a rush.

He swallowed a draught of vesper-milk, restoring the cloudy glass swiftly to his knee and collecting little belated flavourings from the corners of his mouth.

That thing you were saying reminds me of something bloody good. I beg your pardon for interrupting, Mr. Storybook.

In the yesterday, said Finn, the man who mixed his utterance with the honeywords of Finn was the first day put naked into the tree of Coill Boirche with nothing to his bare hand but a stick of hazel. On the morning of the second day thereafter. . . .

Now listen for a minute till I tell you something, said Shanahan, did any man here ever hear of the poet Casey?

Who did you say? said Furriskey.

Casey. Jem Casey.

On the morning of the second day thereafter, he was taken and bound and rammed as regards his head into a black hole so that his white body was upside down and upright in Erin for the gazing thereon of man and beast.

Now give us a chance, Mister Storybook, yourself and your black hole, said Shanahan fingering his tie-knot with a long memory-frown across his brow. Come here for a minute. Come here till I tell you about Casey. Do you mean to tell me you never heard of the poet Casey, Mr. Furriskey?

Never heard of him, said Furriskey in a solicitous manner.

I can't say, said Lamont, that I ever heard of him either.

He was a poet of the people, said Shanahan.

I see, said Furriskey.

Now do you understand, said Shanahan. A plain up-standing labouring man, Mr. Furriskey, the same as you or me. A black hat or a bloody ribbon, no by God, not on Jem Casey. A hard-working well-made block of a working man, Mr. Lamont, with the handle of a pick in his hand like the rest of us. Now say there was a crowd of men with a ganger all working there laying a length of gas-pipe on the road. All right. The men pull off their coats and start shovelling and working there for further orders. Here at one end of the hole you have your men crowded up together in a lump and them working away and smoking their butts and talking about the horses and one thing and another. Now do you understand what I'm telling you. Do you follow me?

I see that.

But take a look at the other end of the hole and here is my brave Casey digging away there on his own. Do you understand what I mean, Mr. Furriskey?

Oh I see it all right, said Furriskey.

Right. None of your horses or your bloody blather for him. Not a bit of it. Here is my nabs saying nothing to nobody but working away at a pome in his head with a pick in his hand and the sweat pouring down off his face from the force of his work and his bloody exertions. That's a quare one!

Do you mind that now, said Lamont.

It's a quare one and one that takes a lot of beating. Not a word to nobody, not a look to left or right but the brain-box going there all the time. Just Jem Casey, a poor ignorant labouring man but head and shoulders above the whole bloody lot of them, not a man in the whole country to beat him when it comes to getting together a bloody pome—not a poet in the whole world that could hold a candle to Jem Casey, not a man of them fit to stand beside him. By God I'd back him to win by a canter against the whole bloody lot of them give him his due.

Is that a fact, Mr. Shanahan, said Lamont. It's not every day in the week you come across a man like that.

Do you know what I'm going to tell you, Mr. Lamont, he was a man that could give the lot of them a good start, pickaxe and all. He was a man that could meet them . . . and meet the best . . . and beat them at their own game, now I'm telling you.

I suppose he could, said Furriskey.

Now I know what I'm talking about. Give a man his due. If a man's station is high or low he is all the same to the God I know. Take the bloody black hats off the whole bunch of them and where are you?

That's the way to look at it, of course, said Furriskey.

Give them a bloody pick, I mean, Mr. Furriskey, give them the shaft of a shovel into their hand and tell them to dig a hole and have the length of a page of poetry off by heart in their heads before the five o'clock whistle. What will you get? By God you could take off your hat to what you'd get at five o'clock from that crowd and that's a sure sharkey.

You'd be wasting your time if you waited till five o'clock if you ask me, said Furriskey with a nod of complete agreement.

You're right there, said Shanahan, you'd be waiting around for bloody nothing. Oh I know them and I know my hard Casey too. By Janey he'd be up at the whistle with a pome a yard long, a bloody lovely thing that would send my nice men home in a hurry, home with their bloody tails between their legs. Yes, I've seen his pomes and read them and . . . do you know what I'm going to tell you, I have loved them. I'm not ashamed to sit here and say it, Mr. Furriskey. I've known the man and I've known his pomes and by God I have loved the two of them and loved them well, too. Do you understand what I'm saying, Mr. Lamont? You, Mr. Furriskey?

Oh that's right.

Do you know what it is, I've met the others, the whole lot of them. I've met them all and know them all. I have seen them and I have read their pomes. I have heard them recited by men that know how to use their tongues, men that couldn't be beaten at their own game. I have seen whole books filled up with their stuff, books as thick as that table there and I'm telling you no lie. But by God, at the heel of the hunt, there was only one poet for me.

On the morning of the third day thereafter, said Finn, he was flogged until he bled water.

Only the one, Mr. Shanahan? said Lamont.

Only the one. And that one poet was a man . . . by the name . . . of Jem Casey. No "Sir", no "Mister", no nothing. Jem Casey, Poet of the Pick, that's all. A labouring man, Mr. Lamont, but as sweet a singer in his own way as you'll find in the bloody trees there of a spring day, and that's a fact. Jem Casey, an ignorant God-fearing upstanding labouring man, a bloody navvy. Do you know what I'm going to tell you, I don't believe he ever lifted the latch of a school door. Would you believe that now?

I'd believe it of Casey, said Furriskey, and

I'd believe plenty more of the same man, said Lamont. You haven't any of his pomes on you, have you, Mr. Shanahan?

Now take that stuff your man was giving us a while ago, said Shanahan without heed, about the green hills and the bloody swords and the bird giving out the pay from the top of the tree. Now that's good stuff, it's bloody nice. Do you know what it is, I liked it and liked it well. I enjoyed that certainly.

It wasn't bad at all, said Furriskey, I have heard worse, by God, often. It was all right now.

Do you see what I'm getting at, do you understand me, said Shanahan. It's good, very good. But by Christopher it's not every man could see it, I'm bloody sure of that, one in a thousand.

Oh that's right too, said Lamont.

You can't beat it, of course, said Shanahan with a reddening of the features, the real old stuff of the native land, you know, stuff that brought scholars to our shore when your men on the other side were on the flat of their bellies before the calf of gold with a sheepskin around their man. It's the stuff that put our country where she stands to-day, Mr. Furriskey, and I'd have my tongue out of my head by the bloody roots before I'd be heard saying a word against it. But the man in the street, where does he come in? By God he doesn't come in at all as far as I can see.

What do my brave men in the black hats care whether he's in or out, asked Furriskey. What do they care? It's a short jump for the man in the street, I'm thinking, if he's waiting for that crowd to do anything for him. They're a nice crowd, now, I'm telling you.

Oh that's the truth, said Lamont.

Another thing, said Shanahan, you can get too much of that stuff. Feed yourself up with that tack once and you won't want more for a long time.

There's no doubt about it, said Furriskey.

Try it once, said Shanahan, and you won't want it a second time.

Do you know what it is, said Lamont, there are people who read that . . . and keep reading it . . . and read damn the bloody thing else. Now that's a mistake.

A big mistake, said Furriskey.

But there's one man, said Shanahan, there's one man that can write pomes that you can read all day and all night and keep reading them to your heart's content, stuff you'd never tire of. Pomes written by a man that is one of ourselves and written down for ourselves to read. The name of that man . . .

Now that's what you want, said Furriskey.

The name of that man, said Shanahan, is a name that could be christianed on you or me, a name that won't shame us. And that name, said Shanahan, is Jem Casey.

And a very good man, said Lamont.

Jem Casey, said Furriskey.

Do you understand what I mean, said Shanahan.

You haven't any of his pomes on you, have you, said Lamont. If there's one thing I'd like. . . .

I haven't one *on* me if that's what you mean, Mr. Lamont, said Shanahan, but I could give one out as quick as I'd say my prayers. By God it's not for nothing that I call myself a pal of Jem Casey.

I'm glad to hear it, said Lamont.

Stand up there and recite it man, said Furriskey, don't keep us waiting. What's the name of it now?

The name or title of the pome I am about to recite, gentlemen, said Shanahan with leisure priest-like in character, is a pome by the name of the "Workman's Friend". By God you can't beat it. I've heard it praised by the highest. It's a pome about a thing that's known to all of us. It's about a drink of porter.

Porter!

Porter.

Up on your legs man, said Furriskey. Mr. Lamont and myself are waiting and listening. Up you get now.

Come on, off you go, said Lamont.

Now listen, said Shanahan clearing the way with small coughs. Listen now.

He arose holding out his hand and bending his knee beneath him on the chair.

When things go wrong and will not come right,
Though you do the best you can,
When life looks black as the hour of night—
A PINT OF PLAIN IS YOUR ONLY MAN.

By God there's a lilt in that, said Lamont.
Very good indeed, said Furriskey. Very nice.
I'm telling you it's the business, said Shanahan. Listen now.

When money's tight and is hard to get
And your horse has also ran,
When all you have is a heap of debt—
A PINT OF PLAIN IS YOUR ONLY MAN.

When health is bad and your heart feels strange,
And your face is pale and wan,
When doctors say that you need a change,
A PINT OF PLAIN IS YOUR ONLY MAN.

There are things in that pome that make for what you call *permanence*. Do you know what I mean, Mr. Furriskey?

There's no doubt about it, it's a grand thing, said Furriskey. Come on, Mr. Shanahan, give us another verse. Don't tell me that is the end of it.

Can't you listen? said Shanahan.

When food is scarce and your larder bare
And no rashers grease your pan,
When hunger grows as your meals are rare—
A PINT OF PLAIN IS YOUR ONLY MAN.

What do you think of that now?

It's a pome that'll live, called Lamont, a pome that'll be heard and clapped when plenty more. . . .

But wait till you hear the last verse, man, the last polish-off, said Shanahan. He frowned and waved his hand.

Oh it's good, it's good, said Furriskey.

> In time of trouble and lousy strife,
> You have still got a darlint plan,
> You still can turn to a brighter life—
> A PINT OF PLAIN IS YOUR ONLY MAN!

Did you ever hear anything like it in your life, said Furriskey. A pint of plain, by God, what! Oh I'm telling you, Casey was a man in twenty thousand, there's no doubt about that. He knew what he was at, too true he did. If he knew nothing else, he knew how to write a pome. A pint of plain is your only man.

Didn't I tell you he was good? said Shanahan. Oh by Gorrah you can't cod me.

There's one thing in that pome, *permanence*, if you know what I mean. That pome, I mean to say, is a pome that'll be heard wherever the Irish race is wont to gather, it'll live as long as there's a hard root of an Irishman left by the Almighty on this planet, mark my words. What do you think, Mr. Shanahan?

It'll live, Mr. Lamont, it'll live.

I'm bloody sure it will, said Lamont.

A pint of plain, by God, eh? said Furriskey.

Tell us, my Old Timer, said Lamont benignly, what do you think of it? Give the company the benefit of your scholarly pertinacious fastidious opinion, Sir Storybook. Eh, Mr. Shanahan?

Conspirators' eyes were winked smartly in the dancing firelight. Furriskey rapped Finn about the knees.

Wake up!

And Sweeny continued, said corn-yellow Finn, at the recital of these staves.

> If I were to search alone
> the hills of the brown world,
> better would I like my sole hut
> in Glen Bolcain.
>
> Good its water greenish-green
> good its clean strong wind,
> good its cress-green cresses,
> best its branching brooklime.

Quick march again, said Lamont. It'll be a good man that'll put a stop to that man's tongue. More of your fancy kiss-my-hand, by God.

Let him talk, said Furriskey, it'll do him good. It has to come out somewhere.

I'm a man, said Shanahan in a sententious fashion, that could always listen to what my fellowman has to say. I'm telling you now, it's a wise man that listens and says nothing.

Certainly said Lamont. A wise old owl once lived in a wood, the more he heard the less he said, the less he said the more he heard, let's emulate that wise old bird.

There's a lot in that, said Furriskey. A little less of the talk and we were right.

Finn continued with a patient weariness, speaking slowly to the fire and to the six suppliant shoes that were

in devotion around it, the voice of the old man from the
dim bed.

> Good its sturdy ivies,
> good its bright neat sallow,
> good its yewy yew-yews,
> best its sweet-noise birch.
>
> A haughty ivy
> growing through a twisted tree,
> myself on its true summit,
> I would lothe leave it.
>
> I flee before skylarks,
> it is the tense stern-race,
> I overleap the clumps
> on the high hill-peaks.
>
> When it rises in front of me
> the proud turtle-dove,
> I overtake it swiftly
> since my plumage grew.
>
> The stupid unwitting woodcock
> when it rises up before me,
> methinks it red-hostile,
> and the blackbird that cries havoc.
>
> Small foxes yelping
> to me and from me,
> the wolves tear them—
> I flee their cries.
>
> They journeyed in their chase of me
> in their swift courses
> so that I flew away from them
> to the tops of mountains.

On every pool there will rain
a starry frost;
I am wretched and wandering
under it on the peak.

The herons are calling
in cold Glen Eila
swift-flying flocks are flying,
coming and going.

I do not relish
the mad clack of humans
sweeter warble of the bird
in the place he is.

I like not the trumpeting
heard at morn;
sweeter hearing is the squeal
of badgers in Benna Broc.

I do not like it
the loud bugling;
finer is the stagbelling stag
of antler-points twice twenty.

There are makings for plough-teams
from glen to glen;
each resting-stag at rest
on the summit of the peaks.

Excuse me for a second, interposed Shanahan in an
urgent manner, I've got a verse in my head. Wait now.
What!

Listen, man. Listen to this before it's lost. When
stags appear on the mountain high, with flanks the colour

of bran, when a badger bold can say good-bye, A PINT OF
PLAIN IS YOUR ONLY MAN!

Well by God Shanahan, I never thought you had it in
you, said Furriskey, turning his wide-eyed smile to the
smile of Lamont, I never thought you had it in you. Take
a look at the bloody poet, Mr. Lamont. What?

The hard Shanahan by God, said Lamont. The hard man.
That's a good one all right. Put it there, Mr. Shanahan.

Hands were extended till they met, the generous grip
of friendship in front of the fire.

All right, said Shanahan laughing in the manner of a
proud peacock, don't shake the handle off me altogether.
Gentlemen, you flatter me. Order ten pints a man till
we celebrate.

My hard bloody Shanahan, said Lamont.

That'll do you now the pair of ye, said Shanahan. Silence
in the court now.

The droning from the bed restarted where it stopped.

> The stag of steep Slieve Eibhlinne,
> the stag of sharp Slieve Fuaid,
> the stag of Eala, the stag of Orrery,
> the mad stag of Loch Lein.

> Stag of Shevna, stag of Larne,
> the stag of Leena of the panoplies
> stag of Cualna, stag of Conachail,
> the stag of two-peaked Bairenn.

> Oh mother of this herd,
> thy coat has greyed,
> no stag is following after thee
> without twice twenty points.

Greater-than-the-material-for-a-little-cloak,
thy head has greyed;
if I were on each little point
littler points would there be on every pointed point.

The stag that marches trumpeting
across the glen to me,
pleasant the place for seats
on his antler top.

After that song, the long one, Sweeny came from
Fiodh Gaibhle to Benn Boghaine, from there to Benn
Faibhne and thence to Rath Murbuilg, attaining no refuge
from the attention of the hag till he came to Dun Sobhairce
in Ulster. Here he went before the hag and threw a leap
from the precise summit of the dun. She followed him in
swift course and dropped on the precipice of Dun Sobhairce
till fine-pulp and small-bits were made of her, falling
lastly into the sea, so that it was thus that she found death
in her chase of Sweeny.

He then travelled and tarried in many places for a month
and a fortnight, on smooth clean delightful hills and on
delicate chill-breezed peaks for a fortnight and a month,
making his abode in the hiding of tree-clumps. And in
leaving Carrick Alaisdar, he delayed there till he had
fashioned these staves as a farewell address, a valediction
on the subject of his manifold sorrow.

Cheerless is existence
without a downy bed,
abode of the shrivelling frost,
gusts of the snowy wind.

Chill icy wind,
shadow of a feeble sun
the shelter of a sole tree
on a mountain-plain.

The bell-belling of the stag
through the woodland,
the climb to the deer-pass,
the voice of white seas.

Forgive me Oh Great Lord,
mortal is this great sorrow,
worse than the black grief—
Sweeny the thin-groined.

Carraig Alasdair
resort of sea-gulls,
sad Oh Creator,
chilly for its guests.

Sad our meeting
two hard-shanked cranes—
myself hard and ragged
she hard-beaked.

Thereafter Sweeny departed and fared till he had crossed the encompassing gullet of the storm-wracked sea till he reached the kingdom of the Britons and fell in with another of a like frenzy, a madman of Briton.

If you are a madman, said Sweeny, tell me your family name.

Fer Caille is my name, he answered.

And the pair of them made a peace and a compact together, talking with each other in a lay of generous staves.

Oh Sweeny, said Fer Caille, let the each watch the other since we have love and trust in each; that is, he who shall first hear the cry of a heron from the blue-watered green-watered water, or the clear call of a cormorant, or the leap of a woodcock from a tree, the note or the sound of a waking plover, or the crack-crackle of withered branches, or he who shall first see the shadow of a bird in the air above the wood, let him call warning and tell the other, so that the two of us can fly away quickly.

At the butt-end of a year's wandering in the company of each other, the madman of Briton had a message for Sweeny's ear.

It is true that we must part to-day, he said, for the end of my life has come and I must go to where I am to die.

What class of a death will you die? asked Sweeny.

Not difficult to relate, said the other, I go now to Eas Dubhthaigh and a gust of wind will get under me until it slams me into the waterfall for drowning, and I shall be interred in the churchyard of a saint, and afterwards I shall attain Heaven. That is my end.

Thereafter, on the recital of valedictory staves, Sweeny fared again in the upper air on his path across sky-fear and rain-squalls to Erin, dwelling here and there in the high places and in the low and nestling in the heart of enduring oaks, never restful till he had again attained ever-delightful Glen Bolcain. There he encountered a demented woman till he fled before her, rising stealthily nimbly lightly from the summit of the peaks till he

reached Glen Boirche in the south and committed himself
to these ranns.

> Chill chill is my bed at dark
> on the peak of Glen Boirche,
> I am weakly, no mantle on me,
> lodged in a sharp-stirked holly.
>
> Glen Bolcain of the twinkle spring
> it is my rest-place to abide in;
> when Samhain comes, when summer comes,
> it is my rest-place where I abide.
>
> For my sustenance at night,
> the whole that my hands can glean
> from the gloom of the oak-gloomed oaks—
> the herbs and the plenteous fruits.
>
> Fine hazel-nuts and apples, berries,
> blackberries and oak-tree acorns,
> generous raspberries, they are my due,
> haws of the prickle-hawy hawthorn.
>
> Wild sorrels, wild garlic faultless,
> clean-topped cress,
> they expel from me my hunger,
> acorns from the mountain, melle-root.

After a prolonged travel and a searching in the skies,
Sweeny arrived at nightfall at the shore of the widespread
Loch Ree, his resting-place being the fork of the tree of
Tiobradan for that night. It snowed on his tree that night,
the snow being the worst of all the other snows he had
endured since the feathers grew on his body, and he was
constrained to the recital of these following verses.

Terrible is my plight this night
the pure air has pierced my body,
lacerated feet, my cheek is green—
O Mighty God, it is my due.

It is bad living without a house,
Peerless Christ, it is a piteous life!
a filling of green-tufted fine cresses
a drink of cold water from a clear rill.

Stumbling out of the withered tree-tops
walking the furze—it is truth—
wolves for company, man-shunning,
running with the red stag through fields.

If the evil hag had not invoked Christ against me that
I should perform leaps for her amusement, I would not
have relapsed into madness, said Sweeny.

Come here, said Lamont, what's this about jumps?

Hopping around, you know, said Furriskey.

The story, said learned Shanahan in a learned explanatory manner, is about this fellow Sweeny that argued
the toss with the clergy and came off second-best at the
wind-up. There was a curse—a malediction—put down
in the book against him. The upshot is that your man
becomes a bloody bird.

I see, said Lamont.

Do you see it, Mr. Furriskey, said Shanahan. What
happens? He is changed into a bird for his pains and he
could go from here to Carlow in one hop. Do you see
it Mr. Lamont?

Oh I see that much all right, said Lamont, but the man

that I'm thinking of is a man by the name of Sergeant
Craddock, the first man in Ireland at the long jump in the
time that's gone.

Craddock?

That was always one thing, said Shanahan wisely, that
the Irish race was always noted for, one place where the
world had to give us best. With all his faults and by God
he has plenty, the Irishman can jump. By God he can
jump. That's one thing the Irish race is honoured for no
matter where it goes or where you find it—jumping.
The world looks up to us there.

We were good jumpers from the start, said Furriskey.

It was in the early days of the Gaelic League, said Lamont.
This Sergeant Craddock was an ordinary bloody bobby
on the beat, down the country somewhere. A bit of a
bags, too, from what I heard. One fine morning he wakes
up and is ordered to proceed if you don't mind to the
Gaelic League Sports or whatever it was that was being
held in the town that fine spring Sunday. To keep his eye
open for sedition do you know and all the rest of it. All
right. In he marches to do his duty, getting the back of
the bloody hand from the women and plenty of guff from
the young fellows. Maybe he was poking around too
much and sticking his nose where it wasn't wanted. . . .

I know what you mean, said Shanahan.

Anyway, didn't he raise the dander of the head of the
house, the big man, the head bottle-washer. Up he
came to my cool sergeant with his feathers ruffled and his
comb as red as a turkeycock and read out a long rigmarole
in Irish to your man's face.

That'll do you, says the sergeant, keep that stuff for them that wants it. I don't know what you're saying, man.

So you don't know your own language, says the head man.

I do, says the sergeant, I know plenty of English.

Your man then asks the sergeant his business in Irish and what he's doing there in the field at all.

Speak English, says the sergeant.

So be damned but your man gets his rag out and calls the sergeant a bloody English spy.

Well maybe he was right, said Furriskey.

Shh, said Shanahan.

But wait till I tell you. The sergeant just looked at him as cool as blazes.

You're wrong, says he, *and I'm as good a man as you or any other man*, says he.

You're a bloody English bags, says your man in Irish.

And I'll prove it, says the sergeant.

And with that your man gets black in the face and turns his back and walks to the bloody platform where all the lads were doing the Irish dancing with their girls, competitions of one kind and another, you know. Oh it was all the fashion at one time, you were bloody nothing if you couldn't do your Walls of Limerick. And here too were my men with the fiddles and the pipes playing away there at the reels and jigs for further orders. Do you know what I mean?

Oh I know what you're talking about all right, said

Shanahan, the national music of our country, Rodney's Glory, the Star of Munster and the Rights of Man.

The Flogging Reel and Drive the Donkey, you can't beat them, said Furriskey.

That's the ticket, said Lamont. Anyway, didn't your man get into a dark corner with his butties till they hatched out a plan to best the sergeant. All right. Back went your man to the sergeant, who was taking it easy in the shade of a tree.

You said a while ago, says your man, that you were a better man than any man here. Can you jump?

I can not, says the sergeant, but I'm no worse than the next man.

We'll see, says your man.

Now be damned but hadn't they a man in the tent there from the county Cork, a bloody dandy at the long jump, a man that had a name, a man that was known in the whole country. A party by the name of Bagenal, the champion of all Ireland.

Gob that was a cute one, said Furriskey.

A very cute one. But wait till I tell you. The two of them lined up and a hell of a big crowd gathering there to watch. Here was my nice Bagenal as proud as a bloody turkey in his green pants, showing off the legs. Beside him stands another man, a man called Craddock, a member of the polis. His tunic is off him on the grass but the rest of his clothes is still on. He is standing as you find him with his blue pants and his big canal-barges on his two feet. I'm telling you it was something to look at. It was a sight to see.

I don't doubt it, said Shanahan.

Yes. Well Bagenal is the first off, sailing through the air like a bird and down in a shower of sand. What was the score?

Eighteen feet, said Furriskey.

Not at all man, twenty-two. Twenty-two feet was the jump of Bagenal there and then and by God the shout the people gave was enough to make the sergeant puke what was inside him and plenty more that he never swallowed.

Twenty-two feet is a good jump any day, said Shanahan.

After the cheering had died down, said Lamont, my man Bagenal strolls around and turns his back on the sergeant and asks for a cigarette and starts to blather out of him to his friends. What does my sergeant do, do you think, Mr. Shanahan.

I'm saying nothing, said knowing Shanahan.

By God you're a wise man. Sergeant Craddock keeps his mouth shut, takes a little run and jumps twenty-four feet six.

Do you tell me that! cried Furriskey.

Twenty-four feet six.

I'm not surprised, said Shanahan in his amazement, I'm not surprised. Go where you like in the wide world, you will always find that the Irishman is looked up to for his jumping.

Right enough, said Furriskey, the name of Ireland is honoured for that.

Go to Russia, said Shanahan, go to China, go to France. Everywhere and all the time it is hats off and a gra-ma-

cree to the Jumping Irishman. Ask who you like they'll
all tell you that. The Jumping Irishman.

It's a thing, said Furriskey, that will always stand to us
—jumping.

When everything's said, said Lamont, the Irishman
has his points. He's not the last man that was made now.

He is not, said Furriskey.

When everything had been said by Sweeny, said droning
dark-voiced Finn, a glimmering of reason assailed the madman till it turned his steps in the direction of his people
that he might dwell with them and trust them. But holy
Ronan in his cell was acquainted by angels of the intention
of Sweeny and prayed God that he should not be loosed
from his frenzy until his soul had been first loosed from
his body and here is a summary of the result. When
the madman reached the middle of Slieve Fuaid, there
were strange apparitions before him there, red headless
trunks and trunkless heads and five stubbly rough grey
heads without trunk or body between them, screaming
and squealing and bounding hither and thither about the
dark road beleaguering and besetting him and shouting
their mad abuse, until he soared in his fright aloft in front
of them. Piteous was the terror and the wailing cries,
and the din and the harsh-screaming tumult of the heads
and the dogsheads and the goatsheads in his pursuit,
thudding on his thighs and his calves and on the nape of
his neck and knocking against trees and the butts of rocks
—a wild torrent of villainy from the breast of a high
mountain, not enough resting for a drink of water for
mad Sweeny till he finally achieved his peace in the tree

on the summit of Slieve Eichneach. Here he devoted his time to the composition and recital of melodious staves on the subject of his evil plight.

After that he went on his career of wild folly from Luachair Dheaghaidh to Fiodh Gaibhle of the clean streams and the elegant branches, remaining there for one year on the sustenance of saffron heart-red holly-berries and black-brown oak-acorns, with draughts of water from the Gabhal, concluding there with the fashioning of this lay.

> Ululation, I am Sweeny,
> my body is a corpse;
> sleeping or music nevermore—
> only the soughing of the storm-wind.

> I have journeyed from Luachair Dheaghaidh
> to the edge of Fiodh Gaibhle,
> this is my fare—I conceal it not—
> ivy-berries, oak-mast.

After that Sweeny in his restlessness came to All Fharannain, a wondrous glen it is with green-streamed water, containing multitudes of righteous people and a synod of saints, heavy-headed apple-trees bending to the ground, well-sheltered ivies, ponderous fruit-loaded branches, wild deer and hares and heavy swine, and fat seals sleeping in the sun, seals from the sea beyant. And Sweeny said this.

> All Fharannain, resort of saints,
> fulness of hazels, fine nuts,
> swift water without heat
> coursing its flank.

Plenteous are its green ivies,
its mast is coveted;
the fair heavy apple-trees
they stoop their arms.

At length Sweeny penetrated to the place the head-saint
Moling was, that is, to speak precisely, House-Moling.
The psalter of Kevin was in Moling's presence and he
reciting it to his students. Sweeny came to the edge of
the well and nibbled at the cresses until Moling said:

Oh madman, that is early eating.

The two of them madman and saint then embarked
on a lengthy dialogue to the tune of twenty-nine elegant
verses; and then Moling spoke again.

Your arrival here is surely welcome, Sweeny, he said,
for it is destined that you should end your life here, and
leave the story of your history here and be buried in the
churchyard there beyant. And I now bind you that,
however much of Erin that you overwander, you will
come to me each evening the way I can write your story.

And so it was, Sweeny returning from his wandering to
and from the celebrated trees of Erin at vespers each
evening, Moling ordering a collation for the mad one at
that hour and commanding his cook to give Sweeny a
share of the day's milking. One night a dispute arose
among the serving-women over the head of Sweeny, the
madman being accused of an act of adultery in the hedge
by the herd's sister as she went with her measure of milk
in the evening to place it in a hole in the cowdung for
Sweeny, the herd's sister putting the dishonourable lie in
the ear of her brother. He immediately took a spear

from the spear-rack in the house and Sweeny's flank being towards him as he lay in the cowdung at his vesper-milk, he was wounded by a spear-cast in the left nipple so that the point went through him and made two halves of his back. An acolyte at the door of the church witnessed the black deed and acquainted Moling, who hastened with a concourse of honourable clerics until the sick man had been forgiven and anointed.

Dark is the deed you have done, Oh herd, said Sweeny, for owing to the wound you have dealt me I cannot henceforth escape through the hedge.

I did not know you were there, said the herd.

By Christ, man, said Sweeny, I have not injured you at all.

Christ's curse on you, Oh herd, said Moling.

Thereafter they had colloquy and talked loudly together until they had achieved a plurality of staves, Sweeny terminating the talking with these verses.

> There was a time when I preferred
> to the low converse of humans
> the accents of the turtle-dove
> fluttering about a pool.

> There was a time when I preferred
> to the tinkle of neighbour bells
> the voice of the blackbird from the crag
> and the belling of a stag in a storm.

> There was a time when I preferred
> to the voice of a fine woman near me
> the call of the mountain-grouse
> heard at day.

There was a time when I preferred
the yapping of the wolves
to the voice of a cleric
melling and megling within.

Thereafter a death-swoon assailed Sweeny so that
Moling and his clerics arose till each man had placed a
stone on Sweeny's tomb.

Dear indeed is he whose tomb it is, said Moling, dear
to me the madman, delightful to behold him at yonder
well. Its name is Madman's Well for often he would feast
on its cresses and its water and the well is named after him
on account of that. Dear to me every other place that
Sweeny was wont to frequent.

And Moling addressed himself to the composition and
the honey-tongued recital of these following poems.

Here is the tomb of Sweeny!
His memory racks my heart,
dear to me therefore are the haunts
of the saintly madman.

Dear to me Glen Bolcain fair
for Sweeny loved it;
dear the streams that leave it
dear its green-crowned cresses.

That beyant is Madman's Well
dear the man it nourished,
dear its perfect sand,
beloved its clear waters.

Melodious was the talk of Sweeny
long shall I hold his memory,
I implore the King of Heaven
on his tomb and above his grave.

Biographical reminiscence, part the sixth: Early one evening I was seated at the large table in the dining-room arranging and perusing my day-papers when I perceived that the hall-door had been opened from without by the means of a latch-key. After a brief interval it was shut again. I heard the loud voice of my uncle from the hallway intermixed with another voice that was not known to me at all; then the shuffling of feet and the thud of gloved palms knocked together in discords of good humour. Hastily I covered such sheets as contained reference to the forbidden question of the sexual relations.

The door of the dining-room was thrown open but nobody entered for the space of fifteen seconds; after that, my uncle came in with a swift heavy stride bearing in his arms before him a weighty object covered with a black water-proof cloth. This he placed on the table without delay and clapped his hands together in a token that his task had been accomplished.

Description of my uncle: Bluff, abounding in external good nature; concerned - that - he - should - be - well - thought - of; holder of Guinness clerkship the third class.

An elderly man of slight build entered, smiling diffidently at me as I sat there at the supervision of my papers. His body was bent sidewise in an awkward fashion and his shoulders appeared to move lithely beneath his coat as if his woollen small-clothes had been disarranged in the divesting of his street-coat. His skull shone clearly in the gaslight under the aura of his sparse hair. His double-breasted jacket bore a vertical ripple in the front, a result of the inexpensive quality of the canvas lining. He nodded to me in friendly salutation.

Fingering his coat-tails, my uncle took a stand near the fire and surveyed us, bisecting between us the benison of his smile. Not terminating it when he addressed me, it imparted a soft husky quality to his voice.

Well, fellow-my-lad, he said, what are *we* at this evening? My nephew, Mr. Corcoran.

I arose. Mr. Corcoran advanced and extended his small hand, exerting considerable strength in a fine man-grip.

I hope we are not disturbing you at your work, he said.

Not at all, I answered.

My uncle laughed.

Faith, he said, you would want to be a clever man to do that, Mr. Corcoran. That would be a miracle certainly. Tell me this, do you ever open a book at all?

This I received in silence, standing quietly by the table.

Nature of silence: Indifferent, contemptuous.

Perceiving that my want of a reply showed me sad and crestfallen before the rebuke of my uncle, Mr. Corcoran moved quickly to my defence.

Oh I don't know about that, he said. I don't know about

that. The people that never seem to exert themselves at all, these are the boys that win the prize. Show me a man that is always fussing and rushing about and I will show you a man that never did a day's work in his life.

My uncle smiled about him without malice.

Maybe true, he said, maybe not.

Now a funny thing I have a young lad at home, said Mr. Corcoran, and I declare to God I am sick sore and tired telling him to stop in at night and do his lessons but you might as well be talking to that, look.

Choosing his boot, the buttoned class, as a convenient example of inanition, he lifted it in the air, slowly describing an arc of forty-five degrees.

Well he came home the other day with a report and I declare to God the little monkey got his own back in great style. He had me where he wanted me. First in Christian doctrine if you please.

My uncle removed his smile in solicitous interrogation.

Your boy Tom?

Young Tom the same boyo.

Well I'm very glad to hear it, I am indeed, said my uncle. A sharp-witted little lad he is too. Christian doctrine of course, it is very nice to see the young lads making that their own. That particular subject, I mean. It is very necessary in the times we live in, it is, faith.

He turned to me.

Now Mister-my-friend, he said, when are we going to hear from you? When are you going to bring home a prize? Certainly you have enough papers there to win a prize at something . . .

He laughed slightly.

. . . if it was only a paper-chase, he added.

His laugh had a dual function, partly to applaud his jest, partly to cloak his anger. Turning to Mr. Corcoran he extracted from him a small smile of concurrence.

I know my catechism, I said in a toneless manner.

That is the main thing, said Mr. Corcoran.

Aye but do you, said my uncle quickly, do you, that's the question. What is meant by sanctifying grace? Why does the bishop give those he confirms a stroke on the cheek? Name the seven deadly sins. Name the one that begins with S.

Anger, I answered.

Anger begins with A, said my uncle.

Mr. Corcoran, in order to achieve diversion, removed the black cloth in a priestly manner, showing that the object on the table was a gramophone.

I think you have the needles, he said.

My uncle had assumed a flushed appearance.

All present and correct, Sir, he said loudly, taking a small canister from his pocket. Oh indeed there is little respect for the penny catechism in Ireland to-day and well I know it. But it has stood to us, Mr. Corcoran, and will please God to the day we die. It is certainly a grand thing to see the young lads making it their own for you won't get very far in the world without it. Mark that, my lad. It is worth a bag of your fine degrees and parchments.

He blew his nose and went to the table in order to assist Mr. Corcoran. The two of them bent together at the adjustment of the machine, extracting a collapsible extensible retractable tone-arm from its interior with the aid of their four hands. I gathered my day-papers silently, hopeful that I might escape without offence. Mr. Corcoran opened a small compartment at the base of the machine by pressing a cleverly hidden spring and brought out a number of records, scraping and whistling them together by a careless manner of manipulation. My uncle was occupied with inserting a cranking device into an aperture in the machine's side and winding it with the meticulous and steady motion that is known to prolong the life and resiliency of springs. Fearing that his careful conduct of the task was not observed, he remarked that fast winding will lead to jerks, jerks will lead to strain and strain to breakage, thus utilizing a figure of speech to convey the importance of taking pains.

Name of figure of speech: Anadipolsis (or Epanastrophe).

Moderation in all things, he said, that is the trick that won the war.

I then recalled that he was a member of an operatic society composed of residents of the Rathmines and Rathgar district, an indifferent voice of the baritone range winning for him a station in the chorus. Mr. Corcoran, I thought, was likewise situated.

My uncle placed a needle finely on the revolving disk and stepped quickly back, his meticulous hands held forth without motion in his expectancy. Mr. Corcoran was waiting in a chair by the fire, his legs crossed, his downcast head supported in position by the knuckles of his right hand, which were resting damply on his top teeth.

The tune came duly, a thin spirant from the *Patience* opera. The records were old and not of the modern electrical manufacture. A chorus intervening, Mr. Corcoran and my uncle joined in it in happy and knowledgeable harmony, stressing the beat with manual gesture. My uncle, his back to me, also moved his head authoritatively, exercising a roll of fat which he was accustomed to wear at the back of his collar, so that it paled and reddened in the beat of the music.

The tune ended.

My uncle shook his head and made a noise of perplexed admiration as he arose with haste to remove the needle.

I could listen to that tune, he said, from early morning to late at night and not a bit of me would tire of it. Ah, it's a lovely thing. I think it's the nicest of the whole lot, I do indeed. There's a great lilt in it, Mr. Corcoran.

Mr. Corcoran, whom by chance I was observing, smiled preliminarily but when about to speak, his smile was transfixed on his features and his entire body assumed a stiff attitude. Suddenly he sneezed, spattering his clothing with a mucous discharge from his nostrils.

As my uncle hurried to his assistance, I felt that my gorge was about to rise. I retched slightly, making a noise with my throat similar to that utilized by persons in the article of death. My uncle's back was towards me as he bent in ministration.

There's a very catching cold going around, Mr. Corcoran, he said. You would need to watch yourself. You would need to keep yourself well wrapped up.

I clutched my belongings and retired quickly as they

worked together with their pocket-cloths. I went to my room and lay prostrate on my bed, endeavouring to recover my composure. After a time the thin music came upon my ear, thinner and hollower through the intervening doors but perceptibly reinforced at the incidence of a chorus. Putting on my grey coat, I made my way to the street.

Such was the degree of my emotional disturbance that I walked down to the centre of the town without adverting to my surroundings and without a predetermined destination. There was no rain but the streets were glistening and people were moving in a quick active manner along the pavements. A slight fog, perforated by the constellation of the street-lamps, hung down on the roadway from the roofs of the houses. Reaching the Pillar, I turned about to retrace my steps when I perceived that Kerrigan had emerged from a side-street and was now walking actively before me. Hastening after him, I dealt him a smart blow with my closed fist in the small of the back, thereby eliciting a coarse expression not infrequently associated with the soldiery. We then saluted in formal fashion and talked on general and academic topics, continuing to walk in the Grafton Street direction.

Where are you going, I asked him.

To Byrne's, he answered. Where are *you* going?

Michael Byrne was a man of diverse intellectual attainments and his house was frequently the scene of scholarly and other disputations.

Description of Michael Byrne: He was tall, middle-aged,

stout. Large eyes moved briskly with attention behind
the windows of his glasses. His upper lip protruded in a
prim bird-like manner. His tones when he spoke were
soothing, authoritative, low, and of delicate texture. He
was painter, poet composer, pianist, master-printer,
tactician, an authority on ballistics.

Nowhere, I answered.

You might as well come along then, he said.

That, I answered, would be the chiefest wisdom.

*The origin of the distinctive adjective, being the wise sayings
of the son of Sirach*: The fear of the Lord is the beginning
and the crown of wisdom. The word of God is the foun-
tain of wisdom, and her ways are everlasting commandments. The fear of the Lord shall delight the heart, and
shall give joy, and gladness, and length of days. It shall
go well with him that feareth the Lord, and in the days
of his end he shall be blessed. My son, from thy youth
up receive instruction, and even to thy grey hairs thou
shalt find wisdom. Come to her as one that plougheth
and soweth, and wait for her good fruits. For in working
about her thou shalt labour a little, and shalt quickly eat
of her fruits. Take all that shall be brought upon thee, and
keep patience, for gold and silver are tried in the fire, but
acceptable men in the furnace of humiliation. Hear the
judgment of your father, and grieve him not in his life.
The father's blessing establisheth the houses of the
children, but the mother's curse rooteth up the foundation. Despise not a man in his old age, for we also shall
become old. Despise not the discourse of them that are

ancient and wise; but acquaint thyself with their proverbs. Praise not a man for his beauty, neither despise a man for his look. The bee is small among flying things, but her fruit hath the chiefest sweetness. Be in peace with many, but let one of a thousand be thy counsellor. Nothing can be compared to a faithful friend, and no weight of gold and silver is able to countervail the goodness of his fidelity. If thou wouldst get a friend, try him before thou takest him, and do not credit him easily. For there is a friend for his own occasion, and he will not abide in the day of thy trouble. A lie is a foul blot in a man. In nowise speak against the truth, but be ashamed of the lie in thy ignorance. Let not the naming of God be usual in thy mouth, and meddle not with the names of saints. A man that sweareth much shall be filled with iniquity, and a scourge shall not depart from his house. Before thou hear, answer not a word, and interrupt not others in the midst of their discourse. Hast thou a word against thy neighbour, let it die within thee, trusting that it will not burst thee. Hedge in thy ears with thorns; hear not a wicked tongue; and make doors and bars of thy mouth. Melt down thy gold and silver, and make a balance for thy words. Flee from sin as from the face of a serpent. All iniquity is like a two-edged sword; there is no remedy for the wound thereof. Observe the time and fly from evil. He that loveth the danger shall perish therein, and he that toucheth pitch shall be defiled with it. In every work of thine regard thy soul in faith, for this is the keeping of the commandments. In all thy works remember thy last end and thou shalt never sin. Conclusion of the foregoing.

We sat there at Byrne's darkly in a dim room, five of us at voice-play on the threads of disputation. A small intense fire glowed from under a dome of slack, a rich roundness being imparted to adjacent or nearby table-legs by red incantation. Byrne was tinkling a spoon in the interior of his glass.

Yesterday, he said, Cryan brought me his complete prose works.

He was seated alone in the darkness beyond the table, dosing himself medicinally with ovoid tablets dissolved in water.

The day before that, he continued, he told me he was *aching* to hear me play Bach. Aching!

He gave a sustained indolent chuckle which he gradually declined in tone, affording a clink of the glass against his teeth in a symbol that he had ended.

Kerrigan unseen put in a voice from his ingle.

Poor Cryan, he said. The poor man.

He is addicted to mental ludo, said Byrne.

We pondered this between us for a time.

The poor man, said Kerrigan.

What is wrong with Cryan and most people, said Byrne, is that they do not spend sufficient time in bed. When a man sleeps, he is steeped and lost in a limp toneless happiness: awake he is restless, tortured by his body and the illusion of existence. Why have men spent the centuries seeking to overcome the awakened body. Put it to sleep, that is a better way. Let it serve only to turn the sleeping soul over, to change the blood-stream and thus make possible a deeper and more refined sleep.

I agree, I said.

We must invert our conception of repose and activity, he continued. We should not sleep to recover the energy expended when awake but rather wake occasionally to defecate the unwanted energy that sleep engenders. This might be done quickly—a five mile race at full tilt around the town and then back to bed and the kingdom of the shadows.

You're a terrible man for the blankets, said Kerrigan.

I'm not ashamed to admit that I love my bed, said Byrne. She was my first friend, my foster-mother, my dearest comforter. . . .

He paused and drank.

Her warmth, he continued, kept me alive when my mother bore me. She still nurtures me, yielding without stint the parturition of her cosy womb. She will nurse me gently in my last hour and faithfully hold my cold body when I am dead. She will look bereaved when I am gone.

This speech did not please us, bringing to each of us our last personal end. We tittered in cynical fashion.

Glass tinkle at his teeth notified a sad concluding drink.

Brinsley gave a loud question.

Wasn't Trellis another great bed-bug?

He was, I answered.

I'm afraid I never heard of Trellis, said Byrne. Who is Trellis?

A member of the author class, I said.

Did he write a book on Tactics? I fancy I met him in Berlin. A tall man with glasses.

He has been in bed for the last twenty years, I said.

You are writing a novel of course? said Byrne.

He is, said Brinsley, and the plot has him well in hand.

Trellis's dominion over his characters, I explained, is impaired by his addiction to sleep. There is a moral in that.

You promised to give me a look at this thing, said Kerrigan.

Brinsley, re-examining his recollection of my spare-time literary work, was chuckling in undertones from his unseen habitation.

He is a great man that never gets out of bed, he said. He spends the days and nights reading books and occasionally he writes one. He makes his characters live with him in his house. Nobody knows whether they are there at all or whether it is all imagination. A great man.

It is important to remember that he reads and writes only green books. That is an important point.

I then gave an account of this quality in order to amuse them and win their polite praise.

Relevant extract from Manuscript: Trellis practised another curious habit in relation to his reading. All colours except green he regarded as symbols of evil and he confined his reading to books attired in green covers. Although a man of wide learning and culture, this arbitrary rule caused serious chasms in his erudition. The Bible, for instance, was unknown to him and much of knowledge of the great mysteries of religion and the origin of man was acquired from servants and public-house acquaintances and was on that account imperfect and in some respects ludicrously garbled. It is for this reason that his well-known work, *Evidences of Christian Religion*, contains the seeds of serious heresy. On being commended by a friend to read a work of merit lately come from the booksellers, he would inquire particularly as to the character of the bindings and on learning that they were not of the green colour would condemn the book (despite his not having perused it), as a work of Satan; this to the great surprise of his friend. For many years he experienced a difficulty in obtaining a sufficiency of books to satisfy his active and inquiring mind, for the green colour was not favoured by the publishers of London, excluding those who issued text-books and treatises on such subjects as fretwork, cookery and parabolics. The publishers of Dublin, however, deemed the colour a fitting one for their many works on the subject of Irish history and antiquities and it is not surprising that Trellis came to be regarded as an authority thereon and was frequently consulted by persons engaged in research, including members of the religious orders, the enclosed class.

On one occasion, his love of learning made him the victim of a melancholy circumstance that continued to cause him spiritual anxiety for many years. He acquired a three-volume work on the subject of the Irish monastic foundations at the time of the Invasion and (being in the habit of sleeping during the day), read it throughout the night by the light of his incandescent petrol lamp. One morning he was recalled from his sleep accidentally by inordinate discords from Peter Place, where rough-mannered labourers were unloading hollow tar-barrels. Turning idly to resume the performance of his sleep, he noticed to his great alarm that the three volumes by his bedside were blue. Perceiving that he had been deluded by a subterfuge of Satan, he caused the books to be destroyed and composed a domestic curriculum calculated to warrant the orthodoxy of all books introduced into his house at any future time. Conclusion of the foregoing.

What happened, asked Brinsley, when the lad was sent to set about the servant or something?

Very unexpected things happened, I said. They fall in love and the villain Furriskey, purified by the love of a noble woman, hatched a plot for putting sleeping-draughts in Trellis's porter by slipping a few bob to the grocer's curate. This meant that Trellis was nearly always asleep and awoke only at predeterminable hours, when everything would be temporarily in order.

This is very interesting, said Byrne an unseen listener.

Well what did Furriskey do when he got the boy asleep? asked Kerrigan.

Oh, plenty, I said. He married the girl. They took a little house in Dolphin's Barn and opened a sweety-shop and lived there happily for about twenty hours out of twenty-four. They had to dash back to their respective stations, of course, when the great man was due to be stirring in his sleep. They hired a girl to mind the shop when they were gone, eight and six a week with dinner and tea.

Polite amusement and approval were expressed at the unsuspected trend of events.

You will have to show me this thing, said Byrne, it involves several planes and dimensions. You have read Schutzmeyer's book, of course?

Well wait now, said Brinsley. What happened Shanahan and that crowd? How did they use their freedom?

Shanahan and Lamont, I answered, were frequent and welcome visitors to the little house in Dolphin's Barn. The girl Peggy made a neat and homely housewife. Tea was dispensed in a simple but cleanly manner. For the rest of their time, they did not use it too well. They consorted with sailors and cornerboys and took to drink and bad company. Once they were very nearly leaving the country altogether. They met two decadent Greek scullions, Timothy Danaos and Dona Ferentes, ashore from the cooking-galley of a strange ship. It happened in one of the low pubs down by the docks there.

The Greeks' names were repeated in admiration by two members of the company.

The two Greeks, I continued, were deaf and dumb but managed to convey, by jerking their thumbs towards the bay and writing down large sums of money in foreign currency, that there was a good life to be lived across the water.

The Greeks were employed, of course, said Kerrigan, as panders by an eminent Belgian author who was writing a saga on the white slave question. They were concerned in the transport of doubtful cargo to Antwerp.

I recall that the dexterity and ready wit of this conversation induced in all of us a warm intellectual glow extremely pleasant to experience.

That is right, I said. I remember that they inscribed

contours in the air by means of gesture to indicate the fulness of the foreign bosom. A very unsavoury pair of rascals if you like.

You will have to show me this thing, said Byrne. It's not fair to be holding things back, you know.

Certainly, I said. The two boys were saved on this occasion by the bell. Trellis was about to waken, so they had to make a dash for it, leaving their half-took drinks behind them.

After enunciating a quiet chuckle, Byrne made a noise in the darkness of a kind associated with the forcible opening of the lid of a tin container. He then moved about the room, a cigarette for each voice in his enterprising hand. Kerrigan declined and remained unseen, the rest of us revealed at intervals, red pale faces with pucker-cheeks at the rear of the glow-points.

A time passed in casual dialectics. Tea was made without and the light flooded suddenly upon us from the roof, showing each for what he was in his own attitude.

Papers and periodicals were perused in a desultory fashion for some time. Afterwards Byrne searched for an old book purchased for a nominal sum upon the quays and read aloud extracts therefrom for the general benefit and or diversion of the company.

Title of Book referred to: *The Athenian Oracle*, being an Entire COLLECTION of all the Valuable QUESTIONS and ANSWERS in the old Athenian Mercuries intermixed with many CASES in Divinity, Hiſtory, Philoſophy, Mathematicks, Love, Poetry, never before publiſhed.

Extract from Book referred to: 1. Whether it be poſſible for a woman ſo carnally to know a Man in her ſleep as to conceive, for I am ſure that this and no way other was I got with Child.

2. Whether it be lawful to uſe Means to put a ſtop to this growing miſchief, and kill it in the Embryo; this being the only way to avert the Thunderclap of my Father's Indignation.

To the firſt Question, Madam, we are very poſitive, that you are luckily miſtaken, for the thing is abſolutely impoſſible if you know nothing of it; indeed, we had an account of a Widow that made ſuch a pretence, and ſhe might have better credit than a maid, who can have no plea but dead drunk, or in ſome ſwooning fit, and our Phyſicians will hardly allow a poſſibility of the thing then. So that you may ſet your heart at reſt, and think no more of the matter, unleſs for your diverſion.

As for the ſecond Queſtion, ſuch practices are murder, and thoſe that are ſo unhappy as to come under ſuch Circumſtances if they uſe the forementioned means, will certainly one day find the remedy worſe than the Diſeaſe. There are wiſer methods to be taken in ſuch Caſes, as a ſmall journey and a Confident. And afterwards, ſuch a pious and good life as may redreſſ ſuch an heavy miſfortune.

Questions, a Selection of Further: Almond, why ſo bitter being taken in the mouth, and yet the Oyl ſo very ſweet? Apprentice, reduced to want, how may he relieve himſelf? Blood, is the eating of it lawful? Baptiſm, adminiſtered by a Mid-wife or Lay Hand, is it lawful? Devil, why called Lucifer; and elfewhere the Prince of Darknefs? Eftate, gotten by felling lewd Books, can it profper? Eyes, what Method muft I take with 'em when weak? Horfe, with a round fundament, why does he emit a fquare Excrement? Happinefs, what is it? Lady, difturbed in her Bed, your thoughts of it? Light, is it a Body? Myftae or Cabalifts, what d'ye think of them? Marriage, is not the End of it, in a great Meafure, loft nowadays? Poem, by Mr. Tate? Virginity, is it a Vertue? Wind, what is it? Wife, is it lawful for a Man to beat her? Wife, if an ill one, may I pray that God wou'd take her to himfelf? Conclusion of the foregoing.

Note to Reader before proceeding further: Before proceeding further, the Reader is respectfully advised to refer to the Synopsis or Summary of the Argument on Page 85.

Further extract from my Manuscript, descriptive of the Pooka MacPhellimey, his journey and other matters: It was the shine of the morning sun, diluted though it was by the tangle of the forest and the sacking on the windows, that recalled the Pooka MacPhellimey from his heavy sleep by the side of his wife. He awoke with a frown and made a magic pass in the air with his thumb, thus awakening also the beetles and the maggots and the other evil creeping things that were slumbering throughout the forest under the flat of great stones. He then lay on his back with his eyes half-closed and his sharp-nailed hands cupped together in the scrub of his poll, uttering his maledictions and his matins in an undertone and reflecting on the hump of his club-foot in the bed in the morning. His shank of a wife beside him was hidden and not easy to discern, a black evil wrinkle in the black sackcloth quilts, a shadow. The Pooka was for taking a hold of his pipe, his pen-knife and his twist of plug-tabacca—he had the three by him— for a morning smoke in bed when the boards of the door were urgently knocked from without and afterwards put in.

Welcome to my house, said the Pooka courteously, tapping his pipe on the bedrail and placing the clubfoot sideways the way no remarks would be passed on the hump. He looked at the empty door with polite inquiry but there was no one there and the party responsible for the knocking could not easily be discerned in any quarter.

Be pleased to come in and welcome, the Pooka said a second time, it is seldom I am honoured by a caller in the morning early.

I am already in the middle of your fine house, said a small voice that was sweeter by far than the tinkle and clap of a waterfall and brighter than the first shaft of day. I am standing here on the flag with the elliptical crack in it.

Welcome to my poor hut, said the Pooka as he surveyed the floor, and it is a queer standing. I do not see you there.

I have come to visit you, said the voice, and to spend an hour in fine talk, and to enter into a colloquy with you.

It is early talking, said the Pooka, but welcome to my house. Your surname, that is a secret that I respect.

My correct name is Good Fairy, said the Good Fairy. I am a good fairy. It is a fine secret but one that is so big that each of us may share it with the other. As to the hour of my advent in your house, it is never too early of a morning for sapient colloquy. Likewise, never is it too late of an evening either.

Under the murk of the bedclothes, the Pooka was fingering the dark hairs of his wife's head—a token that he was engaged in fine thought.

On account of the fact, he said gentlemanly, that I have at all times purposely refrained from an exhaustive exercise of my faculty of vision and my power of optical inspection (I refer now to things perfectly palpable and discernible—the coming of dawn across the mountains is one example and the curious conduct of owls and bats in strong moonlight is another), I had expected (foolishly, perhaps), that I should be able to see quite clearly things that are normally not visible at all as a compensation for my sparing inspection of the visible. It is for that reason that I am inclined to regard the phenomenon of a voice unsupported by a body (more especially at an hour that is acknowledged as inimical to phantasy), as a delusion, one of the innumerable hallucinations which can be traced to lapses from plain diet and to reckless over-eating at bed-time, figments of the large gut rather than of the brain. It is perhaps not altogether irrelevant to mention that last night I finished the last delectable (if indigestible), portion of a queer confection that was prepared in that pan there in the corner. Last night I ate a loins.

Your talk surprises me, said the Good Fairy. Was it the loins of a beetle, or a monkey, or a woman?

Two loinses I ate, replied the Pooka, the loins of a man

and the loins of a dog and I cannot remember which I ate the first or which was tasted sweeter. But two loinses I had in all.

I recognize that that is good eating, said the Good Fairy, though myself I have no body that I could feed. As a feat of eating it is first-rate.

I hear what you say, said the Pooka, but from what quarter are you speaking?

I am sitting here, said the Good Fairy, in a white cup on the dresser.

There are four coppers in that cup, said the Pooka, be careful of them. The truth is that I would ill like to be at the loss of them.

I have no pockets, said the Good Fairy.

That surprises me, said the Pooka raising his thick eyebrows till they were mixed with his hair, that surprises me certainly and by the hokey I do not understand how you can manage without the convenience of a pocket. The pocket was the first instinct of humanity and was used long years before the human race had a trousers between them—the quiver for arrows is one example and the pouch of the kangaroo is another. Where do you keep your pipe?

It is cigarettes I smoke, said the Good Fairy, and I disincline to think that kangaroos are human.

That time you spoke, said the Pooka, it is of course a secret where your voice came from?

When I spoke last, said the Good Fairy, I was kneeling in the cup of your navel but it is bad country and I am there no longer.

Do you tell me that, said the Pooka. This here beside me is my wife.

That is why I left, said the Good Fairy.

There are two meanings in your answer, said the Pooka with his smile of deprecation, but if your departure from my poor bed was actuated solely by a regard for chastity and conjugal fidelity, you are welcome to remain between the blankets without the fear of anger in your host, for there is safety in a triad, chastity is truth and truth is an odd number. And your statement that kangaroos are not human is highly debatable.

Even if it were desirable, replied the Good Fairy, angelic or spiritual carnality is not easy and in any case the offspring would be severely handicapped by being half flesh and half spirit, a very baffling and neutralizing assortment of fractions since the two elements are forever at variance. An act of quasi-angelic carnality on the part of such issue would possibly result in further offspring consisting in composition of a half caro plus half the sum of a half and half caro and spiritus, that is, three-quarters caro and a quarter spiritus. Further carry-on would again halve the spiritual content of the progeny and so on until it becomes zero, thus bringing us by geometric progression to an ordinary love-child with nothing but an unrepresented tradition on the spiritual or angelic side. In regard to the humanity of kangaroos, to admit a kangaroo unreservedly to be a man would inevitably involve one in a number of distressing implications, the kangaroolity of women and your wife beside you being one example.

Your granny, said the Pooka's wife lifting the flap of the blankets the way her voice could be let out.

If we take the view, observed the Pooka, that the angelic element can be eliminated by ordered breeding, it follows that the flesh can be reduced by an opposite process, so that the spectacle of an unmarried mother with a houseful of adult and imperceptible angels is not really the extravagance that it would first appear to be. As an alternative to the commonplace family, the proposition is by no means unattractive because the saving in clothes and doctors' bills would be unconscionable and the science of shop-lifting could be practised with such earnestness as would be compatible with the attainment and maintenance of a life of comfort and culture. I would not be in the least surprised to learn that my wife is a kangaroo, for any hypothesis would be more tenable than the assumption that she is a woman.

Your name, said the Good Fairy, is one thing that you have not related to me privately. There is nothing so important as the legs in determining the kangaroolity of a woman. Is there for example fur on your wife's legs, Sir?

My name, said the Pooka, with an apologetic solicitude, is Fergus MacPhellimey and I am by calling a devil or pooka. Welcome to my poor house. I cannot say whether there is fur on my wife's legs for I have never seen them nor do I intend to commit myself to the folly of looking at them. In any event and in all politeness—nothing would be further from me than to insult a guest—I deem the point you have made as unimportant because there is surely nothing in the old world to prevent a deceitful kangaroo from shaving the hair off her legs, assuming she is a woman.

I knew you were of the Pooka class, said the Good Fairy, but your name, that much escaped me. Taking it for granted that the art of the razor is known to kangaroos as a class, by what subterfuge could the tail be passed off for something different from what it is?

The vocation of the pooka, said the Pooka, is one that is fraught with responsibilities, not the least of these being the lamming and leathering of such parties as are sent to me for treatment by Number One, which is the First Good and the Primal Truth and necessarily an odd number. My own personal number is Two. As regards the second objection you make about the tail, I must state that I personally belong to a class that is accustomed to treat with extreme suspicion all such persons as are un-provided with tails. Myself I have two tails in the bed here, my own tail of loose hair and the tail of my night-shirt. When I wear two shirts on a cold day, you might say that I appear to have three tails in all?

I find your commentary on the subject of your duties a matter of absorbing interest, said the Good Fairy, and I find myself in agreement with your conception of the Good and the Bad Numerals. It is for that reason that I consider the wearing of two shirts by you a deplorable lapse since it must result as you say in three tails in all and truth is an odd number. It is indisputable, whatever about the tail, that a woman kangaroo is provided with a built-in bag where youngsters and trinklets may be stored until such time as they are required—did you ever notice,

Sir, that things were missing about the house where your wife might have put them in her sack for hiding?

I am afraid, replied the Pooka, that you are mistaken in the matter of my tails for I have never worn less than two or more than twenty-four at the one time and together, notwithstanding anything I have confided in you this fine morning. Your personal difficulty will be resolved when I tell you that my second-best day-shirt is fitted with two tails, the one longer than the other, thus enabling me to intermix the physical comfort of two shirts on a cold day with the ceremonial probity of four tails about my bottom (the four of them moving in unison in my trousers when I waggle my hair-tail). I never permit myself to forget that truth is an odd number and that my own personal numerals, the first and the last and all intermediaries, are all inevitably even. I have frequently missed these small things which are necessitous to personal comfort—my glasses and the black glove I use for moving the pan from the hob when it is hot, these are two examples. It is not impossible that my kangaroo has hidden them in her pouch, for by the hoke there was never a child there. To inquire the character of the weather you encountered in your travels here to my poor house from where you were, that would be deplorable violation of your status as a guest?

As regards the vexed question of the little tails, said the Good Fairy, I accept without question your explanation concerning your bi-tailed shirt, a device that I commend as ingenious. By what sophistry of mathematics, however, do you preserve your even numeral when the

exigencies of social etiquette compel you to resort to the
white waistcoat and the tail-coat of an evening? That is
one point that perplexes me. It is very regrettable that
a man of your years can be put to the loss of his glasses
and his black glove for life is very narrow without glasses
and a burnt hand is a bugger. The weather I experienced
was wet and windy but that did not affect me in the least
because I am without a body to be incommoded and I
wear no suit that could be seeped.

There is little substance, said the Pooka, in your difficulty about the dress-coat for the tail of such an elegant
garment has a split through the middle of it that makes it
into two tails, which makes four tails in company with
my own tail and my shirt-tail, or twelve tails in all with
nine shirts. When I come to think of it, I have also
missed a pig-iron coal-scuttle and a horsehair arm-chair
and a ball of twine and a parcel of peats. I am perfectly
sure that spirit though you be you would be troubled by
a fog, for there are few things so spiritual or permeaty as
a wispy fog, or that at least is my experience, because
people who suffer from consumption complain most and
frequently die when there is fog in the air. I make it
a practice to inquire courteously of everyone I meet
whether they can inform me as to the oddity or otherwise
of the last number, I mean, will it be an odd one and
victory for you and your people, or an even one and the
resolution of heaven and hell and the world in my favour.
And the question I ask you in conclusion is this, where
did your talk come from the last time you talked?

Once again, said the Good Fairy, I find myself in the

happy position of being enabled to accept your answer about the tail-coat and I am much beholden to you. But there is this troubling me now, that there might be a heresy in your hair—for the number of such strands might well be odd and the truth is never even. Your enumeration of the matters you have missed about the house, that was an absorbing recital, and I am sure that you can retrieve the lot of them by catching the kangaroo when she is least expectant of rough play and inverting or upturning her the way all that is in her will fall out upon the flags of the kitchen. It is a mistake to think that ghosts and spirits are adversely affected by fogs and vapours (though it is quite possible that a consumptive or weak-chested spirit would find such an atmosphere far from salubrious). I would personally be a happier being if I could solve the riddle that you mention, viz., the character of the last number. When I spoke the last I was skating on that hard lard in the pan and I am now at present resting myself in an egg-cup.

The Pooka's face, at all times flushed and red, now changed to the colour of a withered acorn as he arose and propped himself by the elbows on the pillow.

In referring to my hair, he said with a strain of gentle anger in his voice, are you sure that you are not endeavouring to annoy me, or (worse still) to take a rise out of me? And when you give me the advice to invert my kangaroo the way my lost property will fall out on the hard stones of my poor kitchen, have you a mind to have my glasses smashed? Is it not so that good spirits are very vulnerable when there is fog because they have only one lung as a result of the fact that truth is an odd number? Are you aware of this, that your own existence was provoked by the vitality of my own evil, just as my own being is a reaction to the rampant goodness of Number One, that is, the Prime Truth, and that another pooka whose number will be Four must inevitably appear as soon as your own benevolent activities are felt to require a corrective? Has it never flitted across your mind that the riddle of the last number devolves on the ultimate appearance of a pooka or good spirit who will be so feeble a force for good or bad (as the case may be), that he will provoke no reagent and thus become himself the last and ultimate numeral—all bringing us to the curious and humiliating conclusion that the character of the Last Numeral devolves directly on the existence of a party whose chief characteristics must be anaemia, ineptitude, incapacity, inertia and a spineless dereliction of duty? Answer me that!

As a matter of fact, said the Good Fairy, I do not understand two words of what you have said and I do not know what you are talking about. Do you know how many subordinate clauses you used in that last oration of yours, Sir?

I do not, replied the Pooka.

Fifteen subordinate clauses in all, said the Good Fairy, and the substance of each of them contained matter sufficient for a colloquy in itself. There is nothing so bad as the compression of fine talk that should last for six hours into one small hour. Tell me, Sir, did you ever study Bach?

Where did you say that from? inquired the Pooka.

I was sitting under your bed, replied the Good Fairy, on the handle of your pot.

The fugal and contrapuntal character of Bach's work, said the Pooka, that is a delight. The orthodox fugue has four figures and such a number is in itself admirable. Be careful of that pot. It is a present from my grandmother.

Counterpoint is an odd number, said the Good Fairy, and it is a great art that can evolve a fifth Excellence from four Futilities.

I do not agree with that, said the Pooka courteously. Here is a thing you have not informed me on—that is— the character of your sex. Whether you are a man-angel, that is a conundrum personal to yourself and not to be discussed with strangers.

It seems to me, Sir, said the Good Fairy, that you are again endeavouring to engage me in multi-clause colloquy. If you do not cease from it I will enter into your ear and you will not like it at all, I will warrant you that. My sex is a secret that I cannot reveal.

I only inquired, said the Pooka, because I had a mind to get up and put on my clothes because long bed-hours are enemies and a new day is a thing to be experienced while it is still fresh. I will now do so and if you are of the woman class I must courteously request you to turn your back. And if that piteous itching in my left ear is due to your presence in the inside of it, please take yourself out of there immediately and return to the cup with the four coppers in it.

I have no back that I could turn, said the Good Fairy.

All right, I will rise in that case, said the Pooka, and if it is a useful occupation you desire, you could occupy your time with taking the tree out of my club-boot in the corner there.

By Hickory, said the Good Fairy in an earnest voice, it is full time that I gave you tidings concerning the purpose and the reason for my morning visit to your fine house here. I have come to inform you, Sir, about a party by the name of Sheila Lamont.

The Pooka had arisen with modest grace and was removing his silk nightshirt and reaching for his well-cut suit of seaman's kerseymere.

Where did you say that from? he inquired.

I am reclining in the key-hole, replied the Good Fairy.

The Pooka had put on his black underdrawers and his grey trousers and his old-world cravat and was engaged with his hands behind him in a fastidious adjustment of his tail of hair.

You did not inform me, he remarked politely, as to the sex of Miss Lamont.

As a matter of fact, said the Good Fairy, she is a woman.

That is very satisfactory, said the Pooka.

She is suffering at the moment, said the Good Fairy with the shadow of a slight frown on the texture of his voice, from a very old complaint. I refer now to pregnancy.

Do you tell me so? said the Pooka with a polite interest. That is very satisfactory.

The child is expected, said the Good Fairy, to-morrow evening. I shall be there and shall endeavour to put the child under my benevolent influence for life. To go there alone, however, without informing you of the happy event, that would be a deplorable breach of etiquette. Let the pair of us go therefore, and let the best man of us win the day.

That is a fine saying and a noble sentiment, said the Pooka, but tell me where it came from in the name of Goodness.

From your wife's hair, replied the Good Fairy. I am here in the dark, and it is a hard and joyless country.

I don't doubt it, said the Pooka. Did you tell me that this Miss Lamont was a man?

I did not, said the Good Fairy. She is a woman and a fine one from the point of view of those that have bodies on them.

That is very satisfactory, said the Pooka.

He carefully arranged the folds of his cravat before a piece of a looking-glass that was nailed to the back of the rough door. He then sprinkled an odorous balsam on his hair.

This party that you talk so much about, he inquired, where does it live?

Over there, said the Good Fairy with a jerk of his thumb, beyant.

If I could only see your thumb the time you jerked it, said the Pooka, I might know what you are talking about.

Hurry, said the Good Fairy.

What will we bring along with us against the journey?

asked the Pooka. I am sure it is a long one and one that will soak our eye-brows with the sweat.

Bring what you like, said the Good Fairy.

Should I bring my shank of a wife—the party in the bed over there beyant?

I would not advise it, said the Good Fairy.

A change of black small-trunks? asked the Pooka.

When I have none at all, said the Good Fairy, it would not be right for you to have more than one pair.

The Pooka nodded courteously and carefully dressed himself in a soberly-cut raincoat of grey kerseymere with a built-in cape and an astrakhan collar and then took a hold of his black velour and his walking-stick. All things were then put in order about the house, pans were heeled up on their ends as a precaution against smuts, the fire was tended with black peats, and fine crocks were settled with their butts in the air. Everything was looked after down to the last acorn, which was retrieved from the floor and thrown out through the window.

Where are you now? asked the Pooka.

I am here, replied the Good Fairy, on the flag with the elliptical crack in it.

Pardon me for a moment if you please, said the Pooka with a small bow towards the cracked flag, I wish to take leave of my family.

He approached the bed with a tender solicitude the way he could put his hand in under the clothes. He caressed her rough cheek, hanging his stick on the rail.

Good-bye, my dear, he said tenderly.

Your granny, Fergus, she said in her queer muffled voice.

Where are you, asked the Pooka again.

I am in the pocket of your coat, said the Good Fairy.

You are a nice pocketful if I may say so, said the Pooka, but no matter. How will I know the way to go unless you proceed in front, cracking twigs and disturbing the leaves the way I will know the right direction?

There is no need for the like of that, said the Good Fairy. I will sit here in your pocket and look through the cloth and tell you when you make a wrong step.

You will not look through *that* cloth, said the Pooka, that is the best cloth that could be had. The cloth of that coat when it was new cost me five and sixpence a yard. That was before the War.

I could see through my lids if I shut my eyes, said the Good Fairy.

There is better stuff in that coat, said the Pooka with an earnest but polite inflexion, than was ever in any angel's eye-lid.

There is little doubt but that you are over-fond of the old talk, said the Good Fairy. Could I trouble you, Sir, to start walking?

I will start now, said the Pooka.

He caught hold of the boards of the door and pulled them open till he passed out into the glory of the morning. He fastened the door carefully with an old rope and strode from the clearing into the murk of the surrounding undergrowth, making short work of all obstacles with terrible batters of his club-boot, demolishing tendrils and

creeper-ropes and severing the spidery suspensions of
yellow and green and blood-red yams with whistling
swats of his ashen stick and treading the lichen with a
heavy tread and a light one, iambic pentameter, a club-
step and a footstep.

There is no need, said the Good Fairy, to walk through
every bed of briars you see. Picking your way, there is
such a thing as that.

That is a matter of opinion, said the Pooka.

You could give yourself a bad jag, said the Good Fairy.
Keep to the left, you are going the wrong way.

The Pooka wheeled in his course without appreciable
loss of pace and went straight to the middle of a thicket
of stout rods, cracking it before him the like of a walnut
in a strong palm. The Fairy turned to survey the ruin of
shattered stirks.

Some of these trees are sharp, he observed, mind or
you will make a tatters of your coat.

There is better stuff in that coat, said the Pooka with a
wilful march on a wall of thornsticks, than they are
putting into clothes nowadays. A coat in the old days
was made to stand up to rough wear and was built to last.

Keep to the left, called the Good Fairy. Do you always
carry on like this when you are out walking?

I do not mind telling you, said the Pooka courteously,
that there is no subterfuge of economy more miscon-
ceived than the purchase of cheap factory-machined
clothing. I was once acquainted with a man who committed himself to the folly of a shoddy suit. What do
you think happened?

Keep well to the left, said the Good Fairy. It was likely torn off his back by a nest of thorns on the roadside.

Not correct, said the Pooka. It lathered in a shower of rain and that is the odd truth. The seams of these inferior garments are secured with soap. It frothed on him in the street the like of a pan of new milk boiling over.

One thing is certain, observed the Good Fairy, if you walk through that clump you are now heading for, you will make ribbons of your coat and a tatters of your skin, you will kill the two of us. Discretion, there is such a thing as that.

I will not, said the Pooka. There was small else for him to do but to enter a barber's shop and have the suit shaved. Do you know how much that cost him in silver coin?

The Good Fairy gave a cry in the gloom of the pocket as the Pooka strode in his career through the mad rending and crackling of the thorn-fraught branch-thick tangle.

I do not, he said.

Ten and sevenpence, said the Pooka, and that was a lot of money before the War. Would it be a discourtesy to ask you whether I am travelling in the right direction at all.

You are doing very well, said the Good Fairy.

Very good, said the Pooka.

Once again he quitted the warm sunlight of the clear morning to smash and shatter a clear path in the suntrellised twilight of the jungle.

The two of them had not journeyed the length of two

perches statute when they saw the two men drinking draughts of cool water from their large hats by the stream-side, the one a tall-boned large fine man and the other a small fleshed man. Around their middles they had the full of two belts of bright bullets as well as a pair of six-guns apiece, and two hatfuls of clear crystal they had drunk before the Pooka approached to the back of them as they knelt there to surprise them with a mouthful of his talk.

Ask them who they are, said the Good Fairy.

Greetings, said the Pooka courteously, to the pair of ye.

God save you, said Slug Willard adroitly donning his wet hat the way he could raise it for politeness, this is my friend and my butty, Mr. Shorty Andrews. How are you?

I am very well said the Pooka. And how are you, Mr. Andrews?

I am grand, said Shorty.

Isn't it wonderful weather, said the Good Fairy from the interior of the pocket, a morning like this is as good as a tonic.

What's that? What did you say, Sir? asked Slug.

I said nothing, said the Pooka.

My mistake, said Slug. Unfortunately, Sir, I suffer from noises in the head and in my sleep I often hear voices. You didn't happen to see a steer anywhere, did you, Sir?

We are searching our legs off looking for a lost steer, explained Shorty.

Lord save us, said the Good Fairy, you will surely have the nice job looking for it in a place like this.

You're right there, said Slug, but, no offence, you have a queer way of talking, Sir.

That time, said the Pooka smiling, I did not talk at all.

Maybe not, said Shorty.

On my word of honour, said the Pooka.

It seemed to come from your clothes, Sir—that voice, said Slug. You are not in the habit of carrying a small gramophone in your pocket, are you, Sir?

I am not, said the Pooka.

Introduce me, the Good Fairy said in his urgent whisper.

You are at it again, said Shorty roughly.

Allow me to explain, said the Pooka, the voice you hear is coming from the pocket of my coat. I have a spirit in my pocket and it is he that is doing the talking.

You have your porridge, said Shorty.

On my solemn word of honour, said the Pooka gravely. He came to my house this morning and the pair of us are now engaged on a private journey. He is very gentlemanly and very good at conversation. The two of us are on our way to assist at a happy event at the Red Swan Hotel.

Your porridge, said Shorty.

Well that's a good one, said Slug. Could you give us a look?

Unfortunately there is nothing to see.

Are you sure it's not a ferret you have in your pocket? asked Shorty. You look like a man that was out after rabbits.

Who's a ferret? asked the Good Fairy sharply.

It's a bloody spirit all right, said Slug. I know a spirit when I hear one talking.

Your porridge, said Shorty, would you be so kind, you in the pocket, as to give us a selection on your harp?

The idea that all spirits are accomplished instrumentalists is a popular fallacy, said the Good Fairy in a cold voice, just as it is wrong to assume that they all have golden tempers. Maybe your doubts would be resolved if I kicked the jaw off your face, Mr. Andrews?

Keep your distance, me man, said Shorty with a quick move to the gun-butts, keep your distance or I'll shoot your lights out!

Put your gun up, man, said Slug, he hasn't got any. Do you not know that much at your time of life. He is all air.

He'll have a damn sight less when I'm through, shouted Shorty, no bloody spirit is going to best me.

Tut, tut, said the Pooka soothingly, there is no necessity to make a scene.

I was called a ferret, said the Good Fairy.

Porridge and parsnips, said Shorty.

You keep your trap shut for five minutes, said Slug with fierce shoulders towering over the head of his friend, shut your bloody mouth now, do you hear me? This gentleman and his spirit are friends of mine, mind that now, and when you insult them you insult me. Don't make any mistake about that if you value your bloody life. H.O., H.A. Hit one, hit all.

Now, gentlemen, *please*, said the Pooka.

Hit one, hit all, repeated Slug.

Pipe down, said Shorty.

I'll pipe you and I'll pipe you down the nearest sewer if you say another word, my fine man, shouted Slug, I'll give you what you won't hold, I'll knock your bloody block off if you say another word. Apologize!

Gentlemen! said the Pooka in a pained manner.

Make your apologies quick, rapped Slug.

All right, all right, said Shorty, apologies all round. Is everybody happy?

I am satisfied, said the Good Fairy.

That is very satisfactory, said the Pooka with a bright re-dawn of courtesy, and now possibly you gentlemen would care to join us in our happy mission. There is a small son being born to Miss Lamont and I have no reason to suspect that guests will be unprovided with refreshment of the right kind.

It's a pleasure, said Slug, we will go and welcome. Did you ever happen to know a party by the name of William Tracy?

I have heard of him, replied the Pooka. Let us take a short-cut through this copse here on the left.

A decent skin if there ever was one, said Slug with warmth, a man that didn't stint the porter. It was a pleasure to work for Mr. Tracy. Isn't the Red Swan where Mr. Trellis lives?

Quite correct, said the Pooka.

What about presents for the bride, asked Shorty, it's only right to bring the full of your pockets when you're going to a hooley.

It's the usual all right, said Slug.

That's a pretty sort of a custom, said the Good Fairy. I wish to God I had a pocket.

The travellers then scattered apart for a bit about the wilderness of the undergrowth till they had filled their pockets with fruits and sorrels and studded acorns, the produce of the yamboo and the blooms of the yulan, blood-gutted berries and wrinkled cresses, branches of juice-slimed sloes, whortles and plums and varied mast, the speckled eggs from the nests of daws.

What do you think I'm made of, asked the Good Fairy sharply, take that thing with the prickles out of your pocket.

Musha, you're very tender, said the Pooka.

I don't wear armour-plated stays, said the Good Fairy.

There's something in there in that clump, called Shorty, I saw something moving.

It's only a rabbit or a black tyke, said the Pooka.

You have your porridge, said Shorty as he peered with his shading hand, there's a trousers on it.

Give us a look, said Slug.

Are you sure it is not a ferret, asked the Good Fairy, chuckling.

Come out of there, roared Shorty with a clasp towards his gun, come out of there or I'll shoot the tail off you!

Steady now, said Slug. Good Day, Sir. Come on out till we see you and don't be afraid.

Its a man and an old one, said the Good Fairy, I can see him through the cloth of the coat here. Advance, Sir, to be recognized!

I don't believe you will see much through *that* cloth, said the Pooka. Five and sixpence a yard it cost.

Give the word, said Shorty with a waving menace of his hand, or it's gunplay and gravestones. Come out of that tree, you bloody bastard you!

There was a prolonged snappling of stiffened rods and stubborn shoots and the sharp agonies of fractured branches, the pitiless flogging against each other of green life-laden leaves, the thrashing and the scourging of a clump in torment, a jaggle of briar-braced tangly-brambled thorniness, incensed, with a demon in its breast. Crack crack crack.

A small man came out of the foliage, a small man elderly and dark with a cloth cap and a muffler around his windpipe.

Jem by God Casey! said Slug Willard. Two emblems of amazement, his limp hands sank down to his waist until the thumbs found fastening in the bullet-studded belt.

Can you beat it? asked Shorty.

Good morning, said the Pooka courteously.

You are a terrible man, Casey, said Slug.

Greetings all round, said the Casey, and the compliments of the season.

All I can say is this, Casey, said Slug, you are the right fly-be-night, the right hop-off-my-thumb, to be stuck in a place like that. Ladies and gentlemen, this is Jem Casey, Poet of the Pick and Bard of Booterstown.

That is very satisfactory, said the Pooka. To meet a poet, that is a pleasure. The morning, Mr. Casey, can only be described as a glorious extravagance.

What sort of a voice is that, asked Casey, high and low like a bloody swingboat?

The remark about the weather, explained the Pooka, was not made by me at all but by a fairy that I have here in my pocket.

It's a fact, said Slug.

I believe you, said the poet, I believe all that I hear in this place. I thought I heard a maggot talking to me a while ago from under a stone. Good morning, Sir or something he said. This is a very queer place certainly.

My hard Casey, said Slug. Tell me, what were you doing in that clump there?

What do you think, asked Casey. What does any man be doing in a clump? What would *you* be doing?

Here Shorty gave a loud laugh.

By God I know what *I'd* be doing, he laughed.

Approximately half of the company at this stage joined their voices together in boisterous noises of amusement.

We all have to do that, roared Shorty at the end of his prolonged laugh, the best of us have to do that.

He collapsed on his back on the rich grass, shrieking aloud in his amusement. He moved his feet in the air as if operating a pedal cycle.

They have no respect, said the Good Fairy quietly to the Pooka, no respect and no conception of propriety.

The Pooka nodded.

I hope I am broad-minded, he said, but I draw the line at vulgarity and smut. Talk the like of that reflects on them and on the parents that brought them up. It speaks very poorly for their home life.

Suddenly Casey turned round and presented a stern face to the company.

What was I doing? he asked. What was I doing then?

The only answer was a loud laugh.

Well I will tell you what I was doing, he said gravely, I will tell you what I was at. I was reciting a pome to a selection of my friends. That's what I was doing. It is only your dirty minds.

Poetry is a thing I am very fond of, said the Good Fairy. I always make a point of following the works of Mr. Eliot and Mr. Lewis and Mr. Devlin. A good pome is a tonic. Was your pome on the subject of flowers, Mr. Casey? Wordsworth was a great man for flowers.

Mr. Casey doesn't go in for that class of stuff, said Slug.

Dirty minds be damned, said Shorty.

None of your soft stuff for Mr. Casey, said Slug.

I am very fond of flowers, too, said the Good Fairy. The smell of a nice flower is like a tonic. Love of flowers, it is a great sign of virtue.

The stuff that I go in for, said Casey roughly, is the real stuff. Oh, none of the fancy stuff for me.

He spat phlegm coarsely on the grass.

The workin' man doesn't matter, of course, he added.

But why? asked the Pooka courteously. He is surely the noblest of all creatures.

What about all these strikes? asked the Good Fairy. I don't know about him being the noblest. They have the country crippled with their strikes. Look at the price of bread. Sixpence halfpenny for a two-pound loaf.

Dirty minds be damned, said Shorty again. Oh, by God I know what you were doing in that clump, me boyo.

And look at bacon, said the Good Fairy. One and ninepence if you please.

To hell with the workin' man, said Casey. That's what you hear. To bloody hell with him.

I have a great admiration for the worker, said the Pooka.

Well so have I, said Casey loudly. I'll always stand up for my own. It's about the Workin' Man that I was reciting my pome.

And then you have the Conditions of Employment Act, said the Good Fairy, class legislation, that's what it is. Holidays with full pay if you please. No wonder the moneyed classes are leaving the country. Bolshevism will be the next step.

I admire the working man immensely, said the Pooka, and I will not hear a word against him. He is the back-bone of family life.

I'd advise that man in the pocket to keep his mouth shut, said Casey roughly. He wouldn't be the first of his kind that got a hammering.

It would take more than you to hammer me then, the Good Fairy answered.

The Pooka spread out his long-nailed hands and made a long soothing noise through his haired nostrils.

Please, gentlemen, he said, no need for acrimony.

If that's what you were at in the clump, said Shorty, stand out there and give us a couple of verses. Go on now.

The poet removed his frown.

I will if you want me to, he said.

Not everybody can recite poetry, said the Good Fairy. It is an art in itself. Verse-speaking they call it in London.

Don't mind him, said Slug. Off you go, Casey. One two, three. . . .

Casey then made a demonstration with his arm and gave out his poetical composition in a hard brassy voice, free from all inflexion.

> Come all ye lads and lassies prime
> From Macroom to old Strabane,
> And list to me till I say my rhyme—
> THE GIFT OF GOD IS A WORKIN' MAN.
>
> Your Lords and people of high degree
> Are a fine and a noble clan,
> They do their best but they cannot see
> THAT THE GIFT OF GOD IS A WORKIN' MAN.
>
> From France to Spain and from Holland gay
> To the shores of far Japan,
> You'll find the people will always say
> THE GIFT OF GOD IS A WORKIN' MAN.
>
> He's good, he's strong and his heart is free
> If he navvies or drives a van,
> He'll shake your hand with a gra-macree—
> THE GIFT OF GOD IS A WORKIN' MAN.
>
> Your Lords and ladies are fine to see
> And they do the best they can,
> But here's the slogan for you and me—
> THE GIFT OF GOD IS A WORKIN' MAN.

Good man! called Slug, good man yourself. Certainly that's a great bit of writing.

Bravo, said the Pooka politely.

Casey put out his two hands to make silence and then waved them up and down.

Here's the last verse, he shouted. All together, boys.

> A WORKIN' MAN, A WORKIN' MAN,
> Hurray Hurray for a Workin' Man,
> He'll navvy and sweat till he's nearly bet,
> THE GIFT OF GOD IS A WORKIN 'MAN!

Oh, good man, said Slug. He started clapping in the sun-drenched clearing of the wild jungle and the applause was completed by the rest of the company.

That is what they call a ballad, observed the Good Fairy. Did you ever read the Ballad of Father Gilligan? he asked the Pooka.

That would be an Intermediate book, of course, replied the Pooka. I'm afraid I never read that. Unfortunately, I left school at Third Book.

A very nice spiritual thing, said the Good Fairy.

A workin' man, eh? said Shorty. He got up from the ground and brushed at his garments.

Now that we've heard and enjoyed Mr. Casey's poetry, said Slug, maybe we should be moving.

Moving where? asked Casey.

We are going to a hooley, said Shorty, fill your pockets, man, and fall in. The fruits of the earth, you know.

The party then moved slowly on, the poet taking a last look at the clump where he had sat in conclave with a synod of tinkers, thimble-riggers, gombeen-men, beggars, channel-rakers, bacaughs, broom-men, and people from every walk in the lower order, singing and reciting a selection of his finer lyrics.

You in the pocket, said the poet, can you fly?

Maybe I can, replied the Good Fairy.

Would you go and tell my wife that I won't be home for dinner? Would you ever do that?

What do you take me for? asked the Good Fairy in a thin testy voice, a carrier-pigeon?

If you want to make him mad, said Shorty, call him a ferret. When I called him that he gave me any God's own thanks.

Can you tell me, Mr. Casey, said the Pooka interposing quickly, whether my wife is a kangaroo?

The poet stared in his surprise.

What in the name of God, he asked, do you mean by throwing a question like that at me? Eh?

I was wondering, said the Pooka.

A kangaroo? She might be a lump of a carrot for all I know. Do you mean a marsupial?

That's the man, said Slug. A marsupial.

Stop the talk, said the Good Fairy quickly. I see a man in a tree.

Where? asked Shorty.

Too far away for you to see. I see him through the trunks and the branches.

Pray what is a marsupial? asked the Pooka.

I cannot see him too well, said the Good Fairy, there is about a half a mile of forest in between. A marsupial is another name for an animal that is fitted with a built-in sack the way it can carry its young ones about.

If you have wings, said the poet sharply, why in the name of barney don't you take a flight in the air and have a good look instead of blathering out of you in the pocket there and talking about what the rest of us can't see?

If that is what a marsupial is, said the Pooka courteously, where is the difference? Surely the word kangaroo is more descriptive?

What do you take me for, asked the Good Fairy, a kite? I will fly away in the air when it suits me and no sooner. There is this distinction between marsupial and kangaroo, that the former denotes a genus and the latter a class, the former is general and the latter particular.

I don't believe there is any kangaroo in the tree, said Slug. Kangaroos don't go up trees in this country.

Possibly, said the Pooka, it is my wife that is up there in the tree. She shares this much with the birds, that she can journey through the air on the shaft of a broomstick. It would not be hard for her to be thus in front of us in our journey.

Who in the name of God, asked Shorty, ever heard of a bird flying on a broomstick?

I did not say my wife was a bird.

You said she was a broomstick this morning, said the Good Fairy, a shank, that's what you called her.

What I was talking about, said the Pooka slowly, was kangaroos. Kangaroos.

It might be a bird in the tree, said Shorty, a big bird.

There's a lot in that, Slug said.

Very well, said the Good Fairy in a displeased way. No doubt I was mistaken. It is not a man. It is a tit. A tit or a bloody wren.

Shorty with a quick gesture gripped his six-gun.

Is that the tree you mean, he shouted, that tree over there? Is it? There's something in *that* tree all right.

The Good Fairy nodded.

Answer me, you bloody little bowsy you! roared Shorty.

Be pleased to answer yourself less vigorously, said the Pooka nervously, there is no need for language the like of that. That is the tree he means. I felt him nodding his head against my hip.

Well why couldn't he say so, said Shorty, taking out his second gun.

If I get out of this pocket, said the Good Fairy in a thin voice, I will do damage. I have stood as much as I will stand for one day.

Come down out of that tree, roared Shorty, come down out of that, you bloody ruffian!

Keep your dander down, said Slug, you can't shoot anything that's sitting.

Whatever it is, observed the poet, it's not a man. It hasn't got a trousers on it. It's likely a marsupial.

I still fail to see the distinction, said the Pooka quietly, or why marsupial should be preferred to the more homely word.

If you don't come down out of that tree in two seconds, bellowed Shorty with a cock of his two hammers, you'll come out a corpse in three! I'll count to ten. One, two. . . .

I'm glad I have no body, said the Good Fairy. With that demented bully flourishing his irons every time he gets the sight of something he can shoot, nobody is safe. The term kangaroo, being the lesser, *is contained* in marsupial, which is a broader and more comprehensive word.

Five, six, seven . . .

I see, said the Pooka, you mean that the marsupial carries a kangaroo in its pouch?

TEN, said Shorty in decision. For the last time, are you coming down?

There was a gentle rustle in the thick of the green branches, a slow caress like the visit of a summer breeze in a field of oats, a faint lifeless movement: and a voice descended on the travellers, querulous and saddened with an infinite weariness, a thin voice that was occupied with the recital of these staves:

> Sweeny the thin-groined it is
> in the middle of the yew;
> life is very bare here,
> piteous Christ it is cheerless.
>
> Grey branches have hurt me
> they have pierced my calves,
> I hang here in the yew-tree above,
> without chessmen, no womantryst.
>
> I can put no faith in humans
> in the place they are;
> watercress at evening is my lot,
> I will not come down.

Lord save us! said Slug.

Shorty waved his guns about him in the air, swallowing at his spittle.

You won't come down?

I think I know the gentleman, said the Pooka courteously interposing, I fancy (it is possible that I may be wrong), that it is a party by the name of Sweeny. He is not all in it.

Do I shoot or don't I, asked Shorty presenting the orb of his puzzled face for the general inspection of the company.

Do you mean the Sweenies of Rathangan, inquired the Good Fairy, or the Sweenies of Swanlinbar?

Keep that bloody gun down, said Casey sharply, the voice that spoke was the voice of a bloody poet. By God I know a bloody poet when I hear one. Hands off the poets. I can write a verse myself and I respect the man that can do the same. Put that gun up.

I do not, replied the Pooka.

Or the flaxen Sweenies from Kiltimagh?

It's an old man, observed Slug, and you can't leave a man roosting in a tree like that. After we're gone he might get sick or have a fit or something and then where are you?

He might puke his porridge, said Shorty.

Not them either, said the Pooka courteously.

Then the MacSweenies of Ferns and Borris-in-Ossory?

With these words there came the rending scream of a shattered stirk and an angry troubling of the branches as the poor madman percolated through the sieve of a sharp yew, a wailing black meteor hurtling through green clouds, a human prickles. He came to the ground with his right nipple opened to the wide and a ruined back that was packed with the thorns and the small-wood of the trees of Erin, a tormented cress-stained mouth never halting from the recital of inaudible strange staves. There were feathers on his body here and there, impaired and shabby with vicissitude.

By God he's down! shouted Slug.

I don't mean them either, said the Pooka above the noise.

Then the O'Sweenies of Harold's Cross?

Jem Casey was kneeling at the pock-haunched form of the king pouring questions into the cup of his dead ear and picking small thorns from his gashed chest with absent thoughtless fingers, poet on poet, a bard unthorning a fellow-bard.

Give him air, said Slug.

Will you walk over there, said the Good Fairy to the Pooka, the way I can see this man that has been bird-nesting?

Certainly, said the Pooka courteously.

What is the man's name, asked the Good Fairy.

The Pooka made a sharp pass in the air with his thumb, a token of annoyance.

Sweeny, he answered. There is only one remedy for a bleeding hole in a man's side—moss. Pack him with moss the way he will not bleed to death.

That's the number, said Slug, plenty of moss.

Damp sponges of lichen and green moss were plied in

the gapes of Sweeny's flank, young shoots and stalks and
verdure in his ruined side till they were reddened and
stiffened with the bleeding of his thick blood. He fell to
muttering discordant verses.

> As I made the fine throw at Ronan
> from the middle of the hosts,
> the fair cleric said that I had leave
> to go with birds.
>
> I am Sweeny the slender-thin,
> the slender, the hunger-thin,
> berries crimson and cresses green,
> their colours are my mouth.
>
> I was in the centre of the yew
> distraught with suffering,
> the hostile branches scourged me,
> I would not come down.

You're all right man, said Casey with kindly pats of
his hand on the mossy side, you'll get over that. You'll
be all right, don't you worry.

A bullet would put him out of his pain, said Shorty, it
would be a merciful act of Providence.

I wish to Goodness, said the Pooka with a courteous
insistence, that you would replace that shooting-iron and
repress this craving for bloodshed. Can you not see the
poor man is unwell?

What is wrong with him? inquired the Good Fairy.

He took a sore fall, said Slug kindly, he might have
broken his bloody neck, eh, Mr. Casey?

He might have split his arc, said Casey.

Maybe he is drunk, suggested the Good Fairy, I don't believe in wasting my sympathy on sots, do you?

There is no harm in an odd drop now and then, replied the Pooka, drink in moderation is all right. Drunkenness, of course—that is another pair of shoes altogether.

The invalid man stirred in his earthen couch and murmured:

> Our wish is at Samhain, up to Maytime,
> when the wild ducks come
> in each dun wood without stint
> to be in ivy-trees.
>
> Water of Glen Bolcain fair
> a listening to its horde of birds,
> its tuneful streams that are not slow,
> its islands, its rivers.
>
> In the tree of Cell Lughaidh,
> it was our wish to be alone,
> swift flight of swallows on the brink of summer—
> take your hands away!

It's drink all right, said the Good Fairy, leave him be.

Nonsense, man, said Slug, a little touch of fever and the best will rave, the strongest will go to the wall with one little dart of double-pneumonia, I had an uncle once that was shouting the walls of the house down two hours after he got his head wet in a shower of rain. Has anybody got a thermometer till we take his pulse?

Would a sun-glass be of any assistance to you? inquired the Pooka politely.

A shandy is what he wants, said the Good Fairy, a glass of gin and a bottle of stone beer, a curer.

That'll do you, said Casey, help me with him, somebody. We'll have to bring him along with us, by God I'd die of shame if we left the poor bastard here on his tod. Give us a hand, somebody.

I'm your man, said Slug.

Together the two strong men, joyous in the miracle of their health, put their bulging thews and the fine ripple of their sinews together at the arm-pits of the stricken king as they bent over him with their grunting red faces, their four heels sinking down in the turf of the jungle with the stress of their fine effort as they hoisted the madman to the tremulous support of his withered legs.

Mind his feathers, said Shorty in a coarse way, never ruffle a cock's feathers.

The madman fluttered his lids in the searchlight of the sun and muttered out his verses as he tottered hither and thither and back again backwards in the hold of his two keepers.

> Though my flittings are unnumbered,
> my clothing to-day is scarce,
> I personally maintain my watch
> on the tops of mountains.
>
> O fern, russet long one,
> your mantle has been reddened,
> there's no bedding for an outcast
> on your branching top.

Nuts at terce and cress-leaves,
fruits from an apple-wood at noon,
a lying-down to lap chill water—
your fingers torment my arms.

Put green moss in his mouth, said the Good Fairy
querulously, are we going to spend the rest of our lives
in this place listening to talk the like of that? There is a
bad smell in this pocket, it is not doing me any good.
What are you in the habit of keeping in it, Sir?

Nothing, replied the Pooka, but tabacca.

It's a queer smell for tabacca, said the Good Fairy.

One and sixpence I pay in silver coin for an ounce of
it, said the Pooka, and nice as it is for the wee pipe, it is
best eaten. It is what they call shag tabacca.

Notwithstanding all that, said the Good Fairy, there is
a queer hum off it. It would be the price of you if I got
sick here in your pocket.

Now be very careful, said the Pooka.

Quick march my hard man, said Casey briskly to the
king, put your best leg forward and we will get you a
bed before the sun goes down, we'll get a sup of whisky
into you to make you sleep.

We'll get you a jug of hot punch and a packet of cream
crackers with plenty of butter, said Slug, if you'll only
walk, if you'll only pull yourself together, man.

And getting around the invalid in a jabbering ring, they
rubbed him and cajoled and coaxed, and plied him with
honey-talk and long sweet-lilted sentences full of fine
words, and promised him metheglin and mugs of viscous
tar-black mead thickened with white yeast and the spoils

183

from hives of mountain-bees, and corn-coarse nourishing
farls of wheaten bread dipped in musk-scented liquors and
sodden with Belgian sherry, an orchard and a swarm of
furry honey-glutted bees and a bin of sun-bronzed grain
from the granaries of the Orient in every drop as it dripped
at the lifting of the hand to the mouth, and inky quids of
strong-smoked tabacca with cherrywood pipes, hubble-
bubbles, duidins, meerschaums, clays, hickory hookahs
and steel-stemmed pipes with enamel bowls, the lot of
them laid side by side in a cradle of lustrous blue plush, a
huge pipe-case and pipe-rack ingeniously combined and
circumscribed with a durable quality of black imitation
leather over a framework of stout cedarwood dovetailed
and intricately worked and made to last, the whole being
handsomely finished and untouched by hand and packed
in good-quality transparent cellophane, a present calculated to warm the cockles of the heart of any smoker.
They also did not hesitate to promise him sides of hairy
bacon, the mainstay and the staff of life of the country
classes, and lamb-chops still succulent with young
blood, autumn-heavy yams from venerable stooping trees,
bracelets and garlands of browned sausages and two
baskets of peerless eggs fresh-collected, a waiting hand
under the hen's bottom. They beguiled him with the
mention of salads and crome custards and the grainy disorder of pulpy boiled rhubarb, matchless as a physic for
the bowels, olives and acorns and rabbit-pie, and venison
roasted on a smoky spit, and mulatto thick-lipped delphy
cups of black-strong tea. They foreshadowed the felicity
of billowy beds of swansdown carefully laid crosswise on

springy rushes and sequestered with a canopy of bear-skins and generous goatspelts, a couch for a king with fleshly delectations and fifteen hundred olive-mellow concubines in constant attendance against the hour of desire. Chariots they talked about and duncrusted pies exuberant with a sweat of crimson juice, and tall crocks full of eddying foam-washed stout, and wailing prisoners in chains on their knees for mercy, humbled enemies crouching in sackcloth with their upturned eye-whites suppliant. They mentioned the leap of a fire on a cold night, long sleeps in the shadows and leaden-eyed forget-fulness hour on hour—princely oblivion. And as they talked, they threaded through the twilight and the sudden sun-pools of the wild country.

It is a scourge, said the Good Fairy, the hum in this pocket.

If that is the case, said the Pooka, you can change to another or get out and walk and welcome.

The smell of another pocket, replied the Good Fairy, that might be far worse.

The company continued to travel throughout the day, pausing at evening to provide themselves with the suste-nance of oakmast and cocoanuts and with the refreshment of pure water from the jungle springs. They did not cease, either walking or eating, from the delights of colloquy and harmonized talk contrapuntal in character nor did Sweeny desist for long from stave-music or from the recital of his misery in verse. On the brink of night they halted to light faggots with a box of matches and continued through the tangle and the grasses with flaming brands above

their heads until the night-newts and the moths and the
bats and the fellicaun-eeha had fallen in behind them in a
gentle constellation of winking red wings in the flair of
the fires, delightful alliteration. On occasion an owl or
an awkward beetle or a small coterie of hedgehogs,
attracted by the splendour of the light, would escort them
for a part of the journey until the circumstances of their
several destinations would divert them again into the
wild treachery of the gloom. The travellers would sometimes tire of the drone of one another's talk and join
together in the metre of an old-fashioned song, filling
their lungs with fly-thickened air and raising their voices
above the sleeping trees. They sang *Home on The Range*
and the pick of the old cowboy airs, the evergreen favourites
of the bunkhouse and the prairie; they joined together
with a husky softness in the lilt of the old come-all-ye's,
the ageless minstrelsy of the native-land, a sob in their
voice as the last note died; they rendered old catches with
full throats, and glees and round-songs and riddle-me-
raddies, *Tipperary* and *Nellie Deane* and *The Shade of the Old
Apple Tree*. They sang Cuban love-songs and moonsweet
madrigals and selections from the best and the finest
of the Italian operas, from the compositions of Puccini
and Meyerbeer and Donizetti and Gounod and the
Maestro Mascagni as well as an aria from *The Bohemian
Girl* by Balfe, and intoned the choral complexities of
Palestrina the pioneer. They rendered two hundred and
forty-two (242) songs by Schubert in the original German
words, and sang a chorus from *Fidelio* (by Beethoven of
Moonlight Sonata fame) and the *Song of the Flea*, and a long

excerpt from a Mass by Bach, as well as innumerable tuneful pleasantries from the able pens of no less than Mozart and Handel. To the stars (though they could not see them owing to the roofage of the leaves and the branches above them), they gave with a thunderous spirit such pieces by Offenbach, Schumann, Saint-Saens and Granville Bantock as they could remember. They sang entire movements from cantatas and oratorios and other items of sacred music, *allegro ma non troppo*, *largo*, and *andante cantabile*.

They were all so preoccupied with music that they were still chanting spiritedly in the dark undergrowth long after the sun, earlier astir than usual, had cleaned the last vestige of the soiling night from the verdure of the tree-tops—rosy-fingered pilgrim of the sandal grey. When they suddenly arrived to find mid-day in a clearing, they wildly reproached each other with bitter words and groundless allegations of bastardy and low birth as they collected berries and haws into the hollows of their hats against the incidence of a late breakfast. Temporary discontinuance of the foregoing.

Biographical reminiscence, part the seventh: I recall that I went into my uncle's house about nine p.m. one evening in the early spring, the sharp edge of my perception dulled somewhat by indulgence in spirituous liquors. I was standing in the middle of the dining-room floor before I had properly adverted to my surroundings. The faces I found there were strange and questioning. Searching among them, I found at last the features of my uncle.

Nature of features: Red, irregular, coarse, fat.

He was situated in a central position in the midst of four others and looked out from them in my direction in a penetrating attentive manner. I was on my way backwards towards the door when he said to me:

No need to go. Gentlemen, my nephew. I think we require a secretary. Take a seat.

After this I heard a murmur of polite felicitation. It was represented that my continued presence was a keen source of pleasure to the company without exception. I sat down at the table and took my blue pencil from a chest-pocket. My uncle studied a black note-book for a moment and then pushed it across to me and said:

I think that should be enough.

I took the book and read the legend inscribed on the front page in the square unambiguous writing of my uncle.

Nature of legend: Eighteen loaves. Two pan-loaves (? one pan). Three pounds cheese. Five pounds cooked ham. Two pounds tea (one and four). Tin floor-powder. Fancy cakes 2d. and 3d. (? 4d.). Eighteen rock-buns. Eight pounds butter. Sugar, milk (? each bring supply?). Rosin. Bottle D.W.D. ?????????. Hire of crockery £1. ? Breakages Speak re necessity care. ? Lemonade. Say £5.

My uncle made an urgent noise with the case of his spectacles.

You were saying, Mr. Connors . . . ? he said.

Ah, yes, said Mr. Connors.

A big loose man to my left drew himself together and

braced his body for the ordeal of utterance. He wore on the upper lip a great straggling moustache and heavy tired eyes moved slowly as if belated in adjustment to his other features. He struggled to an attitude of upright attention.

Now I think it's a great mistake to be too strict, he said. We must make allowances. One old-time waltz is all I ask. It's as Irish as any of them, nothing foreign about the old-time waltz. We must make allowances. The Gaelic League . . .

I don't agree, said another man.

My uncle gave a sharp crack on the table.

Order, Mr. Corcoran, he said in reprimand, order if you please. Mr. Connors has the floor. This is a Committee meeting. I'm sick sore and tired saying this is a Committee meeting. After all there is such a thing as Procedure, there is such a thing as Order, there is such a thing as doing things in the right way. Have you a Point of Order, Mr. Corcoran?

I have, said Mr. Corcoran. He was tall and thin and fair. I found that his face was known to me. His hair was sparse and sandy.

Very well. If you have a Point of Order, well and good. Well and good if you have a Point of Order. Proceed.

Eh? said Mr. Corcoran.

Proceed. Continue.

Oh, yes. Old-time waltzes. Yes. I don't agree with the old-time waltz at all. Nothing *wrong* with it, of course, Mr. Connors, nothing actually *wrong* with it. . . .

Address the Chair, address the Chair, said my uncle.

But after all a Ceilidhe is not the place for it, that's all.

A Ceilidhe is a Ceilidhe. I mean, we have our own. We have plenty of our own dances without crossing the road to borrow what we can't wear. See the point? It's all right but it's not for us. Leave the waltz to the jazz-boys. By God they're welcome as far as I'm concerned.

Mr. Connors to reply, said my uncle.

Oh, settle it any way you like, said Mr. Connors. It was only a suggestion. There's nothing wrong with the old-time waltz. Nothing in the wide world. I've danced it myself. Mr. Hickey here has danced it. We have all danced it. Because a thing is foreign it does not stand to reason that it's bad.

When did I dance it? asked Mr. Hickey.

Description of Mr. Hickey: Old, yellow, dark, lean. Pendulous flesh at eyes and jaws. Of utterance precise and slow. A watching listener.

On a Point of Personal Explanation? asked my uncle.

Yes, said Mr. Hickey.

Very well.

Twenty-three years ago at the Rotunda Gardens, said Mr. Connors. Haven't I a good memory?

You certainly have, said Mr. Hickey.

He smiled, mollified. He pursed his lips in the exercise of a retrospect across the years, absently playing with his loose plates. Bushy brows hid his eyes as they gazed on his white knuckles.

Mr. Fogarty? said my uncle.

Mr. Fogarty was a middle-aged man but with a round satisfied face. He smiled evenly on the company. He was attired in good-quality expensive clothing and wore an air of assurance.

Settle it between ye, he said lightly. Leave Mr. Fogarty alone now.

The Gaelic League is opposed to the old-time waltz, said Mr. Corcoran. So are the clergy.

Now, now, I don't think that's right, said Mr. Connors.

Order, order, said my uncle.

I never heard that said, said Mr. Connors. Which of the clergy now?

My uncle gave another crack.

Order, he repeated. *Order*.

Chapter and verse, Mr. Corcoran. Which of the clergy.

That will do, Mr. Connors, said my uncle sharply, that is quite sufficient. This is a Committee Meeting. We won't be long settling it. All those in favour of the old-time waltz say Aye.

Aye!

Those against say No.

No!

I declare the Noes have it.

Division, called Mr. Connors.

A division has been challenged. I appoint Mr. Secretary teller. All those in favour raise one hand.

The total that I counted in favour of each proposition was one; certain parties abstained from voting.

My casting vote, said my uncle loudly, is in favour of the negative.

Well that's that, said Mr. Connors sighing.

If things are done in the right way, said my uncle,

there is no question of wasting time. Now when does he arrive? You have the details, Mr. Hickey.

Mr. Hickey bestirred himself with reluctance and said:

He will be in Cork from the liner at ten, that means Kingsbridge about seven.

Very well, said my uncle, that means he reaches the hall about nine, making allowance for a wash and a bite to eat. By nine o'clock—yes, we will be in full swing by nine o'clock. Now a Reception Committee. I appoint Mr. Corcoran and Mr. Connors and myself.

I still challenge Mr. Corcoran to give the name of the clergyman, said Mr. Connors.

That is not a Point of Order, said my uncle. He turned to me and said: Have you the names of the Reception Committee?

Yes, I answered.

Very good. Now I think I should read a brief address when he is at the door. Something short and to the point. A few words in Irish first, of course.

Oh, certainly, said Mr. Corcoran. Not forgetting a red carpet on the steps. That is the recognized thing.

My uncle frowned.

Well I don't know, he said. I think a red carpet would be a bit. . . .

I agree with you, said Mr. Hickey.

A bit, you know . . . well, a little bit. . . .

I see your point, I see your point, said Mr. Corcoran.

You understand me? We don't want to be too formal. After all he is one of our own, an exile home from the foreign clime.

Yes, he might not like it, said Mr. Corcoran.

It was quite proper, of course, to raise the point if it was on your mind, said my uncle. Well that is settled. Just a friendly Irish welcome, céad mile fáilte. Now there is another very important matter that we'll need to see to. I refer to the inner man. The honourable secretary will now read out my estimate of what we want. The secretary has the floor.

In my thin voice I enunciated the contents of the black note-book given over to my charge.

I think you might put down another bottle and a couple of dozen stout, said Mr. Hickey. I don't think they would go to waste.

Oh, Lord yes, said Mr. Fogarty. We would want that.

I don't think he touches anything, said my uncle. A very strict man, I believe.

Well, of course, there are others, said Mr. Hickey sharply.

Who? asked my uncle.

Who! Well dear knows! said Mr. Hickey testily.

Mr. Fogarty gave a loud laugh in the tense air.

Oh, put it down, Mr. Chairman, he laughed. Put it down man. A few of us would like a bottle of stout and we might have friends in. Put it down and say no more about it.

Oh, very well, said my uncle. Very good, very good.

I entered these further items in my ledger.

Oh, talking about the clergy—on a Point of Order, Mr. Chairman—talking about the clergy, said Mr. Connors suddenly, I heard a good one the other day. A P.P. down in the County Meath.

Now, Mr. Connors, please remember that your audience is a mixed one, said my uncle severely.

It's all right now, said Mr. Connors smiling in reassurance. He invited two young priests down to the house for dinner. Two young priests from Clongowes or somewhere, you understand, smart boys, doctors and all the rest of it. Well the three of them went in to dinner and here were two fine fat chickens on the table. Two chickens for the three of them.

Fair enough, said Mr. Fogarty.

Now no disrespect, warned my uncle.

It's all right, said Mr. Connors. Just when they were sitting down for a good tuck-in, the P.P. gets a sick call and away with him on his white horse after telling the two visitors to eat away and not to mind him or to wait for him.

Fair enough, said Mr. Fogarty.

Well after an hour back came his reverence the P.P. to find a heap of bones on the plate there. Not a pick of the two chickens left for him. He had to swallow his anger for damn the thing else was there left for him to swallow.

Well dear knows they were the nice pair of curates, said my uncle in facetious consternation.

Weren't they, said Mr. Connors. Well after a bit the two said they were very full and would like to stretch their legs. So out went the three of them to the farmyard. It was in the summer, you understand.

Fair enough, said Mr. Fogarty.

Over comes the P.P.'s cock, a grand big animal with feathers of every colour in his tail. Isn't that the fine proud cock you have, says one of the curates. The P.P. turns and looks at him. And why wouldn't he be proud, says he, and him with two sons in the Jesuits!

Oh, fair enough, roared Mr. Fogarty laughing.

There was general acclamation and amusement in which I inserted perfunctorily my low laugh.

Isn't it good? laughed Mr. Connors. The P.P. turns on the curate and looks him straight in the eye. *And why wouldn't he be proud*, says he, *and him with two sons in the Jesuits!*

Very good indeed, said my uncle. Now we want three clean respectable women to cut the bread.

Let me see, said Mr. Corcoran. You have Mrs. Hanafin and Mrs. Corky. Poor of course, but good clean respectable women.

Cleanliness is all-important, said my uncle. Lord save us, thumb-marks on bread, there is nothing so disgusting. Are they clean, Mr. Corcoran?

Oh, very clean and respectable.

Very good, said my uncle, we will leave that to you.

He put up the four fingers of a hand in the air and identified by a finger the cares of each member of the assembly.

Sandwiches and refreshments Mr. Corcoran, he said. Mr. Hickey is attending to the band and will oblige in the interval. Mr. Fogarty will be M.C. and will also oblige with a hornpipe. I will look after our friend. That is everything, I think. Any questions, gentlemen?

A vote of thanks to our efficient young secretary, said Mr. Fogarty smiling.

Oh, certainly, said my uncle. Passed unanimously. Nothing else?

No.

Very good. I declare the meeting adjourned seeny day. Conclusion of reminiscence.

Penultimum continued. A further account of the journey of the Pooka and party: At approximately twenty past four p.m. they arrived at the Red Swan Hotel and entered the premises, unnoticed, by the window of the maids' private bed-room on the ground floor. They made no noise in their passage and disturbed no dust of the dust that lay about the carpets. Quickly they repaired to a small room adjoining Miss Lamont's bedroom where the good lady was lying-in, and deftly stacked the papered wall steads with the colourful wealth of their offerings and their fine gifts—their golden sheaves of ripened barley, firkins of curdy cheese, berries and acorns and crimson yams, melons and marrows and mellowed mast, variholed sponges of crisp-edged honey and oaten breads, earthenware jars of whey-thick sack and porcelain pots of lathery lager, sorrels and short-bread and coarse-grained cake, cucumbers cold and downy straw-laced cradles of elderberry wine poured out in sea-green egg-cups and urn-shaped tubs of molasses crushed and crucibled with the lush brown-heavy scum of pulped mellifluous mushrooms, an exhaustive harvesting of the teeming earth, by God.

Sit down and make yourselves happy, boys, said Slug, put a match to the fire, somebody. Give the door a knock, Mr. Casey. See if the hour has come if you know what I mean.

These bogberries, said Shorty with a motion of his brown thumb, would it be against the rules to eat a few of them?

Certainly it would, said the Good Fairy, you won't touch them. In any case they are not bogberries.

Aren't they bogberries, mister smarty, asked Shorty, aren't they though, you little pimp!

The door is locked, said Casey.

No they are not, said the Good Fairy.

That is a pity, said the Pooka civilly. I suppose we can only wait until we are asked in. Has anybody got an American master-key?

A bullet would put the lock in in half a tick, said Shorty.

I don't doubt that, said Slug, but there is going to be no gun-play here, remember that.

I have not got a key anyway, said the Good Fairy, except an old-fashioned watch-key, a very good instrument for taking out blackheads.

The new-lit fire was maturing with high leaps which glowed for red instants on the smooth cheeks of the inky grapes and on the long tenuous flanks of the marrows.

Our policy, said the Pooka with his careful statesman's smile as he sat in his arm-chair with his clubfoot hidden beneath the seat, must be an open one, a policy of wait and see.

What about a hand of cards? asked Shorty.

Eh?

Just to pass the time. . . .

Not a bad idea at all, said the Good Fairy.

I don't hold with gambling, said the Pooka, for money.

With quiet industry he filled at his pipe, his face averted.

Of course a small stake to keep one's interest from flagging, he said, there is no great harm in that. That is a different thing.

It will pass the time for a start, said Casey.

Deal out for a round of Poker, said the Good Fairy, there is nothing like a good game of cards.

Have you a pack, Shorty? asked Slug.

I have the cards in my hand, said Shorty, gather in closer, my arm isn't a yard long. How many hands now?

Is Sweeny playing, asked Casey, are you, Sweeny?

Have you any money, Sweeny? asked Slug.

Six hands, said the Good Fairy placidly, everybody is playing.

You in the pocket, barked Shorty, if you think you are going to play cards you are making a bloody big mistake.

Mad Sweeny was sprawled on a chair in an attitude of inadvertence, idly plucking the blood-stiffened lichen from the gash in his nipple with an idle finger. His eyelids fluttered as he addressed himself to the utterance of this stave.

They have passed below me in their course, the stags

across Ben Boirche, their antlers tear the sky, I will take a hand.

Tell me, said the Pooka putting his hand in his pocket, are *you* going to play?

Of course I am going to play, said the Good Fairy loudly; certainly I am going to play, why shouldn't I play?

We are playing for money, said Shorty roughly, what guarantee have we that you will . . . pay?

My word of honour, said the Good Fairy.

You have your porridge, said Shorty.

How are you going to take the cards if you have no hands and where do you keep your money if you have no pocket, answer me that, asked Slug sharply.

Gentlemen, interposed the Pooka civilly, we really must learn to discuss difficulties without a needless resort to acrimony and heat. The party in my pocket would not be long there if I were not satisfied that he was of unimpeachable character. The charge of cheating or defaulting at cards is a vile one and a charge that cannot be lightly levelled in the present company. In every civilized community it is necessary that the persons comprising it shall accept one another at their face value as honest men until the contrary is proved. Give me the cards and I will deal out six hands, one of which I will pass into my pocket. Did I ever tell you the old story about Dermot and Granya?

Take the cards if you want them, snapped Shorty, and talk about face-value, that fellow has no face. By God it's a poor man that hasn't that much.

We'll try anything once, said Casey.

No, said the Good Fairy, I never heard that particular story. If it is dirty, of course, etiquette precludes me from listening to it at all.

The Pooka shuffled clumsily with his long-nailed fingers.

Go on, man, deal, said Slug.

It is not dirty, said the Pooka, it is one of the old Irish sagas. I played a small part in it in the long ago. The card-playing here brings it all back—how many hands did I say I would deal?

Six.

Six fives are thirty, one of the even numerals. Where women were concerned, this Dermot was a ruffian of the worst kind. Your wife was never safe if you happened to live in the same town with Dermot.

Don't waste so much time, man, said Slug.

You don't mean to tell me, said the Good Fairy, that he ran away with your kangaroo? Hurry and pass my cards in to me here. Come on now.

There you are now, said the Pooka, six hands. No he did not, all this happened before the happy day of my marriage. But what he did do, he ran away with Granya, the woman of Finn MacCool. By Golly it took a good man to do that.

The light is very bad in here, said the Good Fairy, I can hardly see my cards at all.

Don't be striking matches in there, that's all, said the Pooka, fire is one thing that I don't like at all. Throw your cards on the floor, gentlemen. How many cards can I give you, Mr. Casey?

Three.

Three gone over, said the Pooka. He had not gone far
I need not tell you when Finn had started off behind him
in full chase. It was hard going in the depth of winter
for the fleeing lovers.

A knot of green-topped bunch-leaves, said Sweeny, is
our choice from a bed of sorrel, acorns and nuts and cresses
thick, and three cards we desire.

Three for you, said the Pooka.

Put your hand in your pocket, said the Good Fairy,
take out the two cards on the left-hand side and give me
two new ones.

Certainly, said the Pooka. One dark night the woman
and Dermot strayed into my cave in their wanderings,
looking if you please for a night's lodging. I was working
at that time, you understand, in the west of Ireland.
My cave was by the seaside.

What in the name of God are you talking about? asked
Shorty. It's up to me, I go threepence.

One thing led to another, continued the Pooka, till
Dermot and myself agreed to play a game of chess for
the woman. Granya was certainly a very fine-looking
lump of a girl. I will advance the play to fivepence.

I cannot hear right, said the Good Fairy querulously,
what are we playing for—a woman. What use is a woman
to me?

Fivepence, you dumb-bell, shouted Shorty.

I will double that, said the Good Fairy. Tenpence.

At this stage certain parties signified that they were
retiring from the game.

So we sat down to the chessboard the two of us, said the Pooka. My guest succeeded in getting white and opened with pawn to king's bishop four, apparently choosing the opening known as Byrd's, so much favoured by Alekhine and the Russian masters. I will make it a shilling.

One and sixpence, said Shorty quickly.

I will see one and sixpence, said the Good Fairy.

I replied with a simple pawn to king's three, a good temporizing move until my opponent disclosed the line he was to follow. The move has received high praise from more than one competent authority. I will also see Mr. Andrews for the sum of one and sixpence.

All right, the two of you are seeing me for one and six, said Shorty, there you are, three kings, three royal sovereigns.

Not good enough I am afraid, said the Good Fairy in a jubilant manner, there is a nice flush in hearts here in the pocket. Take it out and see it for yourselves. A flush in hearts.

None of your bloody miracles, shouted Shorty, we're playing for money! None of your trick-o'-the-loop, none of your bloody quick ones! If you try that game I'll take you out of that pocket by the scruff of the bloody neck and give you a kick in the waterworks!

What was his next move do you think? asked the Pooka. You would hardly credit it—pawn to king's knight's four! I have a full house here, by the way.

Give us a look at it.

Three tens and two twos, said the Pooka quietly. All

I had to do was to move my queen to rook five and I had him where I wanted him. Pay up, gentlemen, and look pleasant.

A good-looking one and sixpence, growled Shorty as he groped in the interior of his fob-pocket.

Queen to rook five was mate, of course, said the Pooka, mate in two, a world record. Stop tugging like that or you will tear my little pocket.

One moment, said the Good Fairy in a whisper, could I see you alone in the hallway for a couple of minutes. I want to discuss something private.

Hurry up for barney's sake till we have another round, said Slug rubbing his hands, give the luck a chance to circulate.

There you are, one and sixpence, said Shorty.

Most certainly, said the Pooka courteously, pray excuse us for a moment, gentlemen, the Fairy and myself have a private matter to discuss in the hallway, though itself it is a draughty place for colloquy and fine talk. We will be back again directly.

He arose with a bow and left the room.

What is it, he asked politely in the passage.

When you won the woman, said the Good Fairy, what did you do with her is it any harm to ask?

Is that all you require to know?

Well no. As a matter of fact . . .

You have no money!

Exactly.

What explanation have you to offer for such conduct?

You see, I always win at cards. I . . .

What is your explanation?

Don't talk so loud, man, said the Good Fairy in alarm, the others will hear you. I cannot be disgraced in front of a crowd like that.

I am sorry, said the Pooka coldly, but I am afraid it is my duty to make the matter public. If it were my own personal concern solely, it would be otherwise, of course. In the present circumstances I have no alternative. The others allowed you to play on my recommendation and you have callously dishonoured me. I cannot be expected to stand by and see them exploited further. Therefore . . .

For God's sake don't do that, don't do that under any circumstances, I would never get over it, it would kill my mother. . . .

Your concern for your family does you credit but I'm afraid it is too late to think of that.

I will pay back every penny I owe you.

When?

Give me time, give me a chance. . . .

Nonsense! You are merely wriggling, merely . . .

For God's sake, man . . .

I will give you one alternative to instant exposure and you can take it or leave it. I will forget the debt and advance you an extra sixpence—making two shillings in all—provided you relinquish absolutely your claim to influence the baby that is expected inside.

What!

You can take your choice.

You cad, you bloody cad!

The Pooka twitched his pocket with a profound shrug of his gaunt shoulders.

Which is it to be? he inquired.

I'll see you damned first, said the Good Fairy excitedly.

Very well. It is all the same to me. Let us go inside.

Stop a minute, you, you. . . . Wait.

Well?

All right, you win. But by God I'll get even with you yet, if it takes me a thousand years, I'll get my own back if I have to swing for it, don't forget that!

That is very satisfactory, said the Pooka with a grateful re-dawn of his urbanity, you have undoubtedly done the right thing and I offer you my congratulations on your pertinacity. Here is the extra sixpence. Let us rejoin the ladies.

You wait! Even if it is a thousand years, you wait!

In regard to the little question you asked me about the lady I won as a result of my skill at chess, it is a long story and a crooked one—shall we go in?

Go in and be damned to you!

The Pooka re-entered the room with his civil smile.

There's your hand, said Slug, hurry up, we haven't all day, man.

I'm sorry for the delay, said the Pooka.

The company again fell to card-play.

After a moderately lengthy interval a good-quality Yale key grated in the lock and the door of the bedroom was thrown open, a broad beam of gaslight pouring in on the players as they turned their questioning faces from their cards to the light. The pallor of the glare was tempered about the edges by a soft apparently-supernatural radiance of protoplasmic amethyst and spotted with a twinkling pattern of red and green stars so that it poured into the ante-room and flowed and eddied in the corners and the shadows like the spreading tail of a large male peacock, a glorious thing like muslin or iridescent snow or like the wispy suds of milk when it is boiling over on a hob. Temporary discontinuance of foregoing.

Note on Constructional or Argumentive Difficulty: The task of rendering and describing the birth of Mr. Trellis's illegitimate offspring I found one fraught with obstacles and difficulties of a technical, constructional, or literary character—so much so, in fact, that I found it entirely beyond my powers. This latter statement follows my decision to abandon a passage extending over the length of eleven pages touching on the arrival of the son and his sad dialogue with his wan mother on the subject of his father, the passage being, by general agreement, a piece of undoubted mediocrity.

The passage, however, served to provoke a number of discussions with my friends and acquaintances on the subject of aestho-psycho-eugenics and the general chaos which would result if all authors were disposed to seduce their female characters and bring into being, as a result, offspring of the quasi-illusory type. It was asked why Trellis did not require the expectant mother to make a violent end of herself and the trouble she was causing by the means of drinking a bottle of disinfectant fluid usually to be found in bathrooms. The answer I gave was that the author was paying less and less attention to his literary work and was spending entire days and nights in the unremitting practice of his sleep. This explanation, I am glad to say, gave instant satisfaction and was represented as ingenious by at least one of the inquirers concerned.

It may be usefully mentioned here that I had carefully considered giving an outward indication of the son's semi-humanity by furnishing him with only the half of a body. Here I encountered further difficulties. If given the upper half only, it would be necessary to provide a sedan-chair or litter with at least two runners or scullion-boys to operate it. The obtrusion of two further characters would lead to complications, the extent of which could not be foreseen. On the other hand, to provide merely the lower half, *videlicet*, the legs and lumbar region, would be to narrow unduly the validity of the son and confine his activities virtually to walking, running, kneeling and kicking football. For that reason I decided ultimately to make no outward distinction and thus avoided any charge that my work was somewhat far-fetched. It will be observed that the omission of several pages at this stage does not materially disturb the continuity of the story.

Penultimum, continued: Momentarily shutting out the richness of the beam with his stout form furrily outlined in the glow, a stocky young man had entered the ante-room and stood looking with polite inquiry at the group of card-players about the fire. His dark well-cut clothing was in sharp contrast to the healthless rubiness of his face; there were pimples on his forehead to the size of sixpences and his languorous heavy eyelids hung uneasily midway over the orbs of his eyes; an air of slowness and weariness and infinite sleep hung about him like a cloak as he stood there standing.

The Pooka arose with a slight bow and pushed back his chair.

Three hundred thousand welcomes, he said in his fine voice, we are honoured to be here at the hour of your arrival. We are honoured to be able to present you with these offerings on the floor there, the choicest and the rarest that the earth can yield. Please accept them on behalf of myself and my friends. One and all we have the honour to wish you good day, to trust that you had a pleasant journey and that your dear mother is alive and well.

Gentlemen, said the newcomer with gratitude in his deep voice, I am deeply touched. Your kind gesture is one of these felicities that banish for a time at least the conviction that wells up in the heart of every newcomer to this world that life is empty and hollow, disproportionately trivial compared with the trouble of entering it. I thank you with all my heart. Your gifts, they are . . .

He searched for a word with his red hand as if to pull one from the air.

Oh, that is all right, said the Good Fairy, these things are plentiful and it was small trouble to bring them here. You are very welcome.

How much of that tack did you carry? snapped Shorty.

Fighting in front of strangers, said the Good Fairy, that, of course, is the height of vulgarity. The parents that brought you up must have had a terrible cross to bear.

You have your porridge, said Shorty.

The world is wonderful all the same, said Orlick. Everybody has a different face and a separate way of talking. That is a very queer little mouth you have in your clothes, Sir, he added to the Pooka. I have only one mouth, this one in my face.

Do not worry or wonder about that, said the Pooka. That is a little angel that I carry in my pocket.

Glad to know you, Sir, said the Good Fairy pleasantly.

A little angel? said Orlick in wonder. How big?

Oh, no size at all, said the Pooka.

I am like a point in Euclid, explained the Good Fairy, position but no magnitude, you know. I bet you five pounds you could not put your finger on me.

Five pounds that I would not put my finger on you? repeated Orlick in imperfect comprehension.

If you don't mind, said the Pooka, let us confine ourselves for the moment to what is visible and palpable. Let us proceed by degrees. Now look at these fruits and jars on the floor there. . . .

Yes, said the Good Fairy, Irish apples, go where you will in the wide world you won't get better. There's a great flavour off them certainly.

We are honoured that you accept our poor offerings, said the Pooka humbly. You are very kind, Mr. . . .

According to my mother, said Orlick, my little name is Orlick.

Orlick Trellis? said the Pooka. That is very satisfactory.

Shorty tore his sombrero from his head and waved it in the air.

Three cheers for little Orlick, he shouted, three cheers for Orlick Trellis!

Not too loud, counselled the Pooka with a motion of his head towards the door of the bedroom.

Hip Hip . . . Hurray! Hurray! Hurray!

There was a short pleased silence.

May I ask, said Slug civilly, what your plans are, Sir?

I have nothing settled yet, said Orlick. I shall have to have a good look round first and find out where I stand. I must say I was very surprised to find that my father was not present here to welcome me. One expects that, you know, somehow. My mother blushed when I asked her about it and changed the subject. It is all very puzzling. I shall have to make some inquiries. Could anyone oblige me with a cigarette?

Certainly, said Slug.

These things in the baskets, they are bottles, said Shorty.

Why not open them and have a drink, said Orlick.

A modest celebration is undoubtedly called for, concurred the Good Fairy.

I say, said the Pooka in a whisper putting his hand in his pocket, I must ask you to leave my pocket for a minute. I wish to talk alone with our host. You remember our agreement?

That is all very well, said the Good Fairy querulously, but where am I to go? Put me on the floor and I'll be walked on, trampled to my death. I am not a door-mat.

Eh? asked Slug.

Be quiet, whispered the Pooka, what is wrong with the mantelpiece?

Nothing, I suppose, said the Good Fairy sulkily, I am not a door-mat.

Very well, you can lean on the clock until I am ready to take you back, said the Pooka.

He approached the fireplace with a few aimless paces and then turned courteously to his host. Shorty, stooping among the offerings, was engaged with earthen jars and kegs and wax-crusted green bottles, fondling and opening them and pouring dusky libations into medhers of old thick pewter.

Don't be all day, said the Good Fairy from the mantel-piece.

By the way, said the Pooka carelessly, could I see you alone for a moment?

Me? said Orlick. Certainly.

Excellent, said the Pooka. Let us go out into the passage for a moment.

He linked an arm in polite friendship and walked towards the door, endeavouring to match his club-step to the footstep.

Don't be too long now, said Casey, the drink is cool-ing.

The door closed. And for a long time the limping beat of the Pooka's club could be heard, and the low hum of his fine talk as they paced the passage, the Pooka and his Orlick. Conclusion of the foregoing.

Biographical reminiscence, part the eighth: While I was engaged in the spare-time literary activities of which the preceding and following pages may be cited as more or less typical examples, I was leading a life of a dull but not uncomfortable character. The following approximate schedule of my quotidian activities may be of some interest to the lay reader.

Nature of daily regime or curriculum: Nine-thirty a.m. rise, wash, shave and proceed to breakfast; this on the insistence of my uncle, who was accustomed to regard himself as the sun of his household, recalling all things to wakefulness on his own rising.

10.30. Return to bedroom.

12.00. Go, weather permitting, to College, there conducting light conversation on diverse topics with friends, or with acquaintances of a casual character.

2.00 p.m. Go home for lunch.

3.00. Return to bedroom. Engage in spare-time literary activity, or read.

6.00. Have tea in company with my uncle, attending in a perfunctory manner to the replies required by his talk.

7.00. Return to bedroom and rest in darkness.

8.00. Continue resting or meet acquaintances in open thoroughfares or places of public resort.

11.00. Return to bedroom.

Minutiae: No. of cigarettes smoked, average 8·3; glasses of stout or other comparable intoxicant, av. 1·2; times to stool, av. 2·65; hours of study, av. 1·4; spare-time or recreative pursuits, 6·63 circulating.

Comparable description of how a day may be spent, being an extract from "A Conspectus of the Arts and Natural Sciences," from the hand of Mr. Cowper. Serial volume the seventeenth: I am obliged to you for the interest you take in my welfare, and for your inquiring so particularly after the manner in which my time passes here. As to amusements, I mean what the world call such, we have none; but the place swarms with them, and cards and dancing are the professed business of almost all the gentle inhabitants of Huntingdon. We refuse to take part in them, or to be accessories to this way of murthering our time, and by so doing have acquired the name of Methodists. Having told you how we do not spend our time, I will next say how we do. We breakfast commonly between eight and nine; till eleven, we read either the Scripture, or the Sermons of some faithful preacher of these holy mysteries; at eleven, we attend Divine Service, which is performed here twice every day, and from twelve to three we separate, and amuse ourselves as we please. During that interval I either read in my own apartment, or walk, or ride, or work in the garden. We seldom sit an hour after dinner, but if the weather permits, adjourn to the garden, where with Mrs. Unwin, and her son, I have generally the pleasure of religious conversation till tea time. If it rains, or is too windy for walking, we either converse within doors, or sing some hymns of Martin's collection, and by the help of Mrs. Unwin's harpsichord make up a tolerable concert, in which our hearts, I hope, are the best and the most musical performers. After tea, we sally forth to walk in good earnest. Mrs. Unwin is a good walker, and we have generally travelled about four miles before we see home again. When the days are short, we make this excursion in the former part of the day, between church-time and dinner. At night, we read and converse as before, till supper, and commonly finish the evening with either hymns, or a sermon, and last of all the family are called to prayers. Conclusion of the foregoing.

Comparable further description of how a day may be spent, being a day from the life of Finn: It is thus that Finn spends the day: a third of the day watching the boys—three fifties of boys has he at play in his ball-yard; a third of the day drinking sack; and a third of the day in the calm sorcery of chess. Conclusion of foregoing.

Further Synopsis, being a summary of what has gone before, for the benefit of new readers: THE POOKA MACPHELLIMEY, having won dominion over Orlick by virtue of superior card-play, brings him home to his hut in the fir-wood and prevails upon him to live there as a P.G. (Paying Guest), for a period not exceeding six months, sowing in his heart throughout that time the seeds of evil, revolt, and non-serviam. Meanwhile, TRELLIS, almost perpetually in a coma as a result of the drugs secretly administered by Mr. Shanahan, makes little progress with the design of his story, with the result that

JOHN FURRISKEY is enabled to enjoy almost uninterrupted marital bliss with his wife (Mrs. Furriskey), while

MESSRS. LAMONT & SHANAHAN continue to live a dissolute if colourful life. Now read on.

Extract from Manuscript, being description of a social evening at the Furriskey household: the direct style: The voice was the first, Furriskey was saying. The human voice. The voice was Number One. Anything that came after was only an imitation of the voice. Follow, Mr. Shanahan?

Very nicely put, Mr. Furriskey.

Take the fiddle now, said Furriskey.

By hell the fiddle is the man, said Lamont, the fiddle is the man for me. Put it into the hand of a lad like Luke MacFadden and you'll cry like a child when you hear him at it. The voice was number one, I don't deny that, but look at the masterpieces of musical art you have on the fiddle! Did you ever hear the immortal strains of the Crutch Sonata now, the whole four strings playing there together, with plenty of plucking and scales and runs and a lilt that would make you tap the shoe-leather off your foot? Oh, it's the fiddle or nothing. You can have your voice, Mr. Furriskey,—and welcome. The fiddle and the bow is all I ask, and the touch of the hand of Luke MacFadden, the travelling tinsmith. The smell of his clothes would knock you down, but he was the best fiddler in Ireland, east or west.

The fiddle is there too, of course, said Furriskey.

The fiddle is an awkward class of a thing to carry, said Shanahan, it's not what you might call a handy shape. They say you get a sort of a crook in the arm, you know. . . .

But the fiddle, continued Furriskey slow and authoritative of articulation, the fiddle comes number two to the voice. Do you mind that, Mr. Lamont? Adam sang . . .

Aye, indeed, said Lamont.

But did he play? By Almighty God in Heaven he didn't. If you put your fiddle, Mr. Lamont, into the hands of our first parents in the Garden of Eden in the long ago . . .

They'd hang their hats on it, of course, said Lamont, but still and all it's the sweetest of the lot. Given a good player, of course. Could I trouble you, Mr. Furriskey?

A sugar-bowl containing sugar was passed deftly from hand to hand in the pause. Tea was stirred and bread was buttered swiftly and trisected; at the same time there were adjustments as to trouser-crease, chair-stance and seat. The accidental gong of a cream-jug and a milk-plate was the signal for a resumption of light conversation.

John is very musical, said Mrs. Furriskey. Her eyes followed closely the movements of her ten fingers as they prepared between them a tasteful collation. I'm sure he has a good voice only it's not trained. He sings a lot when he thinks I amn't listening.

A small laugh was initiated and gently circulated.

Do you mind that, eh, said Lamont. What does he sing now, Mrs. F.? Is it the songs of the native land?

The songs he sings, said Mrs. Furriskey, have no words to them. The bare air just.

When do you hear me at it? asked the prisoner, a meek inquiry on the changing contours of his face. Then stern and immobile, he waited for an answer.

Don't mind him, Mrs. F., said Shanahan loudly, don't mind him, he's only an old cod. Don't give him the satisfaction.

Sometimes when you're down there shaving. Oh, I'm up to all his tricks, Mr. Shanahan. He can sing like a lark when he feels like it.

Because when you were listening to my singing this morning, my good woman, said Furriskey stressing with his finger the caesura of his case, I was blowing my nose in the lavatory. That's a quare one for you.

Oh, that's a shame for you, said Mrs. Furriskey contributing her averted giggle to an arpeggio of low sniggers. You shouldn't use language like that at table. Where are your manners, Mr. Furriskey?

Clearing my head in the bowl of the W.C., he repeated with coarse laughing, that's the singing I was at. I'm the right tenor when it comes to that game.

It's a poor man that doesn't sing once in a while, anyway, observed Lamont continuing the talk with skill, we all have our little tunes. We can't all be Luke Mac-Faddens.

That's true.

Of all the musical instruments that have been fashioned by the hand of man, said Furriskey, the piano is far and away the most . . . useful.

Oh, everybody likes the piano, said Lamont. Nobody can raise any objection to that. The piano and the fiddle, the two go well together.

Some of the stuff I've heard in my time, said Shanahan is no joke to play for the man that has only two hands. It was stuff of the best make I don't doubt, classical tack and all the rest of it, but by God it gave me a pain in my bandbox. It hurt my head far worse than a pint of whisky.

It's not everyone can enjoy it, said Furriskey. Every man to his taste. As I was saying, the piano is a fine instrument. It comes number two to the human voice.

My sister, I believe, said Lamont, knew a lot about the piano. Piano and French, you know, it's a great thing at the convents. She had a nice touch.

Furriskey angled idly for the floating tea-leaf with the lip of his tea-spoon, frowning slightly. He was sprawled crookedly on his chair, his left thumb tucked in the arm-hole of his waistcoat.

You have only half the story when you say piano, he announced, and half the notes as well. The word is pianofurty.

I heard that before, said Shanahan. Correct.

The furty stands for the deep notes on your left hand side. Piano, of course, means our friends on the right.

Do you mean to say it is wrong to call it piano? asked Lamont. His attitude was one of civil perplexity; his eyelids fluttered and his lower lip drooped as he made his civil inquiry.

Well, no . . . It's not *wrong*. Nobody is going to say you're *wrong*. But . . .

I know what you mean. I see the point.

By virtue of enlightenment, culture, and a spirit of give-and-take, the matter was amicably settled to the satisfaction of all parties.

Do you understand, Mr. Lamont?

I do indeed. You are quite right. Pianofurty.

There was a pleased pause in which the crockery, unopposed, clinked merrily.

I believe, said Shanahan in a treacherous manner, I believe that you can do more in the line of music than give out a song. I'm told—no names, of course—I'm told the fiddle is no stranger to your hand. Now is that a fact?

What's this good God? asked Lamont. His surprise, as a matter of fact, was largely pretence. He became upright and attentive.

You never told me, John, said Mrs. Furriskey. She sadly reproached him with her weak blue eyes, smiling.

Not a word of truth in that yarn, boys, said Furriskey moving his chair noisily. Who told you that one? Is this another of your stories, woman?

Dear knows it's not.

It's a thing you want an ear for, I may tell you, told Lamont. For the hundred that takes it up, it's a bare one that lives to play it right. Do you play the violin, though, honest to God?

By God I don't, said Furriskey with a sincere widening of the eyes, no Sir. I was half thinking of trying it, you know, give it a short trial and see do I like it. Of course it would mean practice. . . .

And practice means work, Shanahan said.

The ear is the main thing, observed Lamont. You can wear the last tatter of skin off your knuckles with a fiddle and a bow and you won't get as far as your own shadow if you haven't got the ear. Have the ear and you're half-way there before you start at all. Tell me this. Did you ever hear of a great fiddler, a man by the name of Pegasus? I believe he was the business.

That's one man I never met, said Shanahan.

He wasn't in our time, of course, said Lamont, but the tale was told that himself and the Devil had arrived at an understanding. What you call a working agreement.

Dear dear, said Furriskey. He gave a frown of pain.

Well now that's a fact. Your man becomes fiddler Number One for the whole world. Everybody has to toe the line. But when the hour comes for him to die, My Nabs is waiting by the bed!

He has come to claim his own, said Mrs. Furriskey, nodding.

He has come to claim his own, Mrs. Furriskey.

Here there was a pause for the purpose of heart-searching and meditation.

That's a queer story certainly, said Shanahan.

But the queerest part of it is this, said Lamont, in all the years he lived, man, never once did he do his scales, never once did he practise. It happened that his fingers were in the pay of who-you-know.

That's very queer, said Shanahan, there's no doubt about it. I'm sure that man's mind was like a sewer, Mr. Lamont?

Very few of the fiddlers had their heads on the right

way, said Lamont. Very few of them indeed. Saving, of course, the presence of our host.

Furriskey gave a sound of coughing and laughing, groped quickly for his handkerchief and waved a hand high in the air.

Leave me out of it, now, he said, leave the host alone boys. The biggest ruffian of the lot, of course, was our old friend Nero. Now that fellow was a thorough bags, say what you like.

He was a tyrant, said Mrs. Furriskey. She brought her light repast to a dainty and timely conclusion and built her vessels into a fine castle. She leant forward slightly, her elbows on the table and her chin on the trestle of her interlocking hands.

If everything I hear is true, ma'am, said Furriskey, you praise him very high up when you call him a tyrant. The man was a bowsy, of course.

He was certainly not everything you look for in a man, said Shanahan, I'll agree with you there.

When the city of Rome, continued Furriskey, the holy city and the centre and the heart of the Catholic world was a mass of flames, with people roasting there in the streets by the God Almighty dozen, here is my man as cool as you please in his palace with his fiddle at his jaw. There were people there . . . roasting . . . alive . . . not a dozen yards from his door, men, women and children getting the worst death of the bloody lot, Holy God can you imagine it!

The like of him would have no principles, of course, said Mrs. Furriskey.

Oh, he was a terrible drink of water. Death by fire, you know, by God it's no joke.

They tel¹ me drowning is worse, Lamont said.

Do you know what it is, said Furriskey, you can drown me three times before you roast me. Yes, by God and six times. Put your finger in a basin of water. What do you feel? Next to nothing. *But put your finger in the fire!*

I never looked at it that way, agreed Lamont.

I'm telling you, now, it's a different story. A very very different story, Mr. Lamont. It's a horse of another colour altogether. Oh, yes.

Please God we'll all die in our beds, said Mrs. Furriskey.

I'd rather live myself, I'll say that, said Shanahan, but if I had to go I'd choose the gun. A bullet in the heart and you're right. You're polished off before you know you're hurt at all. There's no nonsense about the gun. It's quick, it's merciful, and it's clean.

I'm telling you now, fire's a fright, said Furriskey.

In the old days, recalled Lamont, they had what you call a draught. It was brewed from weeds—deadly nightshade, you know. It got you at the guts, at the pit of the stomach, here, look. You took it and you felt grand for a half an hour. At the end of that time, you felt a bit weak, do you know. At the heel of the hunt, your inside is around you on the floor.

Lord save us!

A bloody fact now. Not a word of a lie. At the finish you are just a bag of air. You puke the whole shooting gallery.

If you ask me, said Shanahan quickly, inserting the shaft

of his fine wit in the midst of the conversation, I've had an odd pint of that tack in my time.

A laugh was interposed neatly, melodiously, retrieved with skill and quietly replaced.

They called the dose a draught of hemlock, Lamont said, they made it from garlic and other things. Homer finished his days on earth with his cup of poison. He drank it alone in his cell.

That was another ruffian, said Mrs. Furriskey. He persecuted the Christians.

That was all the fashion at one time, Furriskey said, we must make allowances, you know. You were nothing if you didn't let the Christians have it. *Onward Christian Soldiers, to your doom!*

No excuse, of course, said Lamont. Ignorance of the law is no excuse for the law, I've often heard that said. Homer was a great poet altogether and that made up for a lot of the rascality. His Iliad is still read. Wherever you go on the face of the civilized globe you will hear of Homer, the glory that was Greece. Yes, indeed. I'm told there are some very nice verses in the Iliad of Homer, very good stuff, you know. You have never read it, Mr. Shanahan?

He was the daddy of them all, said Shanahan.

I believe, said Furriskey with a finger to his eye, that he was as blind as the back of your neck. Glasses or no glasses, he could see nothing.

You are perfectly right, Sir, said Lamont.

I saw a blind beggerman the other day, said Mrs. Furriskey rummaging with a frown in the interior of her memory, in Stephens Green I think it was. He was heading straight for a lamp-post. When he was about a yard away from it, he turned to the one side and made a bee-line around it.

Oh, he knew it was there, said Furriskey, he knew it was there. He knew what he was about the same man.

The Compensations of Nature, that's what they call it, explained Shanahan. It's as long as it's broad. If you can't speak, you can listen twice as good as the man that can. Six of one and half a dozen of the other.

It's funny, said Mrs. Furriskey. Curiously examining it, she replaced her reminiscence.

The blind are great harpers, said Lamont, great harpers altogether. I knew a man once by the name of Searson, some class of a hunchback that harped for his living about the streets. He always wore a pair of black glasses.

Was he blind, Mr. Lamont?

Certainly he was blind. From the day of his birth he hadn't a light in his head. But don't worry it was all made up to him. My brave man knew how to take it out of his old harp. I'll swear by God he did. He was a lovely harper certainly. It would do you good to listen to him. He was a great man altogether at the scales.

Is that so?

Oh, by God he was a treat.

Music is a wonderful thing when you come to think of it, observed Mrs. Furriskey, raising her gentle countenance until its inspection had been duly accomplished by the company.

Here's a thing I was going to ask for a long time, said Shanahan, is there any known cure for blackheads?

Plenty of sulphur, said Mrs. Furriskey.

Do you mean pimples? inquired Lamont. Pimples take time, you know. You can't clean pimples up in one night.

Sulphur's very good, of course, Mrs. Furriskey, but it's for the bowels they give you sulphur unless I'm thinking of something different.

To clear away pimples in the one go-off, continued Lamont, you'll have to get up early in the morning. Very early in the morning, I'm thinking.

They tell me if you steam the face, said Shanahan, the pores will—you know—open. That's the man for blackheads, plenty of steam.

I'll tell you what it is, explained Lamont, bad blood is the back of the whole thing. When the quality of the blood isn't first class, out march our friends the pimples. It's Nature's warning, Mr. Shanahan. You can steam your face till your snot melts but damn the good it will do your blackheads if you don't attend to your inside.

I always heard that sulphur was the best thing you could take, said Mrs. Furriskey, sulphur and a good physic.

There would be less consumption in this country, continued Lamont, if the people paid more attention to their blood. Do you know what it is, the nation's blood is getting worse, any doctor will tell you that. The half of it is poison.

Blackheads are not so bad, said Furriskey. A good big boil on the back of your neck, that's the boy that will make you say your prayers. A boil is a fright. It's a fright now.

A boil is a fright if you get it in the wrong place.

You walk down the street and here you are like a man with a broken neck, your snot hopping off your knees. I know a man that never wore a collar for five years. Five years, think of that!

Well sulphur is good for that complaint, said Mrs. Furriskey, people who are subject to that complaint are never without a pot of sulphur in the house.

Sulphur cools the blood, of course, concurred Lamont.

There was a girl that I knew once, said Mrs. Furriskey rummaging anew in the store of her recollections. She worked in a house where they had a lot of silver, pots, you know, and that kind of thing. She used to polish them with sulphur.

Ah, but the boil's the boy, said Furriskey with a slap of his knee, the boil's the boy that will bend your back.

I'll tell you what's hard, too, said Shanahan, a bad knee. They say a bad knee is worse than no knee at all. A bad knee and an early grave.

Water on the knee do you mean?

Yes, water on the knee is a bad man, I believe. So I'm told. But you can have a bad cap too, a split knee. Believe me that's no joke. A split knee-cap.

Where are you if you are gone in the two knees? asked Furriskey.

I knew a man and it's not long ago since he died, Bartley Madigan, said Shanahan. A man by the name of Bartley

Madigan. A right decent skin too. You never heard a bad word about Bartley.

I knew a Peter Madigan once, said Mrs. Furriskey, a tall well-built man from down the country. That was about ten years ago.

Well Bartley got a crack of a door-knob in the knee. . . .

Eh! Well dear knows that's the queer place to get the knob of a door. By God he must have been a bruiser. A door-knob!—Oh, come here now. How high was he?

It's a question I am always asked, ladies and gentlemen, and it's a question I can never answer. But what my poor Bartley got was a blow on the crown of the cap. . . . They tell me there was trickery going on, trickery of one kind or another. Did I tell you the scene is laid in a public-house?

You did not, said Lamont.

Well what happened, asked Furriskey.

I'll tell you what happened. When my hard Bartley got the crack, he didn't let on he was hurt at all. Not a word out of him. On the way home in the tram he complained of a pain. The same night he was given up for dead.

For goodness sake!

Not a word of a lie, gentlemen. But Bartley had a kick in his foot still. A game bucko if you like. Be damned but he wouldn't die!

He wouldn't die?

Be damned but he wouldn't die. I'll live, says he, I'll live if it kills me, says he. I'll spite the lot of ye. And live he did. He lived for twenty years.

Is that a fact?

He lived for twenty years and he spent the twenty years on the flat of his back in bed. He was paralysed from the knee up. That's a quare one.

He was better dead, said Furriskey, stern in the certainty of his statement.

Paralysis is certainly a nice cup of tea, observed Lamont. Twenty . . . bloody . . . years in bed, eh? Every Christmas he was carried out by his brother and put in a bath.

He was better dead, said Furriskey. He was better in his grave than in that bed.

Twenty years is a long time, said Mrs. Furriskey.

Well now there you are, said Shanahan. Twenty summers and twenty winters. And plenty of bedsores into the bargain. Oh, yes, bags of those playboys. The sight of his legs would turn your stomach.

Lord help us, said Furriskey with a frown of pain. That's a blow on the knee for you. A blow on the head would leave you twice as well off, a crack on the skull and you were right.

I knew a man, said Lamont, that was presented with an accidental skelp of a hammer on the something that he sits on—the important what you may call it to the rear, you will understand. How long did he live?

Is this a man I know? asked Mrs. Furriskey.

He lived for the length of a split second, long enough to fall in a heap in his own hall. Something, you understand, gave way. Something—I forget what they call it —but it was badly burst, so the doctors said when they examined him.

A hammer is a dangerous weapon, said Shanahan, if you happen to get it in the wrong place. A dangerous instrument.

The cream of the joke is this, but, continued Lamont, that he got the hammer on the morning of his birthday. That was the present *he* got.

The poor so-and-so, said Furriskey.

Shanahan gave a whisper from the screen of his flat hand and a privy laugh, orderly and undertoned, was offered and accepted in reward.

He died by the hammer—did you ever hear that said? A finger of perplexity straying to her lip, Mrs. Furriskey presented the troubled inquiry of her face to each in turn.

I never heard that, ma'am, said Furriskey.

Well maybe I am thinking of something else, she reflected. *He died by the hammer*. I see they have great coal-hammers in that place in Baggot Street for one and nine.

A shilling is plenty to pay for a coal-hammer, said Furriskey.

There's another gentleman that I advise ye all to avoid, counselled Shanahan, cross the road if you see him coming. Our old friend pee-eye-ell-ee-ess.

Who might he be? asked Mrs. Furriskey.

He's a man that'll make you sit up and take notice if you let him into the house, explained Furriskey, a private wink for the entertainment of his male companions. Eh, Mr. Shanahan?

Oh, a bad man, said Shanahan. I met him once but I may tell you he got his orders. Out he went.

It's the blood again, said Lamont.

Here a loud knocking at the door became audible to the company. Mrs. Furriskey moved quietly from the room in response.

That'll be Mr. Orlick, said Shanahan. I was talking to him to-day. I think he is going to do a bit of writing to-night. Conclusion of the foregoing.

Biographical reminiscence, part the ninth: It was the late summer, a humid breathless season that is inimical to comfort and personal freshness. I was reclining on my bed and conducting a listless conversation with Brinsley, who was maintaining a stand by the window. From the averted quality of his voice, I knew that his back was towards me and that he was watching through the window without advertence the evening boys at ball-throw. We had been discussing the craft of writing and had adverted to the primacy of Irish and American authors in the world of superior or better-class letters. From a perusal of the manuscript which has just been presented in these pages, he had expressed his inability to distinguish between Furriskey, Lamont and Shanahan, bewailed what he termed their spiritual and physical identity, stated that true dialogue is dependent on the conflict rather than the confluence of minds and made reference to the importance of characterization in contemporary literary works of a high-class, advanced or literary nature.

The three of them, he said, might make one man between them.

Your objections are superficial, I responded. These gentlemen may look the same and speak the same but actually they are profoundly dissimilar. For example, Mr. Furriskey is of the brachycephalic order, Mr. Shanahan of the prognathic.

Prognathic?

I continued in this strain in an idle perfunctory manner, searching in the odd corners of my mind where I was accustomed to keep words which I rarely used. I elaborated the argument subsequently with the aid of dictionaries and standard works of reference, embodying the results of my researches in a memorandum which is now presented conveniently for the information of the reader.

Memorandum of the respective diacritical traits or qualities of Messrs. Furriskey, Lamont and Shanahan:

Head: brachycephalic; bullet; prognathic.

Vision: tendencies towards myopia; wall-eye; nyctalopia.

Configuration of nose: roman; snub; mastoid.

Unimportant physical afflictions: palpebral ptosis; indigestion; German itch.

Mannerisms: tendency to agitate or flick fingers together in prim fashion after conveying bread or other crumbling substance to mouth; tooth-sucking and handling of tie-knot; ear-poking with pin or match, lip-pursing.

Outer clothing: D.B. indigo worsted; S.B. brown serge, two button style; do., three button style.

Inner or under-clothing: woollen combinations, front buttoning style; home-made under-tabard of stout moreen-cloth (winter) or paramatta (summer); abdominal belt or corset with attached unguinal protective appliance.

Fabric of shirt: tiffany; linen; tarlatan.

Pedal traits: hammer-toes; nil; corns.

Volar traits: horniness; callosity; nil.

Favourite flower: camomile; daisy; betony.

Favourite shrub: deutzia; banksia; laurustinus.

Favourite dish: loach; caudle; julienne. Conclusion of memorandum.

The door opened without warning and my uncle entered. From his manner it was evident that he had seen the note-books of Brinsley below-stairs on the hall-stand. He wore a genial and hostly manner. His cigarette-box, the ten-for-sixpence denomination, was already in his hand. He stopped with a polite ejaculation of his surprise at the presence of a guest by the window.

Mr. Brinsley! he said.

Brinsley responded according to the practices of polite society, utilizing a formal good evening for the purpose.

My uncle conferred a warm handshake and immediately placed his cigarettes at the disposal of the company.

Well it isn't often we see you, he said.

He forestalled our effort to find matches. I had arisen from the supine attitude and was seated on the bed-edge in an uneasy manner. As he came round to me tendering his flame, he said:

Well, mister-my-friend, and how are *we* this evening? I see you're as fond of the bed as ever. Mr. Brinsley, what are we going to do with this fellow? Dear knows I don't know what we'll do with him at all.

Without addressing my uncle I made it known that there was but one chair in the room.

You mean this lying in bed during the day? said Brinsley. His voice was innocent. He was intent on discussing my personal habits in a sympathetic manner with my uncle in order to humiliate me.

I do, Mr. Brinsley, said my uncle in an eager earnest manner, I do certainly. Upon my word I think it is a very bad sign in a young lad. I don't understand it at all. What would you say is the meaning of it? The lad is healthy as far as I can see. I mean, you would understand an old person or an invalid. He looks as fit as a fiddle.

Putting his cigarette-hand to his head, he shut his right eye and rubbed the lid in perplexity with the crook of his thumb.

Dear knows it is more than I can understand, he said.

Brinsley gave a polite laugh.

Well we're all lazy, he said in a broad-minded manner, it's the legacy of our first parents. We all have it in us. It is just a question of making a special effort.

My uncle gave a rap of concurrence on the washstand.

We all have it in us, he repeated loudly, from the highest to the lowest we all have it in us. Certainly. But tell me this, Mr. Brinsley. Do we make the effort?

We do, said Brinsley.

Oh, we do indeed, said my uncle, and faith it would be a very nice world to live in if we didn't. Oh, yes.

I agree with you, said Brinsley.

We can say to ourselves, continued my uncle, I have now rested. I have had enough. I will now rise and use my God-given strength to the best of my ability and according to the duties of my station in life. To the flesh we say: Thus far and no further.

Yes, said Brinsley nodding.

Sloth—Lord save us—sloth is a terrible cross to carry in this world. You are a burden to yourself . . . to your friends . . . and to every man woman and child you meet and mix with. One of the worst of the deadly sins, there is no doubt about it.

I'd say it is the worst, said Brinsley.

The worst? Certainly.

Turning to me, my uncle said:

Tell me this, do you ever open a book at all?

I open and shut books several times a day, I replied in a testy manner. I study here in my bedroom because it is quiet and suitable for the purpose. I pass my examinations without difficulty when they arise. Is there any other point I could explain?

That will do you now, there is no need for temper, said my uncle. No need at all for temper. Friendly advice no wise man scorns, I'm sure you have often heard that said.

Ah don't be too hard on him, said Brinsley, especially about his studies. A little more exercise would do the trick. *Mens sana in corpore sano*, you know.

The Latin tongue was unknown to my uncle.

There is no doubt about it, he said.

I mean, the body must be in good condition before the mind can be expected to function properly. A little more exercise and study would be less of a burden, I fancy.

Of course, said my uncle. Lord knows I am sick sore and tired telling him that. Sick, sore, and tired.

In the speech of Brinsley I detected an opening for crafty retaliation and revenge. I turned to him and said:

That is all very well for you. You are fond of exercise —I am not. You go for a long walk every evening because you like it. To me it is a task.

I am very glad to hear you are fond of walking, Mr. Brinsley, said my uncle.

Oh, yes, said Brinsley. His tone was disquieted.

Well, indeed, you are a wise man, said my uncle. Every evening in life I go for a good four-mile tramp myself. Every evening, wet or fine. And do you know what I am going to tell you, I'm the better for it too. I am indeed. I don't know what I would do without my walk.

You are a bit late at it this evening, I observed.

Never you fear, late or early I won't forget it, he said. Would you care to join me, Mr. Brinsley?

They went, the two of them. I lay back in the failing light in a comfortable quiet manner. Conclusion of the foregoing.

Synopsis, being a summary of what has gone before, for the benefit of new readers: ORLICK TRELLIS, having concluded his course of study at the residence of the Pooka Mac-Phellimey, now takes his place in civil life, living as a lodger in the house of

FURRISKEY, whose domestic life is about to be blessed by the advent of a little stranger. Meanwhile,

SHANAHAN and LAMONT, fearing that Trellis would soon become immune to the drugs and sufficiently regain the use of his faculties to perceive the true state of affairs and visit the delinquents with terrible penalties, are continually endeavouring to devise A PLAN. One day in Furriskey's sitting-room they discover what appear to be some pages of manuscript of a high-class story in which the names of painters and French wines are used with knowledge and authority. On investigation they find that Orlick has inherited his father's gift for literary composition. Greatly excited, they suggest that he utilize his gift to turn the tables (as it were) and compose a story on the subject of Trellis, a fitting punishment indeed for the usage he has given others. Smouldering with resentment at the stigma of his own bastardy, the dishonour and death of his mother, and incited by the subversive teachings of the Pooka, he agrees. He comes one evening to his lodgings where the rest of his friends are gathered and a start is made on the manuscript in the presence of the interested parties. Now read on.

Extract from Manuscript by O. Trellis. Part One. Chapter One: Tuesday had come down through Dundrum and Foster Avenue, brine-fresh from sea-travel, a corn-yellow sun-drench that called forth the bees at an incustomary hour to their day of bumbling. Small house-flies performed brightly in the embrasures of the windows, whirling without fear on imaginary trapezes in the lime-light of the sun-slants.

Dermot Trellis neither slept nor woke but lay there

in his bed, a twilight in his eyes. His hands **he rested** emptily at his thighs and his legs stretched loose-jointed and heavily to the bed-bottom. His diaphragm, a metronome of quilts, heaved softly and relaxed in the beat of his breathing. Generally speaking he was at peace.

A cleric, attaining the ledge of the window with the help of a stout ladder of ashplant rungs, round and seasoned, quietly peered in through the glass. The bar of the sunbeams made a great play of his fair hair and burnished it into the appearance of a halo. He civilly unloosed the brass catch on the window by inserting the blade of his pen-knife between the sashes. He then raised up the bottom sash with a strong arm and entered into the room without offence, one leg first for all the hobble of his soutane, and afterwards the other. He was meek and of pleasing manners and none but an ear that listened for it could perceive the click of the window as it was shut. The texture of his face was mottled by a blight of Lent-pocks, but—stern memorials of his fasts—they did not lessen the clear beauty of his brow. Each of his features was pale and hollow and unlivened by the visits of his feeble blood; but considering them together in the manner in which their Creator had first arranged them, they enunciated between them a quiet dignity, a peace like the sad peace of an old grave-yard. His manner was meek. The cuffs, the neck and the fringes of his surplice were intricately crocheted in a pattern of stars and flowers and triangles, three diversities cunningly needle-worked to a white unity. His fingers were wax pale and translucent and curled resolutely about the butt of a club of the mountain-ash that can be found in practically every corner of the country. His temples were finely perfumed.

He examined the bedroom without offence and with plenty of diligence, for it was the first room he was in. He drew a low sound from a delph wash-jug with a blow of his club and a bell-note was the sound he brought forth with the two of them, his sandal and a chamber.

Trellis arose and made a hypotenuse of his back, his weight being supported on his elbows. His head was sunken in the cup of his collar-bones and his eyes stared forth like startled sentries from their red watch-towers.

Who are you? he asked. A quantity of dried mucous had been lodged in a lump in his wind-pipe and for this reason the tone of his voice was not satisfactory. He followed his question without delay with a harsh coughing noise, presumably in order to remedy his defective articulation.

I am Moling, said the cleric. A smile crossed his face without pausing on its way. I am a cleric and I serve God. We will pray together after.

On the outer edge of the cloud of wonder that was gathered in the head of Trellis, there was an outer border of black anger. He brought down his lids across his eye-balls until his vision was confined to slits scarcely wider than those in use by houseflies when flying in the face of a strong sun, videlicet, the thousandth part of an inch statute. He ascertained by trial that his windpipe was clear before he loudly put this question:

How did you get in here? What do you want?

I was acquainted of the way by angels, said the cleric,

and the ladder I have climbed to your window-shelf was fashioned by angelic craftsmen from pitch pine of the best quality and conveyed to my college in a sky-carriage in the middle of last night, at two of the clock to speak precisely. I am here this morning to make a bargain.

You are here to make a bargain.

To make a bargain between the pair of us, yourself and me. There is fine handwork in that thing on the floor. Too delightful the roundness of its handle.

What? said Trellis. Who did you say you were? What was that noise? What is the ringing for?

The bells of my acolyte, said the cleric. His voice was of a light quality and was unsupported by the majority of his wits, because these were occupied with the beauty of the round thing, its whiteness, its star-twinkle face.

Eh?

My acolytes are in your garden. They are taping the wallsteads of a sunbright church and ringing their bells in the morning.

I beg your pardon, Sir, said Shanahan, but this is a bit too high up for us. This delay, I mean to say. The fancy stuff, couldn't you leave it out or make it short, Sir? Couldn't you give him a dose of something, give him a varicose vein in the bloody heart and get him out of that bed?

Orlick placed his pen in the centre of his upper lip and exerted a gentle pressure by a movement of his head or hand, or both, so that his lip was pushed upwards.

Result: baring of teeth and gum.

239

You overlook my artistry, he said. You cannot drop a man unless you first lift him. See the point?

Oh, there's that too, of course, said Shanahan.

Or a varicose vein across the scalp, said Furriskey, near the brain, you know. I believe that's the last.

I saw a thing in a picture once, said Shanahan, a concrete-mixer, you understand, Mr. Orlick, and three of your men fall into it when it is working full blast, going like the hammers of hell.

The mixture to be taken three times after meals, Lamont said laughing.

You must have patience, gentlemen, counselled Orlick, the whiteness of a slim hand for warning.

A concrete-mixer, said Shanahan.

I'm after thinking of something good, something very good unless I'm very much mistaken, said Furriskey in an eager way, black in the labour of his fine thought. When you take our hero from the concrete-mixer, you put him on his back on the road and order full steam ahead with the steam-roller. . . .

And a very good idea, Shanahan agreed.

And a very good idea as you say, Mr. Shanahan. But when the roller passes over his dead corpse, be damned but there's one thing there that it can't crush, one thing that lifts it high offa the road—a ten ton roller, mind! . . .

Indeed, said Orlick, eye-brow for question.

One thing, said Furriskey, sole finger for true counting. They drive away the roller and here is his black heart sitting there as large as life in the middle of the pulp of his banjaxed corpse. *They couldn't crush his heart!*

Very . . . very . . . good, intoned Lamont. A winner,
Mr. Orlick. Well that will ring the bell certainly.

Admirable, concurred Orlick, honey-word for peace.

They couldn't crush the heart!

Steam-rollers are expensive machines but, remarked
Shanahan, what about a needle in the knee? He kneels
on it by mistake, drives it in and then it breaks and leaves
nothing to get a grip on. A knitting needle or a hat-pin.

A cut of a razor behind the knee, said Lamont with a
wink of knowledge, try it and see.

Orlick had been quietly occupied with the arrangement of a paragraph of wisdom in his mind; he now inserted
it with deftness in the small gap which he discovered in
the disputations.

The refinements of physical agony, he enunciated, are
limited by an ingenious arrangement of the cerebral
mechanism and the sensory nerves which precludes from
registration all emotions, sensations and perceptions
abhorrent to the fastidious maintenance by Reason of its
discipline and rule over the faculties and the functions
of the body. Reason will not permit of the apprehension
of sensations of reckless or prodigal intensity. Give me
an agony within reason, says Reason, and I will take it,
analyse it, and cause the issue of vocal admission that it
has been duly received; I can deal with it and do my other
work as well. Is that clear?

Very well put, Sir, said Shanahan.

But go beyond the agreed statutory limit, says Reason
and I won't be there at all. I'll put out the light and pull
down the blinds. I will close the shop. I will come back

later when I think I will be offered something I can deal with. Follow?

And back he'll come too. When the fun is over, back he'll come.

But the soul, the ego, the *animus*, continued Orlick, is very different from the body. Labyrinthine are the injuries inflictable on the soul. The tense of the body is the present indicative; but the soul has a memory and a present and a future. I have conceived some extremely recondite pains for Mr. Trellis. I will pierce him with a pluperfect.

Pluperfect is all right, of course, said Shanahan, anybody that takes exception to that was never very much at the bee-double-o-kay-ess. I wouldn't hear a word against it. But do you know, this tack of yours is too high up in the blooming clouds. It's all right for you, you know, but the rest of us will want a ladder. Eh, Mr. Furriskey?

A forty-foot ladder, said Furriskey.

At the conclusion of a brief interval, Lamont spread out his hand and addressed Mr. Orlick in a low earnest voice.

A nice simple story would be very nice, Sir, he said, you take a lot of the good out of it when you start, you know, the other business. A nice simple story with plenty of the razor, you understand. A slash of the razor behind the knee, Oh, that's the boy!

The right hand of Orlick was fastened about his jaw.

Interpretation of manual attitude mentioned: a token of extreme preoccupation and intense thought.

I admit, gentlemen, he said at last, I admit that there is a certain amount to be said for your point of view. Sometimes. . . .

There's this, too, said Shanahan with a quick continuance of his argument, there's this, that you have to remember the man in the street. *I* may understand you, *Mr. Lamont* may understand you, *Mr. Furriskey* may understand you—but the man in the street? Oh, by God you have to go very *very* slow if you want *him* to follow you. A snail would be too fast for him, a snail could give him yards.

Orlick detached his hand from his jaw and passed it slowly about his brow.

I could begin again, of course, he said with a slight weariness, but it would mean wasting some very good stuff.

Certainly you can begin again, said Shanahan, there's no harm done, man. I've been longer in this world and I can tell you this: *There's nothing to be ashamed of in a false start.* We can but try. Eh, boys? We can but try.

We can but try, said Furriskey.

Well, well, well, said Orlick.

Tuesday had come down through Dundrum and Foster Avenue, brine-fresh from sea-travel, a corn-yellow sun-drench that called forth the bees at an incustomary hour to their day of bumbling. Small house-flies performed brightly in the embrasures of the windows, whirling without a fear on imaginary trapezes in the lime-light of the sun-slants.

Dermot Trellis neither slept nor woke but lay there in his bed, a twilight in his eyes. His hands he rested emptily at his thighs and his legs stretched loose-jointed and heavily to the bed-bottom. His diaphragm, a metronome of quilts, heaved softly and relaxed in the beat of his breathing. Generally speaking he was at peace.

His home was by the banks of the Grand Canal, a magnificent building resembling a palace, with seventeen windows to the front and maybe twice that number to the rear. It was customary with him to remain in the interior of his house without ever opening the door to go out or let the air and the light go in. The blind of his bedroom window would always be pulled down during the daytime and a sharp eye would discover that he had the gas on even when the sun was brightly shining. Few had ever seen him in the flesh and the old people had bad memories and had forgotten what he looked like the last time they had laid their eyes on him. He paid no attention to the knocking of mendicants and musicians and would sometimes shout something at people passing from behind his blind. It was a well-known fact that he was responsible for plenty of rascality and only simple people were surprised at the way he disliked the sunshine.

He paid no attention to the law of God and this is the short of his evil-doing in the days when he was accustomed to go out of his house into the air:

He corrupted schoolgirls away from their piety by telling impure stories and reciting impious poems in their hearing.

Holy purity he despised.

Will this be a long list do you think, Sir, asked Furriskey.

Certainly, answered Orlick, I am only starting.

Well what about a Catalogue, you know?

A Catalogue would be a very cute one, Lamont concurred. Cross-references and double-entry, you know. What do you think, Mr. Orlick? What do you say?

A catalogue of his sins, eh? Is that what you mean? asked Orlick.

Do you understand what I mean? asked Furriskey with solicitude.

I think I do, mind you. DRUNKENNESS, was addicted to. CHASTITY, lacked. I take it that's what you had in mind, Mr. Furriskey?

That sounds very well, gentlemen, said Lamont, very well indeed in my humble opinion. It's the sort of queer stuff they look for in a story these days. Do you know?

Oh, we'll make a good job of this yarn yet.

We will see, said Orlick.

He paid no attention to the laws of God and this is the short of his evil-doing in the days when he was accustomed to go out of his house into the light.

ANTHRAX, paid no attention to regulations governing the movements of animals affected with.

BOYS, corner, consorted·with.

CONVERSATIONS, licentious, conducted by telephone with unnamed female servants of the Department of Posts and Telegraphs.

DIRTINESS, all manner of spiritual mental and physical, gloried in.

ECLECTICISM, practised amorous.

The completion of this list in due alphabetical order, observed Orlick, will require consideration and research.

We will complete it later. This is not the place (nor is the hour appropriate), for scavenging in the cesspools of iniquity.

Oh, you're a wise man, Mr. Orlick, and me waiting without a word to see what you would do with x. You're too fly now, said Shanahan.

E for evil, said Furriskey.

He is quite right, said Lamont, can't you see he wants to get down to business. Eh? Mr. Orlick. Can't you see that it means delay?

Quite right, said Shanahan. Silence!

On a certain day this man looked out accidentally through a certain window and saw a saint in his garden taping out the wallsteads of a new sun-bright church, with a distinguished concourse of clerics and acolytes along with him, discoursing and ringing shrill iron bells and reciting elegant latin. For a reason he was angry. He gave the whoop of a world-wide shout from the place he was and with only the bareness of time for completing the plan he was engaged with, made five strides to the middle of his garden. The brevity of the tale is this, that there was a sacrilege in the garden that morning. Trellis took the saint by a hold of his wasted arm and ran (the two of them), until the head of the cleric had been hurt by a stone wall. The evil one then took a hold of the saint's breviary—the one used by holy Kevin—and tore at it until it was a tatters in his angry hand; and he added this to his sins, videlicet, the hammering of a young clergyman, an acolyte to confide precisely, with a lump of a stone.

There now, he said.

Evil is the work you have accomplished here this morning, said the saint with a hand to the soreness of his head.

But the mind of Trellis was darkened with anger and evil venom against the saintly band of strangers. The saint smoothed out the many-lined pages of his ruined book and recited a curse in poetry against the evil one, three stanzas in devvy-metre of surpassing elegance and sun-twinkle clearness. . . .

Do you know, said Orlick, filling the hole in his story with the music of his voice, I think we are on the wrong track again. What do you say, gentlemen?

Certainly you are, said Shanahan, no offence but that class of stuff is all my fanny.

You won't get very far by attacking the church, said Furriskey.

I gather my efforts are not approved, said Orlick. He gave a small smile and took advantage of the parting of his lips for a brief spell of pen-tap at the teeth.

You can do better, man, said Lamont, that's the way to look at it. You can do twice as good if you put your mind to it.

I think, said Orlick, we might requisition the services of the Pooka MacPhellimey.

If you don't hurry and get down to business, Sir, said Furriskey, Trellis will get *us* before we get him. He'll hammer the lights out of us. Get him on the run, Mr. Orlick. Get the Pooka and let him go to work right away. God, if he catches us at this game. . . .

What about this for a start, asked Shanahan, a big boil

247

on the small of his back where he can't get at it. It's a well-known fact that every man has a little square on his back that he can't itch with his hand. Here, look.

There's such a thing as a scratching-post, observed Lamont.

Wait now! said Orlick. Silence please.

Tuesday had come down through Foster Avenue and Dundrum, brine-fresh from sea-travel, a corn-yellow sun-drench that called forth the bees at an incustomary hour to their day of bumbling. Small, house-flies performed brightly in the embrasures of the windows, whirling without fear on imaginary trapezes in the lime-light of the sunslants.

Dermot Trellis neither slept nor woke but lay there in his bed, a twilight in his eyes. His hands he rested emptily at his thighs and his legs stretched loose-jointed and heavily to the bed-bottom. His diaphragm, a metronome of quilts, heaved softly and relaxed in the beat of his breathing. Generally speaking, he was at peace.

The utterance of a civil cough beside his ear recalled him to his reason. His eyes, startled sentries in red watch-towers on the brink of morning, brought him this intelligence, that the Pooka MacPhellimey was sitting there beside him on the cabinet of his pots, a black walking-stick of invaluable ebony placed civilly across the knees of his tight trousers. His temples were finely scented with an expensive brand of balsam and fine snuff-dust could be discerned on the folds of his cravat. A top-hat was inverted on the floor, with woven gloves of black wool placed neatly in its interior.

Good morning to you, Sir, said the Pooka with melodious intonation. No doubt you have awakened to divert yourself with the refreshment of the dawn.

Trellis composed his pimples the way they would tell of the greatness of the surprise that was in his mind.

Your visit to my house this morning, he said, that surprises me. A bull may sometimes be a cow, a jackdaw may discourse, cocks have established from time to time the hypothesis that the egg is impeculiar to the she-bird, but a servant is at all times a servant notwithstanding. I do not recall that I desired you for a guest at an hour when I am accustomed to be unconscious in the shadow of my sleep. Perchance you bring a firkin of sweet ointment compounded for the relief of boils?

I do not, rejoined the Pooka.

Then a potion, herbal and decanted from the juice of roots, unsurpassed for the extirpation of personal lice?

Doubts as to the sex of cattle, observed the Pooka after he had first adjusted the hard points of his fingers one against the other, arise only when the animal is early in its youth and can be readily resolved by the use of a prongs or other probing instrument—or better still, a magnifying glass of twenty diameters. Jackdaws who discourse or who are accustomed to express themselves in Latin or in the idiom of sea-faring men may betray an indication of the nature of their talent by inadvertently furnishing the same answer to all questions, making claim in this manner to unlimited ignorance or infinite wisdom. If a cock may secrete eggs from his interior, equally a hen can crow at four-thirty of a morning. Rats have been observed to fly, small bees can extract honey from dung and agamous mammals have been known to produce by the art of allogamy a curious offspring azoic in nature and arachnoid in appearance. It is not false that a servant is a servant but truth is an odd number and one master is a great mistake. Myself I have two.

Allogamy and arachnoid I understand, said Trellis, but the meaning you attach to azoic is a thing that is not clear to me at all.

Devoid of life, having no organic remains, said the Pooka.

That is an elegant definition, said Trellis, affording an early-morning smile for the enjoyment of his guest. A grain of knowledge with the dawning of the day is a breakfast for the mind. I will now re-enter the darkness of my sleep, remembering to examine it anew on my recovery. My serving-girl, she is the little guide who will conduct you from the confinement of my walls. I have little doubt that the science of bird-flight is known to rats of cunning and resource, but nevertheless I have failed to observe such creatures passing by in the air through the aperture of my window. Good morning, Sir.

Your courteous salutation is one I cannot accept, answered the Pooka, for this reason, that its valedictory character invalidates it. It is my mission here this morning to introduce you to a wide variety of physical scourges, torments, and piteous blood-sweats. The fulness of your suffering, that will be the measure of my personal perfection. A window without rat-flight past it is a backyard without a house.

Your talk surprises me, said Trellis. Furnish three examples.

Boils upon the back, a burst eye-ball, a leg-withering chill, thorn-harrowed ear-lobes, these are four examples.

By God we're here at last, said Furriskey loudly. He made a noise with the two of them, his palm and his knee. We're here at last. From now on it's a fight to the finish, fair field and no favour.

Strop the razor, boys, smiled Shanahan. Mr. Lamont, kindly put the poker in the fire.

Here there was a laugh, immelodious, malicious, high-pitched.

Now, now, boys, said Orlick. Now, now, boys. Patience.

I think we are doing very well, said Furriskey. We'll have the skin off his back yet. He'll be a sorry man.

That is a piteous recital, said Trellis. Provide further examples five in number.

With a slight bow the Pooka arranged the long-nailed fingers of his left hand in a vertical position and then with his remaining hand he pressed a finger down until it was horizontal in respect of each of the agonies he recited.

An anabasis of arrow-points beneath the agnail, razor-cut to knee-rear, an oak-stirk in the nipple, suspension by nose-ring, three motions of a cross-cut athwart the back, rat-bite at twilight, an eating of small-stones and a drinking of hog-slime, these are eight examples.

These are eight agonies, responded Trellis, that I would not endure for a chest of treasure. To say which of them is worst, that would require a winter in a web of thought. A glass of milk, that is the delicacy I offer you before you go.

These and other gravities you must endure, said the Pooka, and the one that you find the worst, that is the thing you must whisper after in the circle of my ear. To see you arise and dressing against the hour of your torment, that would be a courtesy. A glass of milk is bad for my indigestion. Acorns and loin-pie, these are my breakfast-tide delights. Arise, Sir, till I inflict twin nipple-hurts with the bevel of my nails.

An agitation to the seat of the Devil's trousers of decent sea-man's serge betokened that his hair-tail and his shirt-tails were engaged in slow contention and stiff whirly gambols of precise intent. His face (as to colour) was grey.

Colour of the face of Trellis, not counting the tops of pimples: white.

Keep away, you crump, you, he roared. Oh, by God, I'll kick your guts around the room if you don't keep your hands off me!

These piteous visitations shall not accurse you singly, observed the Pooka in a polite tone, nor shall they come together in triads. These hurts shall gather to assail you in their twos or fours or in their sixties; and all for this reason, that truth is one.

It was then that the Pooka MacPhellimey exercised the totality of his strange powers by causing with a twist of his hard horn-thumb a stasis of the natural order and a surprising kinesis of many incalculable influences hitherto in suspense. A number of miracles were wrought as one and together. The man in the bed was beleaguered with the sharpness of razors as to nipples, knee-rear and belly-roll. Leaden-hard forked arteries ran speedily about his scalp, his eye-beads bled and the corrugations of boils and piteous tumuli which appeared upon the large of his back gave it the appearance of a valuable studded shield and could be ascertained on counting to be sixty-four in number. He suffered a contraction of the intestines and a general re-arrangement of his interior to this result, that a meat repast in the process of digestion was ejected on the bed, on the coverlet, to speak precisely. In addition to his person, his room was also the subject of mutations unexplained by any purely physical hypothesis and not to be accounted for by mechanical devices relating to the manipulation of guy-ropes, pulley-blocks, or mechanical collapsible wallsteads of German manufacture, nor did the movements of the room conform to any known laws relating to the behaviour of projectiles as ascertained by a study of gravitation enforced by calculations based on the postulata of the science of ballistics. On the contrary, as a matter of fact, the walls parted, diminished and came back again with loud noises and with clouds of choking lime-dust, frequently forming hexagons instead of squares when they came together. The gift of light was frequently withdrawn without warning and there was a continuous loud vomit-noise offensive to persons of delicate perceptions. Chamber-pots flew about in the aimless parabolae normally frequented by blue-bottles and heavy articles of furniture—a wardrobe would be a typical example—could be discerned stationary in the air without visible means of support. A clock could be heard incessantly reciting the hours, a token that the free flight of time had also been interfered with; while the mumbling of the Pooka at his hell-prayers and the screaming of the sufferer, these were other noises perceptible to the practised ear. The obscure atmosphere was at the same time pervaded by a stench of incommunicable gravity.

The butt of that particular part of the story is this, that Trellis, wind-quick, eye-mad, with innumerable boils upon his back and upon various parts of his person, flew out in his sweat-wet night-shirt and day-drawers, out through the glass of the window till he fell with a crap on the cobbles of the street. A burst eye-ball, a crushed ear and bone-breaks two in number, these were the agonies that were his lot as a result of his accidental fall. The Pooka, a master of the science of rat-flight, fluttered down through the air with his black cloak spread about him like a rain-cloud, down to the place where the stunned one was engaged in the re-gathering of his wits, for these were the only little things he had for defending himself from harm; and this is a précis of the by-play the pair of them engaged in with their tongues:

You hog of hell, you leper's sore you! said Trellis in a queer voice that came through the grid of his bleeding mouth-hiding hand. He reclined on the mud-puddled cobbles, a tincture of fine blood spreading about his shirt. You leper's death-puke!

It was an early-morning street, its quiet distances still

small secrets shared by night with day. Two fingers at the eyes of his nostrils, the Pooka delicately smelt the air, a token that he was engaged in an attempt to predict the character of the weather.

You leper's lights, said Trellis.

To forsake your warm bed, said the other courteously, without the protection of your heavy great-coat of Galway frieze, that was an oversight and one which might well be visited with penalties pulmonary in character. To inquire as to the gravity of your sore fall, would that be inopportune?

You black bastard, said Trellis.

The character of your colloquy is not harmonious, rejoined the Pooka, and makes for barriers between the classes. Honey-words in torment, a growing urbanity against the sad extremities of human woe, that is the further injunction I place upon your head; and for the avoidance of opprobrious oddity as to numerals, I add this, a sickly suppuration at the base of the left breast.

I find your last utterance preoccupying to my intellect, said Trellis, and I am at the same time not unmindful of the incidence of that last hurt upon my person. . . .

Come here for a minute, said Shanahan, there's one thing you forgot. There's one cat in the bag that didn't jump.

Which cat would that be? Orlick asked.

Our man is in the room. Right. The boyo starts his tricks. Right. The room begins to dance. The smell and the noise starts. Right. Everything goes bang bar one thing. That one thing is a very important article of furniture altogether. Gentlemen, I refer to our friend the ceiling. *Is my Nabs too much of a gentleman to get the ceiling on the napper?*

Oh, God that's a terrible thing to get, said Lamont. A friend of mine got a crack of a lump of plaster on the neck here, look. By God Almighty it nearly creased him.

Didn't I tell you it was good, said Shanahan.

Nearly killed him, nearly put the light out for good.

A wallop of the ceiling is all I ask, Sir, Shanahan said. What do you say now? A ton of plaster on the napper.

It's a bit late to think of it now, you know, Orlick answered, table-tap for doubt.

He was in the Mater for a week, said Lamont. People were remarking the scab for the best part of a year—do you know that? Oh, not a bit of him could wear a collar.

It means bringing the whole party into the house again, said Orlick.

And well worth it! said Furriskey, slapping the sun-bright serge of his knee. And well worth it, by God.

Wheel him in man, begged Shanahan. He'd be in and out by now if we had less talk out of us.

A second thought is never an odd thought, said the Pooka with a courteous offering of his snuff-box, and it is for that reason that it would be wisdom for the pair of us to penetrate again to the privacy of your bedroom. The collapse of the ceiling, that is one thing we forgot.

That time you spoke, said Trellis, the sweetness of your words precluded me from comprehending the meaning you attach to them.

It is essential, explained the Pooka, that we return to

your room the way we may perfect these diversions upon which the pair of us were engaged.

That is an absorbing project, said Trellis. In what manner do we re-attain the street?

The way we came, said the Pooka.

Our project is the more absorbing for that, said Trellis, a small tear running evenly from his eye to his chin and a convulsion piteous to behold running the length of his back-bone.

The Pooka thereupon betook himself into the upper air with a graceful retraction of his limbs beneath his cloak in the fashion of a gannet in full flight and flew until he had attained the sill of his window, with Trellis for company and colloquy by his side by the means of a hair-grip; and these were the subjects they held brief discourse on the time they were in flight together, videlicet, the strange aspect of tramway wires which, when viewed from above and from a postulated angle, have the appearance of confining the street in a cage; the odd probity of tricycles; this curious circumstance, that a dog as to his legs is evil and sinful but attains sanctity at the hour of his urination.

It is my intention, said the Pooka in the ear of Trellis, to remain resting here on the stone-work of this window; as for you, to see you regain the security of your bedroom (littered as it is by a coat of lime), that would indeed be a graceful concession to my eccentric dawning-day desires.

Easily accomplished, said Trellis, as he crawled in his crimson robe to the interior of his fine room, but give me time, for a leg that is in halves is a slow pilgrim and my shoulder is out of joint.

When he had crawled on to the floor, the ceiling fell upon his head, hurting him severely and causing the weaker parts of his skull to cave in. And he would have remained there till this, buried and for dead beneath the lime-clouded fall, had not the Pooka given him a quantity of supernatural strength on loan for five minutes, enabling him to raise a ton of plaster with the beam of his back and extricate himself until he achieved a lime-white hurtling through the window and dropped with a crap on the cobbles of the street again, the half of the blood that was previously in him now around him and on his outside.

It was here that Furriskey held up the further progress of the tale with his hand in warning.

Maybe we're going a bit too hard on him, he warned. You can easily give a man a bigger hiding than he can hold.

We're only starting man, said Shanahan.

Gentlemen, I beg of you, leave everything to me, said Orlick with a taste of anger in his words. I guarantee that there will be no untoward fatality.

I draw the line at murder myself, observed Lamont.

I think we are doing very well, said Shanahan.

All right, Sir, away we go again, but don't forget he has a weak heart. Don't give him more than he can carry now.

That will be all right, answered Orlick.

Thereafter the Pooka applied his two horn-hard thumbs together, turning them at incustomary angles and scrubbing them on the good-quality kerseymere of his narrow trousers so that further sorcery was worked to this effect, that Trellis was beleaguered by an anger and a darkness and he was filled with a restless tottering unquiet and with a disgust for the places that he knew and with a desire to go where he never was, so that he was palsied of hand and foot and eye-mad and heart-quick so that he went bird-quick in craze and madness into the upper air, the Pooka at his rat-flight beside him and his shirt, red and blood-lank, fluttering heavily behind him.

To fly, observed the Pooka, towards the east to discover the seam between night and day, that is an aesthetic delight. Your fine overcoat of Galway frieze, the one with the khaki lining, you forgot that on the occasion of your second visit to your bedroom.

The gift of flight without the sister-art of landing, answered Trellis, that is always a doubt. I feel a thirst and the absence of a drink of spring water for a longer period than five minutes might well result in my death. It might be wisdom for the pair of us to attain land, me to lie upon my back and you to pour water from your hat into my interior. I have a hole here in my neck and through it the half of a cupful might escape before it could attain my stomach.

It was here that Orlick laid his pen upon its back.

Talking of water, Mr. Furriskey, he said, pardon my asking but where is the parochial house, the bath-room, you know?

The important apartment to which you refer, Sir, answered Furriskey with gravity, is on your left on the first landing on your way up, you can't miss it.

Ah. In that case there will be a slight intermission. I must retire for meditation and prayer. The curtain will be lowered to denote the passage of time. Gentlemen, adios!

Safe home, cried Shanahan, waving his hand.

Orlick arose stiffly from where he was and left the room, pushing back his hair and running it swiftly through the comb of his fingers. Lamont extracted a small box from his pocket, exhibited it and proved to the company beyond doubt that it contained but one cigarette; he lit the sole cigarette with the aid of a small machine depending for its utility on the combustibility of petroleum vapour when mixed with air. He sucked the smoke to the bottom of his lungs and these following words were mixed with it when he blew it out again on the flat of the table.

Do you know we're doing well. We're doing very well. By God he'll rue the day. He'll be a sorry man now.

A bigger hiding, remarked Furriskey with articulation leisurely in character, no man ever got. A more ferocious beating was never handed out by the hand of man.

Gentlemen, said Shanahan we're taking all the good out of it by giving him a rest, we're letting him get his wind. Now that's a mistake.

He'll get more than his wind.

Now I propose with your very kind permission to give our friend a little hiding on my own. A side-show, you understand. We'll put him back where we found him before the master comes back. Is the motion passed?

Now be careful, warned Lamont. Easy now. You'd

better leave him be. We're doing very nicely so we
are.

Not at all, man. Listen. A little party on our own.

The two lads in the air came to a sudden stop by order
of his Satanic Majesty. The Pooka himself stopped where
he was, never mind how it was done. The other fell
down about a half a mile to the ground on the top of his
snot and broke his two legs in halves and fractured his
fourteen ribs, a terrible fall altogether. Down flew the
Pooka after a while with a pipe in his mouth and the full
of a book of fancy talk out of him as if this was any consola-
tion to our friend, who was pumping blood like a stuck
pig and roaring out strings of profanity and dirty foul
language, enough to make the sun set before the day was
half over.

Enough of that, my man, says the Pooka taking the
pipe from his mouth. Enough of your dirty tongue now,
Caesar. Say you like it.

I'm having a hell of a time, says Trellis. I'm nearly
killed laughing. I never had such gas since I was a
chiseller.

That's right, says the Pooka, enjoy yourself. How would
you like a kick on the side of the face?

Which side? says Trellis.

The left side, Caesar, says the Pooka.

You're too generous altogether, says Trellis. I don't
know you well enough to take a favour like that from
you.

You're welcome, says the Pooka. And with these
words he walked back, took the pipe out of his jaw, came

down with a run and lifted the half of the man's face off his head with one kick and sent it high up into the trees where it got stuck in a blackbird's nest.

Say you like it, says he to Trellis quicklike.

Certainly I like it, says Trellis through a hole in his head—he had no choice because orders is orders, to quote a well-worn tag. Why wouldn't I like it. I think it's grand.

We are going to get funnier as we go along, says the Pooka, frowning with his brows and pulling hard at the old pipe. We are going to be very funny after a while. Is that one of your bones there on the grass?

Certainly, says Trellis, that's a lump out of my back.

Pick it up and carry it in your hand, says the Pooka, we don't want any of the parts lost.

When he had finished saying that, he put a brown tobacco spit on Trellis's snot.

Thanks, says Trellis.

Maybe you're tired of being a man, says the Pooka.

I'm only half a man as it is, says Trellis. Make me into a fine woman and I'll marry you.

I'll make you into a rat, says the Pooka.

And be damned but he was as good as his word. He worked the usual magic with his thumb and changed Trellis by a miracle of magic into a great whore of a buck rat with a black pointed snout and a scaly tail and a dirty rat-coloured coat full of ticks and terrible vermin, to say nothing of millions of plague-germs and disease and epidemics of every description.

What are you now? says the Pooka.

Only a rat, says the rat, wagging his tail to show he was pleased because he had to and had no choice in the matter. A poor rat, says he.

The Pooka took a good suck at his pipe.

Stop, said Furriskey.

What's the matter, amn't I all right man? asked Shanahan.

You're doing very nicely, Sir, said Furriskey, but here's where I contribute my penny to the plate. Here, gentlemen, is my idea of how our story goes on from where you stopped.

The Pooka took a good pull at his pipe. The result of this manœuvre was magic of a very high order, because the Pooka succeeded in changing himself into a wire-haired Airedale terrier, the natural enemy of the rat from the start of time. He gave one bark and away with him like the wind after the mangy rat. Man but it was a great chase, hither and thither and back again, the pair of them squealing and barking for further orders. The rat, of course, came off second best. He was caught by the throat at the heel of the hunt and got such a shaking that he practically gave himself up for lost. Practically every bone and sinew in his body was gone by the time he found himself dropped again on the grass.

That's right, you know, remarked Furriskey, a rat's bones are very weak. Very soft, you know. The least thing will kill a rat.

Noises, peripatetic and external, came faintly upon the gathering in the midst of their creative composition and spare-time literary activity. Lamont handled what promised to be an awkward situation with coolness and cunning.

And the short of it is this, he said, that the Pooka worked more magic till himself and Trellis found themselves again in the air in their own bodies, just as they had been a quarter of an hour before that, none the worse for their trying ordeals.

Orlick came back amongst them, closing the door with care. He was fresh, orderly, civil, and a small cloud of new tobacco fumes was in attendance on his person.

More luck there, said Shanahan, the best story-teller in all the world. We're waiting with our tongues hanging out. The same again, please.

Orlick beamed a smile of pleasure with the suns of his gold teeth. A token of preoccupation, he retained his smile after its purpose had been accomplished.

A further thrilling instalment? Yes, he said.

No delay now, said Lamont.

I have been engaged, said Orlick, in profound thought. It is only now that the profundity of my own thought is dawning on me. I have devised a plot that will lift our tale to the highest plane of great literature.

As long as the fancy stuff is kept down, said Shanahan.

A plot that will be acceptable to all. You, gentlemen, will like it in particular. It combines justice with vengeance.

As long as the fancy stuff is kept down, said Shanahan, well and good.

Bending his head forward as if with the weight of the

264

frown he had arranged on his brow, Lamont said in a dark voice:

Do anything to spoil the good yarn you have made of it so far, and I will arise and I will slay thee with a shovel. Eh, boys?

This was agreed to.

Now listen, gentlemen, said Orlick. Away we go.

That night they rested at the tree of Cluain Eo, Trellis at his birds'-roost on a thin branch surrounded by tufts of piercing thorns and tangles of bitter spiky brambles. By the sorcery of his thumbs the Pooka produced a canvas tent from the seat of his trousers of seaman's serge and erected it swiftly upon the carpet of the soft and daisy-studded sward, hammering clean pegs into the fresh-smelling earth by means of an odorous pine-wood mallet. When he had accomplished this he produced another wonder from the storehouse of his pants videlicet a good-quality folding bed with a hickory framework, complete with intimate bedclothes of French manufacture. He then knelt down and occupied himself with his devotions, making sounds with his tongue and with the hard horn of his thumbs that put the heart across the cripple high above him in the tree. This done, he hid his body in silk pyjamas of elegant oriental cut and provided about the waist of the trousers with gorgeous many-coloured tassels, a garment suitable for wear in the *harem* of the greatest Sultan of the distant East. He then said this to Trellis.

From the manner in which one breeze follows another about the trees, I predict that the day after to-morrow will be a wet one. Good night to you in the place you are, and a salubrious breathing of fresh-air towards the restoration of your strength. Myself, I sleep in a tent because I am delicate.

Trellis's wits were by this time feeble with suffering and by the time his courteous answer had made its way through the cloaks of the heavy leaves, it was barely perceptible.

Rain is badly wanted for the crops, he said. Good night to you. May angels guard you.

The Pooka then knocked the red fire from the interior of his meerschaum pipe and retired to the secrecy of his tent, having first taken good care to extinguish the embers of his pipe with a lump of a flat stone, for fires are extremely destructive and are jealously guarded against by every lover of the amenities of our land. And of the two of them, this much is sure, i.e., that one of them snored soundly through the night.

The night passed and the morning, having first wakened the plains and the open places, came into the fastness of the trees and knocked on the gaberdine flap of the Pooka's tent. He arose, prayed, and scented his temples with a rare balsam which he invariably carried about his person in a small black jar of perfect rotundity. He afterwards extracted a pound of oats and other choice ingredients from the inside of his pockets and baked himself an oaten farl of surpassing lightness and nourishment. He fed on this politely in a shaded corner of the wood he was in, but did not begin his feasting until he had extended to the man upon the branch a courteous invitation to make company with him at eating.

266

Breakfast? said Trellis, his hollow whisper coming from the exterior of the wood, for his tree-top was a high one.

Not incorrect, replied the Pooka. I beg that you will come and eat with me and the better to destroy the oddity of a single invitation, I add this, that you must refuse it.

I will not have any of it, thank you, said Trellis.

That is a pity, rejoined the Pooka, cracking a brown-baked crust in the crook of his clean-shaven jaws. Not to eat is a great mistake.

It was the length of two hours before the Pooka had put the entirety of the farl deep down in the pit of his stomach. At the end of that time the cripple in the tree was abandoned without warning by each of his wits with this unfortunate result, that he fell senseless through the cruel arms of the branches, and came upon the ground with a thud that placed him deeper in the darkness of his sleep. The thorns which were embedded in his person could be ascertained on counting to be no less than 944 in number.

After the Pooka had restored him to his reason with this delicacy videlicet a pint of woodland hogslime, the pair of them went forward on a journey with no more than three legs between them.

Proceeding on a carpet of fallen leaves and rotting acorns they had not travelled a distance longer in length than twenty-six perches when they saw (with considerable surprise, indeed), the figure of a man coming towards them from the secrecy of the old oaks. With a start of pleasure, the Pooka saw that it was none other than Mr. Paul Shanahan, the eminent philosopher, wit and raconteur.

Shanahan at this point inserted a brown tobacco finger in the texture of the story and in this manner caused a lacuna in the palimpsest.

Wait a minute, he said. Just a minute now. Not so fast. What's that you said, Sir?

Orlick smiled.

Nature of smile: innocent, wide-eyed, inquiring.

Mr. Paul Shanahan, he said slowly, the eminent philosopher, wit, and raconteur.

Furriskey adjusted his neck so that his face was close to that of Shanahan.

What's wrong with you man, he asked. What's the matter? Isn't it all right? Isn't it high praise? Do you know the meaning of that last word?

It's from the French, of course, said Shanahan.

Then I'll tell you what it means. It means you're all right. Do you understand me? *I've met this man. I know him. I think he's all right.* Do you see it now?

There's nothing to worry about, boy, said Lamont. Shanahan moved his shoulders and said this:

Well all right. All right. It's a story I'd rather be out of and that's the God's truth. But now that I'm in it, well and good. I trust you, Mr. Orlick.

Orlick smiled.

Nature of smile: satisfied, complacent.

A finer looking man than Mr. Paul Shanahan you would

not hope to meet in a day's walk. The glory of manhood in its prime was stamped on every line of his perfectly proportioned figure and the rhythm of glorious youth was exemplified in every movement of his fine athletic stride. The beam of his shoulders and the contours of his chest made it clear to even the most casual observer or passer-by that here was a tower, a reservoir of strength—not strength for loutish feats or for vain prodigal achievement, no; but strength for the defence of weakness, strength against oppression, strength for the advancement of all that was good and clean and generous. His complexion without blemish, his clear eye, these were the tokens of his clean living. Perfect as he was in physique, however, it would be a mistake to assume that his charms were exclusively of the physical (or purely bodily) variety. To the solution of life's problems and anxieties he brought a ready wit and a sense of humour—an inexhaustible capacity for seeing the bright side of things even when skies were grey and no beam of sun lightened the dull blackness of the clouds. His high education, his wealth of allusion and simile embracing practically every known European language as well as the immortal classics of Greece and Rome, these were gifts that made him the mainspring and the centre of gravity of every conversation irrespective of the matter being discussed or the parties engaged therein. A kindly heart and an unfailing consideration for the feelings of others, these were reasons (if indeed more were needed) as to why he endeared himself to everybody with whom he chanced to come in contact. A man of infinite patience, he was in short, of a fine upstanding type—a type which, alas, is becoming all too rare.

He had barely arrived in the orbit or radius of vision of the two travellers when he was joined by another man, one who resembled him in many respects with striking closeness. The newcomer was a man by the name of John Furriskey, a name happily familiar to all who still account the sanctity of home life and the family tie as among the things that matter in this mundane old world. In appearance and physique, it could not be truly said by an impartial observer that he was in any way inferior to Mr. Shanahan, magnificent specimen of manhood as the latter undoubtedly was. Curiously enough, however, it was not the perfection of his body that impressed one on first seeing him but rather the strange spirituality of his face. Looking at one with his deep eyes, he would sometimes not appear to see one, tho' needless to say, nothing would be further from his mind than to be deliberately rude to a fellow-creature. It was obvious that he was a man who was used to deep and beautiful thinking, for there was no escaping the implications of that calm thoughtful face. It has been wisely said that true strength and greatness can spring only from a study and appreciation of what is small and weak and tiny—the modest daisy raising its meek head in the meadow sward, a robin red-breast in the frost, the gentle wandering zephyrs that temper the genial exuberance of King Sol of a summer's day. Here if ever was a man who carried the repose and grandeur of nature in his face; here was one of whom it might be truly said that he forgave all because he understood all. A learning and an erudition boundless in its universality, an affection phenomenal in its intensity and a quiet sympathy with the innumerable little failings of our common humanity—these were the sterling qualities that made Mr. John Furriskey a man among men and endeared him to the world and his wife, without distinction of creed or class and irrespective of religious or political ties or allegiances of any description or character.

It was more by coincidence than anything else that these gentlemen were now observed to have been joined by a third, who appeared to approach from a direction almost due east. It might at first appear to the *illiterati* or uninitiated that a person devoid of practically all the virtues and excellences just enumerated in respect of the other gentlemen would have but little to recommend him. Such an hypothesis, however, would involve a very serious fallacy and one of which Antony Lamont could be said to constitute a living refutation. His body was neat and compactly built but it had withal a lissom gracefulness and a delicacy that could be almost said to be effeminate without in any way evoking anything of the opprobrious connotation of that word. His features were pale, finely moulded and ascetic, the features of a poet and one addicted almost continuously to thoughts of a beautiful or fragrant nature. The delicate line of his nostrils, his sensitive mouth, the rather wild escapade that was his hair—all were clear indications of a curiously lovely æstheticism, a poetical perception of no ordinary intensity. His fingers were the long tapering fingers of the true artist and one would be in nowise surprised to learn that he was an adept at the playing of some musical instrument (which in fact he was). His voice when he spoke was light and musical, a fact that was more than once commented on by people who had no reason for praising him and indeed by people who had the opposite.

Thanks, said Lamont.

You are welcome, said Orlick.

No need to make a joke of everything, Mr. Lamont, said Furriskey, frowning.

Oh, God I'm not joking, said Lamont.

All right, said Furriskey, prohibiting further utterance by the extreme gravity of his countenance. That will do now. Yes, Mr. Orlick.

The three men, each of them a perfect specimen of his own type, stood together in a group and commenced to converse in low cultured tones. The Pooka, never averse to bettering himself and acquiring fresh knowledge, listened spell-bound from the shadow of a magnificent Indian cashew-tree, feeding absently on the nuts of the lower branches; and as for the crippled man, he rested his body on a bough between the earth and heaven, a bough of the strong medicinal chinchona; and the pair of them revelled in the enchantment of three fine voices mingling together in pleasing counterpoint, each of them sweeter than the dulcet strains of the ocarina (or oval rib-bellied musical instrument of terra cotta), and softer than the sound of the ophicleide, a little-known wind instrument now virtually obsolete.

The fiddle is the man, said Shanahan.

Please be quiet, said Orlick.

The following, imperfect résumé or summary as it is, may be taken as a general indication of the scholarly trend of the conversation sustained without apparent effort by the three of them.

It is not generally known, observed Mr. Furriskey, that the coefficient of expansion of all gases is the same. A gas expands to the extent of a hundred and seventy-third part of its own volume in respect of each degree of increased temperature centrigrade. The specific gravity of ice is 0·92, marble 2·70, iron (cast) 7·20 and iron (wrought) 7·79. One mile is equal to 1·6093 kilometres reckoned to the nearest ten-thousandth part of a whole number.

True, Mr. Furriskey, remarked Mr. Paul Shanahan with a quiet smile that revealed a whiteness of the teeth, but a man who confines knowledge to formulæ necessary for the resolution of an algebraic or other similar perplexity, the same deserves to be shot with a fusil, or old-fashioned light musket. True knowledge is unpractised or abstract usefulness. Consider this, that salt in solution is an excellent emetic and may be administered with·safety to persons who are accustomed to eat poisonous berries or consume cacodyl, an evil-smelling compound of arsenic and methyl. A cold watch-key applied to the neck will relieve nose-bleeding. Banana-skins are invaluable for imparting a gloss to brown shoes.

To say that salt in solution, Lamont objected finely, is a pleasing emetic is a triviality related to inconsequent ephemera—the ever-perishing plasms of the human body.

The body is too transient a vessel to warrant other than perfunctory investigation. Only in this regard is it important, that it affords the mind a basis for speculation and conjecture. Let me recommend to you, Mr. Shanahan, the truer spiritual prophylaxis contained in the mathematics of Mr. Furriskey. Ratiocination on the ordered basis of arithmetic is man's passport to the infinite. God is the root of minus one. He is too great a profundity to be compassed by human cerebration. But Evil is finite and comprehensible and admits of calculation. Minus One, Zero and Plus One are the three insoluble riddles of the Creation.

Mr. Shanahan laughed in a cultured manner.

The riddle of the universe I might solve if I had a mind to, he said, but I prefer the question to the answer. It serves men like us as a bottomless pretext for scholarly dialectic.

Other points not unworthy of mention, mentioned Mr. Furriskey in an absent-minded though refined manner, are the following: the great pyramid at Gizeh is 450 feet high and ranks as one of the seven wonders of the world, the others being the hanging gardens of Babylon, the tomb of Mausolus in Asia Minor, the colossus of Rhodes, the temple of Diana, the statue of Jupiter at Olympia and the Pharos Lighthouse built by Ptolemy the First about three hundred and fifty years B.C. Hydrogen freezes at minus 253 degrees centigrade, equivalent to minus 423 on the Fahrenheit computation.

Everyday or colloquial names for chemical substances, observed Mr. Shanahan, cream of tartar—bitartate of potassium, plaster of Paris—sulphate of calcium, water—oxide of hydrogen. Bells and watches on board ship: first dog—4 p.m. to 6 p.m., second dog—6 p.m. to 8 p.m., afternoon—noon to 4 p.m. Paris, son of Priam, King of Troy, carried off the wife of Menelaus, King of Sparta and thus caused the Trojan War.

The name of the wife, said Lamont, was Helen. A camel is unable to swim owing to the curious anatomical distribution of its weight, which would cause its head to be immersed if the animal were placed in deep water. Capacity in electricity is measured by the farad; one microfarad is equal to one millionth of a farad. A carbuncle is a fleshy excrescence resembling the wattles of a turkey-cock. Sphragistics is the study of engraved seals.

Excellent, remarked Mr. Furriskey with that quiet smile which endeared him to everyone who happened to come his way, but do not overlook this, that the velocity of light *in vacuo* is 186,325 miles per second. The velocity of sound in air is 1,120 feet per second, in tin 8,150 feet per second, in walnut mahogany and heavy timbers 11,000 feet per second approximately; in fir-wood, 20,000 feet per second. Sine 15 degrees is equal to the root of six minus the root of two, the whole divided by four. Percentages of £1: $1\frac{1}{4}$ per cent, threepence; 5 per cent, one shilling; $12\frac{1}{2}$ per cent, a half a crown. Some metric equivalents: one mile equals 1.6093 kilometres; one inch equals 2.54 centimetres; one ounce equals 28.352 grams. The chemical symbol of Calcium is Ca and of Cadmium, Cd. A Trapezoid may be defined as a four-sided figure capable of being transformed into two triangles by the means of a diagonal line.

Some curious facts about the Bible, Mr. Lamont mentioned politely, the longest chapter is Psalm 119 and the briefest, Psalm 117. The Apocrypha contains 14 Books. The first English translation was published in A.D. 1535.

Some notable dates in the history of the world, observed Mr. Shanahan, B.C. 753, foundation of Rome by Romulus, 490 B.C., Battle of Marathon, A.D. 1498, Vasco da Gama sailed around South Africa and reached India, 23 April 1564 Shakespeare was born.

It was then that Mr. Furriskey surprised and indeed, delighted his companions, not to mention our two friends, by a little act which at once demonstrated his resource and his generous urge to spread enlightenment. With the end of his costly malacca cane, he cleared away the dead leaves at his feet and drew the outline of three dials or clock-faces on the fertile soil in this fashion:

How to read the gas-meter, he announced. Similar dials to these somewhat crudely depicted at my feet may be observed on any gas-meter. To ascertain the consumption of gas, one should procure pencil and paper and write down the figures nearest to the indicator on each dial—

thus in the present hypothetical case 963. To this one should add two zeros or noughts, making the number 96,300. This is the answer and represents the consumption of gas in cubic feet. The reading of the electric-meter for the discovery of consumption in Kilowatt-hours is more intricate than the above and would require the help of six dials for demonstration purposes—more indeed than I have room for in the space I have cleared of withered leaves, even assuming the existing dials could be adapted for the purpose.

Thereafter these three savant or wise men of the East began to talk together in a rapid manner and showered forth pearls of knowledge and erudition, gems without price, invaluable carbuncles of sophistry and scholastic science, thomistic maxims, intricate theorems in plane geometry and lengthy extracts from Kant's *Kritik der reinischen Vernunst*. Frequent use was made of words unheard of by illiterates and persons of inferior education *exempli gratia* saburra or foul granular deposit in the pit of the stomach, tachylyte, a vitreous form of basalt, tapir, a hoofed mammal with the appearance of a swine, capon, castrated cock, triacontahedral, having thirty sides or surfaces and botargo, relish of mullet or tunny roe. The following terms relating to the science of medicine were used with surprising frequency videlicet chyme, exophthalmus, scirrhus, and mycetoma meaning respectively food when acted upon by gastric juices and converted into acid pulp, protrusion of the eye-ball, hard malignant tumour and fungoid disease of hand or foot. Aestho-therapy was touched upon and reference made to the duodenum, that is, the primary part of the small intestine, and the cæcum or blind gut. Flowers and plants rarely mentioned in ordinary conversation were accorded their technical or quasi-botanical titles without difficulty or hesitation for instance now fraxinella species of garden dittany, canna plant with decorative blossoms, bifoliate of two leaves (also bifurcate forked), cardamom spice from the germinal capsules of certain East India plants, granadilla passion flower, knapweed hard-stemmed worthless plant, campanulla plant with bell-shaped blossoms, and dittany see fraxinella above. Unusual animals mentioned were the pangolin, chipmuck, echidna, babiroussa and bandicoot, of which a brief descriptive account would be (respectively), scabrous-spined scaly ant-eater, American squirrel *aliter* wood-rat, Australian toothless animal resembling the hedgehog, Asiatic wild-hog, large Indian insectivorous marsupial resembling the rat.

The Pooka made a perfunctory noise and stepped from the shelter of his tree.

Your morning talk in the shadow of the wood, he said with a bow, that has been an incomparable recital. Two plants which you did not mention—the bdellium-tree and the nard, each of which yields an aromatic oleo-resinous medicinal product called balsam which I find invaluable for preserving the freshness of the person. I carry it with me in my tail pocket in a chryselephantine pouncet-box of perfect rotundity.

The three men regarded the Pooka in silence for a while and then conversed for a moment in Latin. Finally Mr. Furriskey spoke.

Good morning, my man, what can I do for you, he asked. I am a Justice of the Peace. Do you wish to be sworn or make a statement?

I do not, said the Pooka, but this man with me is a fugitive from justice.

In that case he should be tried and well tried, said Mr. Lamont courteously.

That is my object in approaching you, said the Pooka.

He looks a right ruffian, observed Mr. Shanahan. What is the charge, pray, he asked taking a small constabulary note-book from his pocket.

There are several counts and charges, replied the Pooka and more are expected. I understand he is wanted in Scotland. The police have not yet completed their inquiries but that small note-book would not contain the half of the present charges, even if taken down in brief and precise shorthand.

In that case we will not bother about the charges at all, said Mr. Shanahan putting away his book. He looks a very criminal type, I must say.

During this conversation the prisoner was stretched on the ground in an unconscious condition.

Let him be brought to trial in due process of law, said Mr. Furriskey.

When his wits returned to Dermot Trellis, they did not come together but singly and at intervals. They came, each with its own agonies, and sat uneasily on the outer border of the mind as if in readiness for going away again.

When the sufferer was strong enough to observe the shape of his surroundings, he saw that he was in a large hall not unlike the Antient Concert Rooms in Brunswick Street (now Pearse Street). The King was on his throne, the satraps thronged the hall, a thousand bright lamps shone, o'er that high festival. Ornate curtains of twilled beaverteen were draped about the throne. Near to the roof there was a *loggia* or open-shaped gallery or arcade supported on thin pillars, each with a *guilloche* on its top for ornament; the *loggia* seemed to be packed with people, each with a cold-watching face. The air was heavy and laden with sullen banks of tobacco smoke; this made respiration an extremely difficult matter for a person like Trellis, who was not in perfect health. He felt a growing queasiness about his stomach and also tormina, griping pains in the region of the bowels. His clothing was disarranged and torn and piteously stained with blood and other fluids discharged probably from his many wounds. Generally speaking he was in very poor condition.

When he raised his eyes again there appeared to be no less than twelve kings on the throne. There was an ornamental bench in front of them like the counter of a good-class public house and they leaned their elbows on it, gazing coldly ahead of them. They were dressed uniformly in gowns of black gunny, an inexpensive material manufactured from jute fibre, and with their jewelled fingers they held the stems of long elegant glasses of brown porter.

In the centre of a shadow to the left-hand side of the bench was the Pooka MacPhellimey, attired in a robe of stout cotton fabric called dimity and seated in an article resembling a prie-dieu with a stout back to it; he appeared to be writing in shorthand in a black note-book.

The sufferer gave an accidental groan and found that the Pooka was immediately at his side and bending over him in a solicitous fashion, making formal inquiries on the subject of the cripple's health.

What is going to happen to me next? asked Trellis.

Shortly you will be judged, replied the Pooka. The judges are before you on the bench there.

I see their shadow, said Trellis, but my face is not in that direction and I cannot turn it. Their names, that would be a boon.

Woe to the man that shall refuse a small kindness, responded the Pooka with the intonation that is required for the articulation of the old proverbs. The names of the judges are easy to relate: J. Furriskey, T. Lamont, P. Shanahan, S. Andrews, S. Willard, Mr. Sweeny, J. Casey, R. Kiersey, M. Tracy, Mr. Lamphall, F. MacCool, Supt. Clohessy.

The jury? asked Trellis.

The same, rejoined the Pooka.

That is the last blow that brings a man to the ground, observed Trellis. His wits then took leave of him and remained at a distance for a long period of time.

That place is a picture-house now of course, said Shanahan's voice as it cut through the pattern of the story, plenty of the cowboy stuff there. The Palace Cinema, Pearse Street. Oh, many a good hour I spent there too.

A great place in the old days, said Lamont. They had tenors and one thing or another there in the old days. Every night they had something good.

And every night they had something new, said Shanahan.

On his smallest finger Orlick screwed the cap of his Waterman fountain-pen, the one with the fourteen-carat nib; when he unscrewed it again there was a black circle about his finger.

Symbolism of the foregoing: annoyance.

I will now continue, he announced.

Certainly man, said Shanahan, a hand to the writer's biceps. We'll get him yet! We'll take the skin off his body.

A little less talk and we were right, said Furriskey.

When Trellis had again re-attained reason, he found that his body was on a large chair and supported by the loan of supernatural strength, for many of the bones requisite for maintaining an upright position were in two halves and consequently unable to discharge their functions. Noiselessly the Pooka came beside him and whispered in his ear.

To be defended by eminent lawyers, he said, that is the right of a man that is accused. There are two men in the court here and you can now be at the choice of them.

I did not expect this, said Trellis. He found that his voice was loud and probably strengthened by the agency of the one that was whispering at his ear. What are their names?

They are Greek citizens, rejoined the Pooka, Timothy Danaos and Dona Ferentes.

The gift of speech, said Trellis, that is one thing they lack.

And a great pity, said the Pooka, for they are fine-looking men and that is a serious blemish.

Trellis in reply to this fashioned a long sentence in his mind, but the words he put on it were lost by the activity of a string orchestra in one of the galleries which struck up a stirring anthem. The players were unseen but two violins, a viola, a piccolo and a violoncello would be a sagacious guess as to their composition. The judges at the long counter listened in a cultured fashion, quietly fingering the stems of their stout-glasses.

Call the first witness, said the voice of Mr. Justice Shanahan, stern and clear as the last bit of music faded from the vast hall and retired to the secrecy of its own gallery. This was the signal for the opening of the great trial. Reporters poised their pencils above their note-books, waiting. The orchestra could be heard very faintly as if at a great distance, playing consecutive fifths in a subdued fashion and tuning their instruments one against the other. The Pooka closed his black notebook and stood up in his prie-dieu.

Samuel ("Slug") Willard, he boomed, take the stand.

Slug Willard hastily swallowed the residue of his stout, drew a cuff across his mouth and disengaging himself from his confreres at the counter, came forward to the witness-box swinging his large hat in his hand. He spat heavily on the floor and inclined his ear in a genial manner towards the Pooka, who appeared to be administering an oath in an undertone.

Trellis noticed that Sweeny was drinking bimbo, a beverage resembling punch and seldom consumed in this country. The stout-glass of Willard was now full again

283

and stood finely on the counter against the back of his vacant chair.

A judge acting as a juryman is bad enough, said Trellis, but to act also as a witness, that is most irregular.

Silence, said Mr. Justice Shanahan severely. Are you legally represented?

I have been assigned two dumb-bells, said Trellis bravely. I have declined their services.

Your ill-conditioned behaviour will avail you nothing, rejoined the judge in a tone even more severe. One more word and I will deal with you summarily for contempt. Proceed with the witness, Mr. MacPhellimey.

I meant no harm, Sir, said Trellis.

Silence.

The Pooka stood up in his prie-dieu and sat on its back staring at the pages of his black note-book. A keen-eyed observer would notice that there was no writing on them.

State your name and occupation, he said to Mr. Willard.

Willard Slug, said Mr. Willard. I am a cattleman and a cowpuncher, a gentleman farmer in the western tradition.

Have you ever been employed by the accused?

Yes.

In what capacity?

As tram-conductor.

Give in your own words a brief statement of the remuneration and conditions of service attaching to the position.

My pay was fifteen shillings per week of seventy-two

hours, non-pensionable emoluments. I was compelled to sleep in an unsanitary attic.

Under what circumstances were your services utilized?

I was instructed to meet and accept his fare from Mr. Furriskey when he was returning one night from Donnybrook. I did so.

In what manner were you compelled to address Mr. Furriskey?

In guttersnipe dialect, at all times repugnant to the instincts of a gentleman.

You have already said that the character or *milieu* of the conversation was distasteful to you?

Yes. It occasioned considerable mental anguish.

Have you any further remarks to make on this subject relevant to the charges now under consideration?

Yes. It was represented that my employment as conductor would commence and terminate on the night in question. I was actually engaged for six months owing to my employer's negligence in failing to instruct me that my employment was at an end.

Was this curious circumstance afterwards explained?

In a way, yes. He attributed his failure to discharge me to forgetfulness. He absolutely refused to entertain a claim which I advanced in respect of compensation for impaired health.

To what do you attribute your impaired health?

Malnutrition and insufficient clothing. My inadequate pay and a luncheon interval of only ten minutes prohibited both the purchase or consumption of nourishing food. When my employment started, I was provided with a shirt, boots and socks, and a light uniform of dyed dowlas, a strong fabric resembling calico. No underdrawers were provided and as my employment was protracted into the depths of the winter, I was entirely unprotected from the cold. I contracted asthma, catarrh and various pulmonary disorders.

That is all I have to ask, said the Pooka.

Mr. Justice Lamont tapped his stout-glass on the counter and said to Trellis.

Do you wish to cross-examine the witness?

I do, said Trellis.

He endeavoured to rise and place his hands in the pockets of his trousers in a casual manner but he found that much of the supernatural strength had been withdrawn. He found that he was now in the grip of a severe myelitis or inflammation of the spinal cord. He crouched on his chair, shuddering in the spasms of a clonus and pressed out words from his mouth with the extremity of his will-power.

You have stated, he said, that you were compelled to sleep in an unsanitary attic. In what respect were the principles of hygiene violated?

The attic was infested by clocks. I found sleep impossible owing to the activities of bed-lice.

Did you ever in your life take a bath?

Mr. Justice Andrews rapped violently on the counter.

Do not answer that question, he said loudly.

I put it to you, said Trellis, that the bed-lice were near relations of other small inhabitants of your own verminous person.

That savours of contempt, said Mr. Justice Lamont in a testy manner, we will not have any more of that. The witness is excused.

Mr. Willard retired to his seat behind the counter and immediately put his stout-glass to his head; Trellis fell back on his chair in a swoon of exhaustion. Distantly the orchestra could be heard in the metre of a dainty toccata.

Call the next witness.

William Tracy, boomed the Pooka, take the stand.

Mr. Tracy, an elderly man, fat, scanty-haired and wearing pince-nez, came quickly from the counter and entered the witness-box. He smiled nervously at the Bench, avoiding the gaze of Trellis, whose head was again bravely stirring amid the ruin of his body and his clothing.

State your name, said the Pooka.

Tracy William James.

You are acquainted with the accused?

Yes, professionally.

At this point the entire personnel of the judges arose in a body and filed out behind a curtain in the corner of the hall over which there was a red-lighted sign. They were absent for the space of ten minutes but the trial proceeded steadily in their absence. The pulse of a mazurka, graceful and lively, came quietly from the distance.

Explain your connections with the accused.

About four years ago he approached me and represented that he was engaged in a work which necessitated the services of a female character of the slavey class. He explained that technical difficulties relating to ladies' dress had always been an insuperable obstacle to his creation of satisfactory female characters and produced a document purporting to prove that he was reduced on other occasions to utilizing disguised males as substitutes for women, a device which he said could scarcely be persisted in indefinitely. He mentioned a growing unrest among his readers. Eventually I agreed to lend him a girl whom I was using in connection with *Jake's Last Throw*, a girl who would not be required by myself for some months owing to my practice of dealing with the action of groups of characters alternately. When she left me to go to him, she was a good girl and attentive to her religious duties. . . .

How long was she in his employment?

About six months. When she returned to me she was in a certain condition.

No doubt you remonstrated with the accused?

Yes. He disclaimed all responsibility and said that his record was better than mine, a remark which I failed to appreciate.

You took no action?

Not so far as the accused was concerned. I considered seeking a remedy in the courts but was advised that my case was one which the courts would be unlikely to understand. I discontinued all social intercourse with the accused.

Did you re-instate the girl in her employment?

Yes. I also created an otherwise unnecessary person to whom I married her and found honest if unremunerative employment for her son with a professional friend who was engaged in a work dealing with unknown aspects of the cotton-milling industry.

Did the introduction of this character to whom you married the girl adversely affect your work?

Assuredly. The character was clearly superfluous and impaired the artistic integrity of my story. I was compelled to make his unauthorized interference with an oil-well the subject of a footnote. His introduction added considerably to my labours.

Is there any other incident which occurs to you explanatory of the character of the accused?

Yes. During his illness in 1924 I sent him—in a charitable attempt to entertain him—a draft of a short story I had written dealing in an original way with banditry in Mexico towards the close of the last century. Within a month it appeared under his own name in a Canadian magazine.

That's a lie! screamed Trellis from his chair.

The judges frowned in unison and regarded the accused in a threatening fashion. Mr. Justice Sweeny, returning from behind the curtain in the corner of the hall said:

You had better conduct yourself, Sir. Your arrogant bearing and your insolence have already been the subject of severe comment. Any further blackguardism will be summarily dealt with. Is it your intention to cross-examine this witness?

Trellis said, Yes.

Very well then. Proceed.

The invalid here gathered his senses closely about him as if they were his overcoat to ensure that they should not escape before his purpose was accomplished. He said to the witness:

Have you ever heard this said: *Dog does not eat dog*.

There was a rattle of glasses at this point and a stern direction from the bench.

Do not answer that question.

Trellis drew a hand wearily across his face.

One other point, he said. You have stated that this person whom you created was entirely unnecessary. If I recollect the tale aright he was accustomed to spend much of his time in the scullery. Is that correct?

Yes.

What was he doing there?

Peeling potatoes for the household.

Peeling potatoes for the household. You said he was unnecessary. You regard that as an entirely wasteful and unnecessary task?

Not at all. The task is necessary and useful. It is the character who carried it out who is stated to be unnecessary.

I put it to you that the utility of any person is directly related to the acts he performs.

There was a potato-peeler in the kitchen, a machine.

Indeed! I did not notice it.

In the recess, near the range, on the left-hand side.

I put it to you that there was no potato-peeler.

There was. It was in the house for a long time.

Here a question from the direction of the counter brought the further examination of the witness to a conclusion.

What is a potato-peeler? asked Mr. Justice Andrews.

A machine, worked by hand, usually used for peeling potatoes, replied the witness.

Very well. Cross-examination concluded. Call the next witness.

Let the Good Fairy take the stand, boomed the Pooka.

I've been in the stand all the time, said the voice, the grand stand.

Where is this woman? asked Mr. Justice Lamphall sharply. If she does not appear quickly I will issue a bench warrant.

This man has no body on him at all, explained the Pooka. Sometimes I carry him in my waistcoat pocket for days and do not know that he is there.

In that case we must declare the Habeas Corpus Act suspended, said Mr. Lamphall. Proceed. Where is the witness now? Come now, no horseplay. This is a court of Law.

I am not very far away, said the Good Fairy.

Are you acquainted with the accused? asked the Pooka.

Maybe I am, said the Good Fairy.

What class of an answer is that to give? inquired Mr. Justice Casey sternly.

Answers do not matter so much as questions, said the Good Fairy. A good question is very hard to answer. The better the question the harder the answer. There is no answer at all to a very good question.

That is a queer thing to say, said Mr. Justice Casey. Where did you say it from?

From the key-hole, said the Good Fairy. I am going

out for a breath of air and I will be back again when it suits me.

That key-hole should have been stuffed, said Mr. Justice Shanahan. Call the next witness before the fly-boy comes back to annoy us.

Paul Shanahan, boomed the Pooka.

It would not be true to say that the sufferer on the chair was unconscious, however much his appearance betokened that happy state, for he was listening to the pulse of a fine theme in three-four time, coming softly to his brain from illimitable remoteness. Darkling he listened. Softly it modulated through a gamut of graduated keys, terminating in a quiet coda.

Paul Shanahan, called and sworn, deposed that he was in the employment of the accused for many years. He was not a party to the present action and had no personal grudge against the accused man. He was thoroughly trained and could serve in any capacity; his talents, however, were ignored and he was compelled to spend his time directing and arranging the activities of others, many of whom were of inferior ability as compared with himself. He was forced to live in a dark closet in the Red Swan Hotel and was allowed little or no liberty. The accused purported to direct witness in the discharge of his religious duties but he (witness) regarded this merely as a pretext for domestic interference and tyranny. His reputed salary was 45s. per week but no allowance was made for travelling and tramfares. He estimated that such expenses amounted to 30s. or 35s. per week. His food was bad and insufficient and required to be supplemented from his own resources. He had wide experience of cow-punching and had served with distinction at the Siege of Sandymount. He was accustomed to handling small-arms and shooting-irons. In company with other parties, he presented a petition to the accused praying relief from certain disabilities and seeking improved pay and conditions of service. The accused violently refused to make any of the concessions sought and threatened the members of the deputation who waited on him with certain physical afflictions, most of which were degrading and involved social stigma. In reply to a question, witness said that the accused was subject to extreme irritability and "tantrums". On several occasions, after reporting to the accused that plans had somewhat miscarried—a circumstance for which witness was in no way to blame—witness found his person infested with vermin. Friends of his (witness's) had complained to him of similar visitations. In reply to a question by the accused, witness said that he was always very careful of personal cleanliness. It was untrue to say that witness was a man of unclean habits.

At this stage a man in the body of the court announced that he had a statement to make and proceeded to read in an indistinct manner from a document which he produced from his pocket. He was immediately set upon by armed cowboys who removed him struggling violently, his words being drowned by a vigorous prestissimo movement of the gavotte class played in a spirited fashion by the orchestra in the secrecy of the gallery. The judges took no notice of the interruption and continued drinking from their long stout-glasses. Four of them at one end of the counter were making movements suggestive of card-play but as a result of their elevated position, no cards or money could be seen.

The next witness was a short-horn cow who was escorted by a black-liveried attendant from a cloakroom marked LADIES at the rear of the hall. The animal, a magnificent specimen of her class, was accorded the gift of speech by a secret theurgic process which had been in the possession of the Pooka's family for many generations. Udder and dewlap aswing in the rhythm of her motion, she shambled forward to the witness-box, turning her great eyes slowly about the court in a melancholy but respectful manner. The Pooka, an expert spare-time dairyman, familiar with the craft of husbandry, watched her with a practised eye, noting the fine points of her body.

State your name, he said curtly.

That is a thing I have never attained, replied the cow. Her voice was low and guttural and of a quality not normally associated with the female mammalia.

Are you acquainted with the accused?

Yes.

Socially or professionally?

Professionally.

Have your relations with him been satisfactory?

By no means.

State the circumstance of your relations with him.

In a work entitled—pleonastically, indeed—*The Closed Cloister*, I was engaged to discharge my natural functions in a field. My milking was not attended to with regularity. When not in advanced pregnancy, a cow will suffer extreme discomfort if not milked at least once in twenty-four hours. On six occasions during the currency of the work referred to, I was left without attention for very long periods.

You suffered pain?

Intense pain.

Mr. Justice Lamont made a prolonged intermittent noise with the butt of his half-empty glass, the resulting vibration providing the porter it contained with a new and considerably improved head. The noise was a token that he desired to put a question.

Tell me this, he said. Can you not milk yourself?

I can not, replied the cow.

Musha, you appear to be very helpless. Why not, pray?

I have no hands and even if I had, the arms would not be long enough.

That savours of contempt, said the Justice sternly. This is a court of justice, not a music-hall. Does the Defendant wish to cross-examine?

Trellis had been listening in a preoccupied manner to a number of queer noises in the interior of his head. He desisted from this occupation and looked at the Justice. The Justice's features were still arranged in the pattern of the question he had asked.

I do indeed, he said, endeavouring to rise and present a spirited exterior to the court. Still sitting, he turned in the direction of the witness.

Well, Whitefoot, he said, you suffered pain because your milking was overlooked?

I did. My name is not Whitefoot.

You have stated that a cow will suffer considerable pain if not milked at regular times. There is, however, another important office discharged by the cowkeeper, a seasonal rite not entirely unconnected with the necessity for providing milk for our great-grandchildren. . . .

I do not know what you are talking about.

The failure of the cowkeeper to attend to this matter, I am given to understand, causes acute discomfort. Was this attended to in your case?

I don't know what you are talking about, shouted the cow excitedly. I resent your low insinuations. I didn't come here to be humiliated and insulted. . . .

There was a loud rapping from the direction of the bench. Mr. Justice Furriskey directed a cold severe finger at the defendant.

Your ill-conditioned attempt to discredit an exemplary witness, he said, and to introduce into the proceedings an element of smut, will be regarded as contempt and punished summarily as such unless immediately discontinued. The witness may go too. A more unsavoury example of the depraved and diseased mind it has rarely been my misfortune to encounter.

Mr. Justice Shanahan concurred. The cow, very much embarrassed, turned and slowly left the court without a stain on her character, her glossy flank the object of expert examination by the practised eye of the Pooka as she passed him on her way. Stretching out a finger, he appraised the pile of her coat with a long nail. The members of the unseen orchestra could be faintly heard practising their scales and arpeggii and rubbing good-quality Italian rosin with a whistling noise on their bows. Three members of the bench had fallen forward in an attitude of besotted sleep as a result of the inordinate quantity of brown porter they had put into their bodies. The public at the back of the hall had erected an impenetrable barrier of acrid tobacco-smoke and had retired behind it, affording coughs and occasional catcalls as evidence that they were still in attendance. The light was somewhat yellower than it had been an hour before.

Call the next witness!

Anthony Lamont, boomed the Pooka, take the stand.

At all times a strict observer of etiquette, the witness laid aside his judicial robe before making his way unsteadily from the bench to the witness-box. Under the cover of the counter the hand of a fellow-judge ran quickly through the pockets of the discarded garment.

You were an employee of the accused? asked the Pooka.

That is so.

Please afford the court a statement of your duties.

My main function was to protect the honour of my sister and look after her generally. People who insulted or assaulted her were to be answerable to me.

Where is your sister now?

I do not know. Dead, I believe.

When did you last see her?

I never saw her. I never had the pleasure of her acquaintance.

You say she is dead?

Yes. I was not even asked to her funeral.

Do you know how she died?

Yes. She was violently assaulted by the accused about an hour after she was born and died indirectly from the effects of the assault some time later. The proximate cause of her death was puerperal sepsis.

Very delicately put, said Mr. Justice Furriskey. You are an exemplary witness, Sir. If every other witness in this court were to give evidence in a similar straightforward and clear manner, the work of the court would be appreciably lightened.

Those of the other judges who were in an upright position concurred with deep nods.

Your Lordship's generous remarks are appreciated and will be conveyed to the proper quarter, said the witness pleasantly, and I need scarcely add that the sentiments are reciprocated.

Mr. F. MacPhellimey, court clerk, paid a tribute to the harmonious relations which had always obtained between the bar and the bench and expressed a desire to be associated with the amiable compliments which had been exchanged. The Justice returned thanks in the course of a witty and felicitous speech.

At this stage, the prisoner, in order to protect his constitutional rights and also in an endeavour to save his life, pointed out that this exchange of pleasantries was most irregular and that the evidence of the witness was valueless, being on his own admission a matter of hearsay and opinion; but, unfortunately, as a result of his being unable to rise or, for that matter, to raise his voice above the level of a whisper, nobody in the court was aware that he had spoken at all except the Pooka, who practised a secret recipe of his grandfather's—the notorious Crack MacPhellimey—for reading the thoughts of others. Mr. Lamont had again donned his judicial robe and was making inquiries about a box of matches which he represented to have been put by him in the right-hand pocket. The members of the unseen orchestra were meticulously picking out an old French tune without the assistance of their bows, a device technically known as pizzicato.

Orlick laid down his pen in the spine-hollow of the red sixpenny copybook he was writing on, the nib pointing away from him. He put his palms to the sides of his head and opened his jaws to an angle of roughly 70 degrees, revealing completely his twin dental horse-shoes. There were four machined teeth at the back and six golden teeth of surpassing richness and twinkle at the front. As his mandibles came together again, a weary moaning sound escaped him and large globules of glandular secretion stood out on the edge of his eyes. Closing the copybook in an idle manner, he read the legend printed legibly on its back.

Nature of legend: Don't run across the road without first looking both ways! Don't pass in front of or behind a standing vehicle without first looking both ways! Don't play at being last across on any road or street! Don't follow a rolling ball into the road while there is traffic about! Don't hang on to a vehicle or climb on to it! Don't forget to walk on the footpath if there is one! Safety First!

He read the last two phrases aloud, rubbing his eyes. Furriskey sat opposite in a downcast manner. His flat hands were fastened along his jaws and, being supported by his arms on the table, were immovable; but the weight of his head had caused his cheeks to be pushed up into an unnatural elevation on a level with his eyes. This caused the outside corners of his mouth and eyes to be pushed up in a similar manner, imparting an inscrutable oriental expression to his countenance.

Do you think it would be safe to go to bed and leave him where he is to the morning? he asked.

I do not, said Orlick. Safety first.

Shanahan took out his thumb from the armhole and straightened his body in the chair.

A false step now, he said, and its a short jump for the lot of us. Do you know that? A false step now and we're all in the cart and that's a fact.

Lamont came forward from a couch where he had been resting and inclined his head as a signal that he was taking an intelligent interest in the conversation.

Will the judges have a bad head to-morrow, he asked.

No, said Orlick.

Well I think the time has come for the black caps.

You think the jury has heard enough evidence?

Certainly they have, said Shanahan. The time for talk is past. Finish the job to-night like a good man so as we can go to bed in peace. God, if we gave him a chance to catch us at this game. . . .

The job should be done at once, said Lamont, and the razor's the boy to do it.

He can't complain that he didn't get fair play, said Furriskey. He got a fair trial and a jury of his own manufacture. I think the time has come.

It's time to take him out to the courtyard, said Shanahan.

A half a minute with the razor and the trick is done, said Lamont.

As long as you realize the importance of the step that is about to be taken, said Orlick, I have no objection. I only hope that nothing will happen to us. I don't think the like of this has been done before, you know.

Well we have had enough of the trial stuff anyhow, said Shanahan.

We will have one more witness for the sake of appearance, said Orlick, and then we will get down to business.

This plan was agreed to, Mr. Shanahan taking advantage of the occasion to pay a spontaneous tribute to the eminence of Mr. O. Trellis in the author world.

The company resumed their former attitudes and the book was re-opened at the page that had been closed.

Conclusion of the book antepenultimate. Biographical reminiscence part the final: I went in by the side-door and hung my grey street-coat on the peg in the shadow under the stone stairs. I then went up in a slow deliberate preoccupied manner, examining in my mind the new fact that I had passed my final examination with a creditable margin of honour. I was conscious of a slight mental exhilaration. When passing through the hallway the door of the dining-room was opened and my uncle's head was put out through the aperture.

I want a word with you, he said.

In a moment, I answered.

His presence in the house was a surprise to me. His talk had ceased and his head had gone before I could appraise the character of his evening disposition. I proceeded to my room and placed my body on the soft trestle of my bed, still nursing in my brain the warm thought of my diligence and scholarship. . . . Few of the candidates had proved themselves of the honours class though many had made it known that they were persons of advanced intelligence. This induced an emotion of comfort and exhilaration. I heard a voice in the interior of my head. Tell me this: Do you ever open a book at all? A delay in my appearance would have the effect of envenoming the character of the interrogation. I took a volume from the mantelpiece and perused many of the footnotes and passages to be found therein, reading in a slow and penetrating manner.

The texts referred to, being an excerpt from "A Conspectus of the Arts and Natural Sciences", volume the thirty-first:
Moral Effects of Tobacco-using: There can be no question but that tobacco has a seriously deteriorating effect upon the character, blunting moral sensibility, deadening conscience, and destroying the delicacy of thought and feeling which is characteristic of the true Christian gentleman. This effect is far more clearly seen, as would be expected, in youths who begin the use of tobacco while the character is receiving its mould, than in those who have adopted the habit later in life, though

too often plainly visible in the latter class of cases. There can be no question but that the use of tobacco is a stepping-stone to vices of the worst character. It is a vice which seldom goes alone. It is far too often accompanied with profanity and laxity of morals, and leads directly to the use of alcoholic drinks. It is indeed the most powerful ally of intemperance; and it is a good omen for the temperance cause that its leaders are beginning to see the importance of recognizing this fact and promulgating it as a fundamental principle in all temperance work. Names of further paragraphs: The Nature of Tobacco; Poisonous Effects of Tobacco; Why All Smokers Do Not Die of Tobacco Poisoning; Effects of Tobacco on the Blood; Tobacco Predisposes to Disease; Smokers' Sore Throat; Tobacco and Consumption; Tobacco a Cause of Heart Disease; Tobacco and Dyspepsia; Tobacco a Cause of Cancer; Tobacco Paralysis; Tobacco a Cause of Insanity.

Moral Effects of Tea-Tasting. The long-continued use of tea has a distinct effect upon the character. This has been too often noticed and remarked to be questioned. There are tea-sots in every great charitable institution—particularly those for the maintenance of the aged. Their symptoms are generally mental irritability, muscular tremors, and sleeplessness. The following is an account of one of the cases observed. The immediate effects upon him are as follows: In about ten minutes the face becomes flushed, the whole body feels warm and heated and a sort of intellectual intoxication comes on, much the same in character, it would seem, as that which occurs in the rarefied air of a mountain. He feels elated, exhilarated, troubles and cares vanish, everything seems bright and cheerful, his body feels light and elastic, his mind clear, his ideas abundant, vivid, and flowing fluently into words. At the end of an hour's tasting a slight reaction begins to set in; some headache comes on, the face feels wrinkled and shrivelled, particularly about the eyes, which also get dark under the lids. At the end of two hours this reaction becomes firmly established, the flushed warm feeling has passed off, the hands and feet are cold, a nervous tremor comes on, accompanied with great mental depression. And he is now so excitable that every noise startles him; he is in a state of complete unrest; he can neither walk nor sit down, owing to his mental condition, and he settles into complete gloom. Copious and frequent urinations are always present, as also certain dyspeptic symptoms, such as eructations of wind, sour taste, and others. His mental condition is peculiar. He lives in a state of dread that some accident may happen to him; in the omnibus fears a collision; crossing the street, fears that he will be crushed by passing teams; walking on the sidewalks, fears that a sign may fall, or watches the eaves of houses, thinking that a brick may fall down and kill him; under the apprehension that every dog he meets is going to bite the calves of his legs, he carries an umbrella in all weathers as a defence against such an attack. Conclusion of the foregoing.

Ibidem, further extract therefrom, being Argument of the poem "The Shipwreck", by William Falconer: 1. Retrospect of the voyage. Season of the year described. 2. Character of the master, and his officers, Albert, Rodmond and Arion. Palemon, son of the owner of the ship. Attachment of Palemon to Anna, the daughter of Albert. 3. Noon. Palemon's history. 4. Sunset. Midnight. Arion's dream. Unmoor by moonlight. Morning. Sun's azimuth taken. Beautiful appearance of the ship, as seen by the natives from the shore.

Canto II. 1. Reflections on leaving shore. 2. Favourable breeze. Waterspout. The dying dolphins. Breeze freshens. Ship's rapid progress along coast. Topsails reefed. Mainsail split. The ship bears up; again hauls upon the wind. Another mainsail bent, and set. Porpoises. 3. The ship driven out of her course from Candia. Heavy gale. Topsails furled. Top gallant yards lowered. Heavy sea. Threatening sunset. Difference of opinion respecting the mode of taking in the main-sail. Courses reefed. Four seamen lost off the lee mainyardarm. Anxiety of the master, and his mates, on being near a lee-shore. Mizzen reefed. 4. A tremendous sea bursts over the deck; its consequences. The ship labours in great distress. Guns thrown overboard. Dismal appearance of the weather. Very high and dangerous sea. Storm lightening. Severe fatigue of the crew at the pumps. Critical situation of the ship near the island Falconera. Consultation and resolution of the officers. Speech and advice of Albert; his devout address to heaven. Order given to scud. The fore-staysail hoisted and split. The head yards braced aback. The mizzen-mast cut away.

Canto III. 1. The beneficial influence of poetry in the civilization of mankind. Diffidence of the author. 2.

Wreck of the mizzen-mast cleared away. Ship puts before the wind—labours much. Different stations of the officers. Appearance of the island of Falconera. 3. Excursion to the adjacent nations of Greece renowned in antiquity. Athens. Socrates, Plato, Aristides, Solon, Corinth—its architecture. Sparta. Leonidas. Invasion by Xerxes. Lycurgus. Epaminondas. Present state of the Spartans. Arcadia. Former happiness, and fertility. Its present distress the effect of slavery. Ithica. Ulysses, and Penelope. Argos and Mycaene. Agamemnon. Macronisi. Lemnos. Vulcan. Delos. Apollo and Diana. Troy. Sestos. Leander and Hero. Delphos. Temple of Apollo. Parnassus. The muses. 4. Subject resumed. Address to the spirits of the storm. A tempest, accompanied with rain, hail and meteors. Darkness of the night, lightning and thunder. Daybreak. St. George's cliffs open upon them. The ship, in great danger, passes the island of St. George. 5. Land of Athens appears. Helmsman struck blind by lightning. Ship laid broadside to the shore. Bowsprit, foremast, and main top-mast carried away. Albert, Rodmond, Arion and Palemon strive to save themselves on the wreck of the foremast. The ship parts asunder. Death of Albert and Rodmond. Arion reaches the shore. Finds Palemon expiring on the beach. His dying address to Arion, who is led away by the humane natives.

Extract from the Poem referred to: The dim horizon lowering vapours shroud, And blot the sun yet struggling in the cloud; Thro' the wide atmosphere condensed with haze,

His glaring orb emits a sanguine blaze. The pilots now their azimuth attend, On which all courses, duly formed, depend: The compass placed to catch the rising ray, The quadrant's shadows studious they survey; Along the arch the gradual index slides, While Phoebus down the vertic-circle glides; Now seen on ocean's utmost verge to swim, He sweeps it vibrant with his nether limb. Thus height, and polar distance are obtained, Then latitude, and declination, gain'd; In chiliads next the analogy is sought, And on the sinical triangle wrought: By this magnetic variance is explored, Just angles known, and polar truth restored. *Conclusion of the foregoing.*

I closed the book and extinguished my cigarette at midpoint by a quick trick of the fingers. Going downstairs with an audible low tread, I opened the door of the dining-room in a meek penitent fashion. My uncle had Mr. Corcoran in attendance by his side. They sat before the fire; having desisted from their conversation at my entry, they held between them a double-sided silence.

How do you do, Mr. Corcoran, I said.

He arose the better to exert the full force of his fine man-grip.

Ah, good evening, Sir, he said.

Well, mister-my-friend, how do you feel to-day, my uncle said. I have something to say to you. Take a seat.

He turned in the direction of Mr. Corcoran with a swift eye-message of unascertained import. He then stretched down for the poker and adjusted the red coals, turning them slowly. The dancing redness on his side-face showed a furrow of extreme intellectual effort.

You were a long time upstairs, he said.

I was washing my hands, I answered, utilizing a voice-tone that lacked appreciable inflexion. I hastily averted my grimy palms.

Mr. Corcoran gave a short laugh.

Well we all have to do that, he said in an awkward manner, we are all entitled to our five minutes.

This much he regretted for my uncle did not answer but kept turning at the coals.

I am sure you will remember, he said at last, that the question of your studies has been a great worry to me. It has caused me plenty of anxiety, I can tell you that. If you failed in your studies it would be a great blow to your poor father and certainly it would be a sore disappointment to myself.

He paused as he turned his head in order to ascertain my listening attitude. I continued following the points of his poker as it continued burrowing among the coals.

And you would have no excuse, no excuse in the wide world. You have a good comfortable home, plenty of wholesome food, clothes, boots—all your orders. You have a fine big room to work in, plenty of ink and paper. That is something to thank God for because there is many a man that got his education in a back-room by the light of a halfpenny candle. Oh, no excuse in the wide world.

Again I felt his inquiring eyes upon my countenance.

As you know yourself, I have strong views on the subject of idling. Lord save us, there is no cross in the world as heavy as the cross of sloth, for it comes to this, that the lazy man is a burden to his friends, to himself and to every man woman or child he'll meet or mix with. Idleness darkens the understanding; idleness weakens the will; idleness leaves you a very good mark for the sinful schemes of the gentleman down below.

I noticed that in repeating idleness, my uncle had unwittingly utilized a figure of speech usually designed to effect emphasis.

Name of figure of speech: Anaphora (or Epibole).

Idleness, you might say, is the father and the mother of the other vices.

Mr. Corcoran, visually interrogated, expressed complete agreement.

Oh, it's a great mistake to get into the habit of doing nothing, he said. Young people especially would have to be on their guard. It's a thing that grows on you and a thing to be avoided.

To be avoided like the plague, said my uncle. Keep on the move as my father, the Lord have mercy on him, used to say—keep on the move and you'll move towards God.

He was a saint, of course, said Mr. Corcoran.

Oh, he knew the secret of life, said my uncle, he did indeed. But wait for a minute now.

He turned to me with a directness that compelled me to meet his eyes by means of imbuing them with almost supernatural intensity.

I've said many a hard word to you for your own good, he said. I have rebuked you for laziness and bad habits of one kind or another. But you've done the trick, you've passed your examination and your old uncle is going to be the first to shake your hand. And happy he is indeed to do it.

Giving my hand to him I looked to Mr. Corcoran in my great surprise. His face bore a circular expression of surpassing happiness and pleasure. He arose in a brisk manner and leaning over my uncle's shoulder, caused me to extract my hand from the possession of the latter and present it to him for the exercise of his honest strength. My uncle smiled broadly, making a pleased but inarticulate sound with his throat.

I don't know you as well as your uncle does, said Mr. Corcoran, but I think I'm a good judge of character. I don't often go wrong. I take a man as I find him. I think you're *all right* . . . and I congratulate you on your great success from the bottom of my heart.

I muttered my thanks, utilizing formal perfunctory expressions. My uncle chuckled audibly in the pause and tapped the grate-bar with his poker.

You have the laugh on me to-night, you may say, he said, and boys there is nobody more pleased than I. I'm as happy as the day is long.

Oh, the stuff was there, said Mr. Corcoran. It was there all the time.

And he would be a queer son of his father if it wasn't, said my uncle.

How did you find out about it? I asked.

Oh, never you mind now, said my uncle with a suitable gesture. The old boys know a thing or two. There are more things in life and death than you ever dreamt of, Horatio.

They laughed at me in unison, savouring the character of their bubbling good-humour in a short subsequent silence.

You are not forgetting something? said Mr. Corcoran.

Certainly not, said my uncle.

He put his hand in his pocket and turned to me.

Mr. Corcoran and myself, he said, have taken the liberty of joining together in making you a small present as a memento of the occasion and as a small but sincere expression of our congratulation. We hope that you will accept it and that you will wear it to remind you when you have gone from us of two friends that watched over you—a bit strictly perhaps—and wished you well.

He again took one hand from me and shook it, putting a small black box of the pattern utilized by jewellers in the other. The edges of the box were slightly frayed, showing a lining of grey linen or other durable material. The article was evidently of the second-hand denomination.

Comparable word utilized by German nation: antiquarisch.

The characters of a watch-face, slightly luminous in the gloom, appeared to me from the interior of the box. Looking up, I found that the hand of Mr. Corcoran was extended in an honest manner for the purpose of manual felicitation.

I expressed my thanks in a conventional way but without verbal dexterity or coolness.

Oh, you are welcome, they said.

I put the watch on my wrist and said it was a convenient article to have, a sentiment that found instant corroboration. Shortly afterwards, on the pretext of requiring tea, I made my way from the room. Glancing back at the door, I noticed that the gramophone was on the table under its black cover and that my uncle had again taken up the poker and was gazing at the fire in a meditative if pleased manner.

Description of my uncle: Simple, well-intentioned; pathetic in humility; responsible member of large commercial concern.

Changed description

I went slowly up the stairs to my room. My uncle had evinced unsuspected traits of character and had induced in me an emotion of surprise and contrition extremely difficult of literary rendition or description. My steps faltered to some extent on the stairs. As I opened my door, my watch told me that the time was five fifty-four. At the same time I heard the Angelus pealing out from far away.

Superiority Complex Challenged

Conclusion of the Book, penultimate: Teresa, a servant employed at the Red Swan Hotel, knocked at the master's door with the intention of taking away the tray but eliciting no response, she opened the door and found to her surprise that the room was empty. Assuming that the master had gone to a certain place, she placed the tray on the landing and returned to the room for the purpose of putting it to rights. She revived the fire and made a good blaze by putting into it several sheets of writing which were littered here and there about the floor (not improbably a result of the open window). By a curious coincidence as a matter of fact strange to say it happened that these same pages were those of the master's novel, the pages which made and sustained the existence of Furriskey and his true friends. Now they were blazing, curling and twisting and turning black, straining uneasily in the draught and then taking flight as if to heaven through the chimney, a flight of light things red-flecked and wrinkled hurrying to the sky. The fire faltered and sank again to the hollow coals and just at that moment, Teresa heard a knock at the hall-door away below. Going down she did her master the unexpected pleasure of admitting him to the house. He was attired in his night-shirt, which was slightly discoloured as if by rain, and some dead leaves were attached to the soles of his poor feet. His eyes gleamed and he did not speak but walked past her in the direction of the stairs. He then turned and coughing slightly, stared at her as she stood there, the oil-lamp in her hand throwing strange shadows on her soft sullen face.

Ah, Teresa, he muttered.

Where were you in your night-shirt, Sir? she asked.

I am ill, Teresa, he murmured. I have done too much thinking and writing, too much work. My nerves are troubling me. I have bad nightmares and queer dreams and I walk when I am asleep. I am very tired. The doors should be locked.

You could easily get your death, Sir, Teresa said.

He reached unsteadily for the lamp and motioned that she should go before him up the stairs. The edge of her stays, lifting her skirt in a little ridge behind her, dipped softly from side to side with the rise and the fall of her haunches as she trod the stairs. It is the function of such garment to improve the figure, to conserve corporal discursiveness, to create the illusion of a finely modulated body. If it betray its own presence when fulfilling this task, its purpose must largely fail.

Ars est celare artem, muttered Trellis, doubtful as to whether he had made a pun.

Conclusion of the book, *ultimate*: Evil is even, truth is an odd number and death is a full stop. When a dog barks late at night and then retires again to bed, he punctuates and gives majesty to the serial enigma of the dark, laying it more evenly and heavily upon the fabric of the mind. Sweeny in the trees hears the sad baying as he sits listening on the branch, a huddle between the earth and heaven; and he hears also the answering mastiff that is counting the watches in the next parish. Bark answers bark till the call spreads like fire through all Erin. Soon the moon comes forth from behind her curtains riding full tilt across the sky, lightsome and unperturbed in her immemorial calm. The eyes of the mad king upon the branch are upturned, whiter eyeballs in a white face, upturned in fear and supplication. His mind is but a shell. Was Hamlet mad? Was Trellis mad? It is extremely hard to say. Was he a victim of hard-to-explain hallucinations? Nobody knows. Even experts do not agree on these vital points. Professor Unternehmer, the eminent German neurologist, points to Claudius as a lunatic but allows Trellis an inverted sow neurosis wherein the farrow eat their dam. Du Fernier, however, Professor of Mental Sciences and Sanitation at the Sorbonne, deduces from a want of hygiene in the author's bed-habits a progressive weakening of the head. It is of importance the most inestimable, he writes, that for mental health there should be walking and not overmuch of the bedchamber. The more one studies the problem, the more fascinated one becomes and incidentally the more one postulates a cerebral norm. The accepted principles of Behaviourism do not seem to give much assistance. Neither does heredity help for his father was a Galwayman, sober and industrious, tried and true in the service of his country. His mother was from far Fermanagh, a woman of grace and fair learning and a good friend to all. But which of us can hope to probe with questioning finger the dim thoughts that flit in a fool's head? One man will think he has a glass bottom and will fear to sit in case of breakage. In other respects he will be a man of great intellectual force and will accompany one in a mental ramble throughout the labyrinths of mathematics or philosophy so long as he is allowed to remain standing throughout the disputations. Another man will be perfectly polite and well-conducted except that he will in no circumstances turn otherwise than to the right and indeed will own a bicycle so constructed that it cannot turn otherwise than to that point. Others will be subject to colours and will attach undue merit to articles that are red or green or white merely because they bear that hue. Some will be exercised and influenced by the texture of a cloth or by the roundness or angularity of an object. Numbers, however, will account for a great proportion of unbalanced and suffering humanity. One man will rove the streets seeking motor-cars with numbers that are divisible by seven. Well-known, alas, is the case of the poor German who was very fond of three and who made each aspect of his life a thing of triads. He went home one evening and drank three cups of tea with three lumps of sugar in each cup, cut his jugular with a razor three times and scrawled with a dying hand on a picture of his wife good-bye, good-bye, good-bye.